A STONE IN TIME

MÓRDHA STONE CHRONICLES, BOOK 1

KIM ALLRED

STORM COAST PUBLISHING, LLC

A Stone in Time
Mórdha Stone Chronicles, Book 1
Kim Allred
Published by Storm Coast Publishing, LLC
Copyright © 2018 by Kim Allred
Cover Design by Amanda Kelsey of Razzle Dazzle Design
ISBN 978-1732241114 (print edition)

For Dad.
It took me a while, but I finally got here.

Life is either a daring adventure or nothing.

Helen Keller

AJ Moore inched higher up the seaside cliff, ignoring the craggy rocks of the Oregon shoreline that glistened with salty spray. A horn from a nearby boat pierced the sound of the early morning surf, cutting through the screeching of the feeding gulls. She tuned out the warring cacophony, the mental connection with her favorite cliff circulating like a mystical chant. Grasping the familiar rock signaling the end of the climb, AJ heaved her straining body over the edge, satisfaction forcing a smile on her face. Her brazen act, daring a forbidden climb that ended on private property, quelled the rebellious demons that haunted her since her father's death.

She wrapped her arms around her legs, bracing herself against the chilled morning air. She watched the sky brighten, the waves shimmering toward the shore as she breathed in the rich smell of salt, sea, and decayed fish. AJ loved alpine starts, the predawn setting of a climb, the sounds of the coast filling the air, encouraging signs of life. The ocean, the danger, and the strenuous exertion on her body brought an inner peace and a true sense of herself she could find no other way since the death of her father.

His unexpected death, a heart attack leading to a car accident, left her world tilted, sometimes past the point of recognition. Her grief had passed, but his irreplaceable loss had left her hollow. His job to guide her left unfinished.

Her family and friends couldn't grasp why AJ had taken climbing lessons, and they would be mortified if they knew how frequently she climbed this wall. But somehow, this place brought her closer to her father. She closed her eyes and let the salty air fill her lungs, the warmth of the morning sun touch her shoulders, and the screams of the gulls penetrate her soul.

After a few moments of peaceful meditation, calmness restoring her inner core, she deliberated her descent. She peered out to the sea below, the view stretching for miles in both directions. To her surprise, a large patch of dense fog rolled in from across the distant waves, covering the sea. Fog could come and go quickly at the shore, yet there hadn't been any hint of precipitation on her drive to the coast or during her climb.

Still somewhat amazed by the speed of the mist, she could only stare at the marvel, a scene she'd never witnessed before. Something from below caught her eye, materializing out of the fog. At first, she couldn't make sense of what she saw, and she leaned forward and squinted. Tall masts pierced the veil of fog, some kind of ship making its way north.

A second later, AJ noticed the myriad ropes draped from the mast, moving gently with the surge of the ship. The sails were down, tied against the arms of the masts, and for a moment, she wondered what powered the ship. Then a ghostly figure appeared, standing on the deck, one hand braced against the tall mast, as if magically steering the ship by sheer touch alone. She blinked. The image faded into the mist.

The fog surged to the beach, riding the waves. It bolted up the cliff and smothered her like a heavy blanket. She remained sitting, her forehead wrinkled, perplexed at the rapidity of this fog. Something else nagged, more than the quickness of its arrival or the glimpse of the wraithlike ship. She couldn't hear anything, not the waves hitting the shore, nor the gulls frenzied with morning feeding.

She closed her eyes, straining to hear a sound, goose bumps rising on her skin, although the temperature hadn't changed. Discomfort wormed through her, not quite panic, more a sense of being out of place. She didn't want to stand, no longer aware of the cliff's edge, although it had been directly in front of her seconds before.

Without warning, she heard a horn in the distance, and her body arched toward the new warmth on her face. Her eyes popped open, and she shielded them with her arm, warding off the sudden glare from the reflection of sun on ocean. Accustomed to the light once more, she turned around, searching for the fog that had enveloped her moments before, but saw nothing. Not one sign the mist had ever been there.

She glanced out to sea, searching for the sailing vessel, but the ocean appeared deserted except for the gulls. No ship. The whole odd experience lasted no more than a minute or two. Where had the ship gone? There were no sails to power it, and even with a motor, it couldn't have vanished from view. Her sense of calm shattered, she chided herself for losing her self-control over a strange bit of fog and what surely must have been a trick of her imagination. She shook herself. Her descent still lay ahead of her. Standing on shaky legs, she looked around once more, saw nothing of the mysterious fog or ship, and prepared the rope for the rappel down the wall.

THE MIST SETTLED around the old house that sat fifty yards from the cliff. Considered a mansion back in its day, the house had fallen into disrepair, remaining vacant for many years. The owner couldn't find a buyer, even with its perfect location on the coast. The dawn light captured the sky and contrasting ocean waters, reflecting them off the tall windows that filled the back of the house, a common architectural feature for contemporary homes, but unusual for its time. The mist rolled in like a freight train, yet tendrils of fog could be seen within the mist, transparent fingers drifting with no particular direction of movement, as if searching for something. Sound all but disappeared, but the temperature never changed as one would expect, no chilling of the air, no dampness from the mist, just the perception that one was standing in a thick bank of fog.

After a few minutes, the mist vanished. The sun once more shed warmth and light on the grasses and trees that landscaped the yard of the house and framed the woman sitting on the edge of the cliff, her short brown tresses stirring gently in the light breeze.

The tall man, dressed in a long black coat, his dark hair slicked back, appeared under a large spruce tree in the yard. He didn't move when the woman at the top of the cliff turned to glance around. A sigh of relief shuddered through him, unseen in the shadows.

She stood, ran her fingers through her hair, gave a last look around, and shrugged her shoulders. The lean muscles along her tall frame stretched when she pulled the rope up from the cliff to lie on the ground next to her. The end of the rope slid into a metal device she attached to a tree, which she tugged several times to confirm the strength of the connection. Placing her back to the edge, hands tight on the rope, she took a step backward and disappeared from view.

Transfixed by the woman's calm demeanor, he surveyed his surroundings and crept to the cliff. He peered over the edge and spotted the woman already a third of the way down. She stopped every few feet to remove metal devices from the crevice that ran down the wall. Impressed by her quick, deliberate movements and mesmerized by her skill, he watched until her foot touched land. He stepped back when she looked up to pull the rope to her. Once the rope disappeared from the anchor at the man's feet, he cautiously peeked over the ledge. The woman finished tying the rope to her pack before she disappeared around a large rock.

Turning from the cliff, the stranger studied the new landscape, reveling in the combined smells of ocean and firs, and listened to the birds bustling about their day. He hadn't traveled as far as he'd expected, and the revelation made him smile as he strolled toward the house.

2

TWO WEEKS LATER

A J ripped the blouse off and replaced it on its hanger, shoving it back into the closet among the array of other neatly hanging items. She turned to her dresser, sighing as she picked out the same sweater she always seemed to wear to these family gatherings, like a well-worn security blanket, a reminder of who she was in the middle of the foreign landscape.

"Did you ever notice there's not much action in this town?" Stella eyed her friend over the top of a newspaper, her forehead scrunched in thought. "The blouse would have been just fine." She had propped herself on AJ's bed, thumbing through the *Baywood Herald*. She closed the paper and tossed it, the inside contents slipping out to sprawl across the bed.

"I suppose you would like to have a murder or two to liven things up." AJ smiled, running her hand over the top of an old wooden box before opening it and picking out a pair of earrings.

"You know it couldn't hurt, but no one nice. Some drug kingpin or abusive husband would be sufficient." Stella returned a smug smile and stretched, like a cat slowly waking up to change position. She tossed her shoulder-length auburn hair and watched AJ complete her adornments.

"Always the optimist." AJ pulled out the top tray of the box and let her fingers run through the pile of jewelry lying below. She picked up a necklace with a large marbled stone mounted in the middle of an ornate silver setting and laid it against the sweater, the accompanying silver chain thick and clunky. She touched the stone, rubbing her thumb over it as she eyed herself in the mirror. Shaking her head, she dropped it back into the box, selecting a thin gold chain with a locket. Giving herself one last perusal in the mirror, she shrugged and closed the box. "Thanks for the wake-up call. I didn't mean to fall asleep."

"You need to slow down. I can't believe I'm saying this, but lately you're even wearing me out." Stella sat up and gave AJ a critical once-over. "I liked the silver necklace. Have I seen that one before? It has a unique stone."

"It was just a catnap that got away from me." AJ shoved on her boots and headed out the door. "I found the necklace at an estate sale a month or so ago. The chain is too heavy for me, and I haven't had time to replace it."

"It would look great on me." Stella followed AJ down the hall. Not thin but not exactly overweight, Stella's ample frame carried all the right curves. She used a selection of flamboyant colors and fashions to bring out the best of her enviable figure, turning heads from both genders. "Why do I always have to be the one to make sure you follow through on your commitments? You know I'm not the best at keeping my own appointments."

AJ rolled her eyes. "When was the last time you were late for anything? I'm not sure why you even keep a day planner since your entire schedule is ingrained in that head of yours. And I didn't ask you to babysit me."

AJ kept her small corner apartment tidy. The walls, painted slate blue, sprouted dozens of wall hangings ranging from abstract to picturesque. White casings bordered the windows with blinds rarely shut. Unimpeded by neighboring buildings, her view from the third floor displayed an overgrown nature park, stretching a good quarter mile before ending at a cozy outdoor amphitheater. She paid more for this view, and it was worth every penny, although she complained to the landlord so he wouldn't think he could easily raise the rent.

The living area overflowed with various sizes and styles of bookcases filled with aged manuscripts, books, magazines, and knickknacks that spoke of history. These small treasures unearthed as a result of AJ's favorite pastime, her small weekend excursions picking through garage or estate sales in search of the past. A few chairs and side tables sat scattered between the bookcases. Some remained as she had found them. Others had been repaired and stained or painted, depending on the type of wood or her mood at the time.

AJ's diverse tastes ran through her entire two-bedroom apartment, with one room functioning as her study, filled with even more bookcases. This room focused on two center pieces. A vintage printer's cabinet, used as a desk, sat against a wall, looking insulted with a laptop and small printer marring its distinguished past. The second piece hung on the other side of the room next to a pastel-yellow chaise. The large painting portrayed a small girl with her dog, standing in a spring meadow with the calm blue sea below. The girl, cast in a hazy morning light, held a bouquet of yellow and white daisies in her hand. Her other hand rested on the dog's head. The painting had been a discovery of her father's. He said it reminded him of her even though she'd never owned a dog. She no longer cared why it made her father think of her—the portrait created a refuge, a strong warm hand that comforted her each time she sank onto the chaise, reading stories of yesteryear from treasured books.

AJ walked past the living room, wishing they had time to sit and catch up on their day, but she was already late. She picked up her purse and waited at the front door for her friend to pass, annoyed with herself for being ungrateful. They were, after all, her own family issues. After locking up behind them, AJ leaned her head against the door and blew out a deep breath. Settled, she turned and followed Stella to their cars.

"Do you want to stop for a quick drink first?" Stella leaned against her sporty red convertible, the top up as it was most of the year.

AJ hovered against her own car, a small white Subaru, perfect for hauling her consignment store treasures. She gazed out to the west, able to catch glimpses of the ocean through the trees and buildings. After a short, almost inaudible sigh, she shook her head. "No, I'm already late." She slid a glance at Stella. "You didn't have to come over just to make sure I'd go."

"I wouldn't have to if you had a permanent date. You've been going solo for a long time."

"I could say the same of you."

"True. But my family get-togethers don't have as much drama." Stella stared back at her, her face softening, the humor gone. "That's what friends do, we have each other's back. I know you don't like these get-togethers. Think of me as your talisman, wishing you well on your journey." Stella unlocked her door and turned to get in the car.

AJ's body relaxed from the tension that had been building all day. She touched Stella's shoulder. "Thanks."

Stella pulled away from the curb, flashing a smile and a wave before slipping into traffic. AJ let out another deep sigh, searched for her own keys, and slumped into the driver's seat.

ounds exploded from the house, threatening to burst the door open before AJ could reach for the knob. She braced herself and pushed her way in. Three small children raced past her. Feet thundered on the cherrywood floor and up the stairs, while screams of "Give it back" and shrieks of laughter assaulted her ears.

The house, an old Cape Cod, carried a coastal style that AJ's mother extended inside, decorated with the same colors Helen had used forever. Yellows, blues and whites combined to battle the gray skies of Oregon winters and prevent the gloom from creeping into her home. The midsize foyer yielded to a wide staircase, framed by family travel pictures that ascended the wall on the left, a white rail banister on the right. Turning her back on the door to her father's study, unchanged over the years, AJ moved into the large living area, an open interior design that swept through the rest of the house.

Her mother's effortless talent always amazed her, the more eclectic taste a stark contrast to her own. Artfully arranged seating areas combined chairs and sofas with the perfect mix of formal and cozy. Several large windows, edged with custom linen drapes, teased muted light from the dull spring day. Crown molding ran along the ceilings, painted a soft white to accent the yellow of the walls, emphasizing the bookcases and table-tops, subtly mixed with classic ornaments and interesting curios purchased during the family's exotic vacations. The unique pieces, gradually and carefully selected by AJ's father, confronted her each time she walked into the house. Helen had arranged each favored piece to fit perfectly in the room.

AJ smirked at the children's assault on Mom's perfect domain. The living room, typically spotless of clutter or dust, lay strewn with toys, sweaters, and overcoats, cast about as if a tornado had burrowed its way under the front door and exploded into action. Before she could regain some composure from the earlier onset of the little people, the same unruly group raced past her again, heading for the noises coming from the kitchen.

AJ approached the jovial sounds. Smells from the kitchen caught up with her, and her stomach announced its own pleasure at the aroma with a light rumbling.

Sure enough, they were all there. AJ stopped at the doorway to watch the domestic play unfold. Helen, light and graceful, pearls resting against her soft coral sweater, moved from stove to oven, making sure one item didn't cook faster than the other. They'd expanded the kitchen a few years before, moving the stove to the island and the oven against the wall. Her mom waltzed back and forth between them, the large spoon in her hand moving in time with the phantom music.

Adam, AJ's older brother, stood next to the marble counter top, surveying his family, the beer in his hand encouraging his growing paunch despite his weekly runs. Yet even with the recent weight gain, he sported the look of the Ivy leaguer he had become. His short-cropped brown hair and soft face still held his charming boyish looks.

Adam's wife, Madelyn, sat at the antique French dining table. Her big blonde hair appeared even larger than normal, and her makeup, while artfully applied, seemed excessive for the weekly family gathering. Their young children sprawled around her, coloring books and small treats finally settling them down in motion if not in sound.

AJ slid to the side counter and poured herself a generous glass of red wine before entering into the fray, keeping her escape route behind her. She couldn't help but smile, even if her family usually grated on her. She leaned against the counter, participating from the margins, silently completing the camaraderie with her mother, her brother, and his family. The only missing link was her father. Yet he still seemed present through the short bouts of laughter, discussions of gardens and home improvements, and the latest antics of the grandchildren.

Suddenly, with the absence of her father, the gap between her and her family widened, leaving her a little empty. An outsider, not fitting into this family scene after all. But before she could turn and sneak out, Helen greeted her with a quick hug, cutting off her escape.

"You've been working too much again," Helen said.

"I know, Mom."

Helen gave her a once-over and tucked a curl behind AJ's ear. Her smile was a little sad as she moved back to the stove, allowing AJ to join the family gathering.

AJ wanted to say something to ease Helen's concern but moved farther into the kitchen instead, edging into the family circle, where her brother's unusually warm greeting threw her off-kilter.

"Sis, what took you so long to get here? Don't tell me, working late again. I'll tell you, this sister of mine doesn't know when to say enough."

AJ rubbed her forehead as Adam blathered on. This was going to be a long evening.

"Come over here and sit, sit. Tell us all about your day in the news world." Adam spread his arms and pointed to a stool close to him.

AJ stiffened at Adam's exuberance. She preferred his normal indifference to her life, but she did as she was told. Curiosity could never hold her back, even when her little voice told her different.

"Nothing much happening in the news today, Adam." Testing the waters.

"Nonsense. I don't believe that for a minute. Not the exciting life of my little sister and the world of headline news at the *Baywood Herald*."

"That's enough, Adam. Let your sister come in and relax," Helen said. "And introduce your friend."

AJ had just grabbed a barstool at the side counter, but the mention of a friend swung her around. That explained Adam's unusually warm greeting. She searched the room, not sure how she had missed him earlier. Adam's notorious attempts at matching her up with some mole of a man annoyed her. He knew she would deplore anyone he trotted out. She suspected he did it to torment her. He couldn't possibly expect her to succumb to the family life with a quiet and boring man.

But when she faced her intended foe, she did a double take. Her skin prickled. Her brother had thrown her for a loop. This stranger exuded a formidable presence that left AJ speechless, and more than a little curious.

Dressed in a dark gray tailored suit, the stranger watched her from across the room, ensconced in a large, cushioned chair. She wouldn't call him pretty-boy handsome. He wore his short dark hair slicked back. His partially hooded eyes, buried deep within his hawkish face, seemed to see everything before coming to rest on her. His long legs stretched out into the room, and his arms relaxed on the arms of the chair. But his penetrating gaze reflected something else. A raw power and control emanated from him, like a stalking panther, waiting for the right moment to pounce.

For a reason AJ couldn't explain, he didn't intimidate her. Instead, she felt a connection to him, not out of desire or magnetism, but something instinctive she couldn't put her finger on, some funky déjà vu. She shrugged it off, irritated with herself. She must be tired. AJ broke away from his stare and turned back to her brother, who, she saw with some annoyance, watched them closely.

"So. Who's your friend?" AJ said.

"Great timing." Adam became more animated. "This is Ethan, fairly new in town. Thought he could use a home-cooked meal."

"And where did you meet Ethan?" AJ spoke to Adam, but she couldn't help glancing at the stranger.

"Through work. He owns the security company we recently signed with." Adam's smile seemed permanently plastered on his face.

"And so, of course, why not bring him to a family dinner." AJ sounded peevish but couldn't stop herself. She could never get the upper hand with her brother without sounding like a whiny schoolgirl, and she wished she had agreed to that drink with Stella.

"You can't blame Adam for it."

The deep voice startled AJ. The stranger rose from the chair, and in one fluid motion, suddenly stood at the counter next to her and Adam. The swift movement triggered AJ's instinct to take a quick step back. His smile at her response lightened his face, making it less severe. She detected an underlying accent.

A blush tinged AJ's face, an annoying emotional reflex she could never control. She had been rude, attempting to thwart her brother at this man's expense. "I'm sorry, it's been a long day and I was caught off guard by a visitor. So you know Adam from work?"

"Yes." Ethan's smile remained, and he studied AJ, making her squirm under the inspection. "Adam and I have been working through the security changes at his firm. I'm afraid it was me that made mention of missing home cooking. I've been living out of a hotel since I arrived."

"So you're not staying long?" AJ regretted the words as soon as she said them, so she busied herself with the tasty appetizer tray her mother had laid out, taking one just to lay it on a napkin.

To her surprise, Ethan laughed. "Just arrived and trying to get rid of me already? Adam did warn me you'd be difficult to win over."

AJ bristled at his response, and a glance at her brother told her Adam had no desire to reduce the friction he'd created after setting the tinder.

"Ethan was telling us he was looking for a place to either rent or buy. Isn't that right?" Helen slid AJ a refreshed glass of wine.

AJ upended the glass, drinking more than she intended. "Sorry." AJ held on to her glass and forced a smile to return. "So, you're moving here? Where from?"

Ethan welcomed a refill of wine from Helen, reducing his height advantage by leaning against the counter. "Here and there over the years. My business takes me to many places."

"So not from anywhere in particular." AJ's reporter instincts, prompted by his elusiveness, begged to be unleashed, especially after the dry spell she'd been having at work. She stared out the kitchen's bay window, her spirits dampened by thoughts of work. Focused on her own thoughts, she missed her mother's question.

"AJ, did you hear me? What do you think?" Helen pulled plates and bowls out of cabinets. "Let's all move into the dining room. We might as well get to know each other over a nice meal before it overcooks."

"I have no doubt Stella would love to jump in and take care of Ethan's needs," said Madelyn, who had observed the exchange of words from the table where her children still colored. "She knows it all, or so she always reminds us."

AJ glared in Madelyn's direction. "I don't know if Stella has time to add another client, but I can ask her."

Picking up steaming bowls of mashed potatoes and green beans, AJ headed for the table. Ethan fell in behind her with another bottle of wine and a basket of rolls. That close, she picked up a whiff of his scent, warm and masculine...and something else, light and barely perceptible, but she couldn't put her finger on it. She almost jumped when he spoke.

"I understand you're an expert on history."

She placed the bowls on the table and settled into her regular spot at the table, startled when Ethan sat next to her, in what had been her father's chair. It was the only chair available, but it vexed her anyway.

"I don't know that I would use that word. I'm no expert, but I do enjoy exploring the past." AJ accepted another glass of wine, but before their discussion could go any further, Adam's kids, forgotten for a while, burst into the room. They chattered away, taking their places at the table, waiting for Madelyn to dole out their portions of dinner.

"Something I also have an interest in. I would like to hear your favorite eras." Ethan gave her a warm smile and filled his plate, oblivious to the noise from the children. "Perhaps we have one in common."

AJ nodded. Any further discussion seemed fruitless until the din of the kids subsided, their voices silenced by the food shoveled into their mouths.

"I have a marvelous idea." Helen controlled the passing of plates and bowls, ensuring Adam and his family had everything they needed. "AJ, you should take Ethan around town. Get him more familiar with the city."

Adam barked a laugh. "Perfect."

AJ considered kicking Adam, but she wasn't twelve. She turned her stare to her mom. Everyone thought themselves a matchmaker. "I'm not sure I'm the right person."

"Who better than a local reporter?" Adam scooped more potatoes onto his plate.

AJ squared her shoulders. She squashed the desire to tell him what those potatoes were doing to his midsection.

"I don't want to intrude on your time," Ethan said. A smile hovered before he sipped his wine.

"I'm just not sure about work." The words squeaked from AJ and she lowered her head, refocused on her plate.

"I'm sure the paper can get by one afternoon without you." Adam winked, the action so swift, AJ might have imagined it.

"Great. That's settled, then." Helen patted AJ's hand before picking up her fork.

Trapped by the family, AJ forced a smile before choking down a bite. Her previous hunger vanished under her new burden, playing guide to Adam's friend. She sneaked a peek at Ethan. He appeared to be enjoying a conversation with her mother about the dishware of all things, a collectible from the early 1900's. She'd heard the story a hundred times.

She couldn't raise the energy to feign interest. She grabbed a roll and caught Adam staring at her. His face filled with complete satisfaction. He had won a perceived battle. AJ stayed on the task of buttering her roll, ignoring whatever game her brother seemed to be playing. She poured a touch more wine, and when she looked back at him, he had fallen into deep conversation with Helen and Ethan.

Certain that she must have misread her brother, she put it behind her, allowing the conversation and meal to erase the tension of the day. She let the evening carry on around her, appreciative of Ethan's command of the group, allowing her to distance herself and glide through the rest of the evening.

AJ OPENED the door to her apartment, greeted by the pleasant sound of silence. After the hectic scene at her mom's, the quiet soothed her, a healing balm to her psyche. She still missed the small sounds of Eleanor, whose slow and aged body would make its way from her blanketed bed to wrap around AJ's legs, her soft purrs tugging on AJ's heart. It had been three months since her death, and the grief still tugged. The cat had been such a part of her since her young teen years, a surprise birthday present from her father. She'd eventually go to the shelter to find another, even though she could hear Stella's warnings labeling her a cat lady in training.

Crossing the small hallway, she dropped her purse on the counter of a high side table discovered years before at some garage sale. This evening, her exhaustion overwhelmed her, and she wished for nothing more than her usual routine. Tempted to pour herself a glass of wine, she decided on a cup of tea instead and crashed into the soft brown couch. She dragged a worn old afghan over her lap and listened to the clicking of her grandfather clock. Frazzled from an unproductive day at the office, her earlier catnap interrupted by Stella, and the boisterous family dinner, she relished the comforting silence.

With a cup of tea in her lap, AJ leaned her head back, her fingers wrapped around a pen in case a story crept in. Her mind had just settled when a memory from dinner jerked her upright, spilling a small drop of tea onto her blanket.

"Damn." The word tumbled from her mouth, and she wiped away the spot of tea, now remembering the foolish acceptance of a date with Adam's new friend. She blamed it on the onslaught of screaming kids and her mother's pleading glances. She didn't know anything about this man. Would never have agreed to another meeting had she met him elsewhere. Worse, AJ would never base her opinion of someone simply on her brother's assessment. In fact, she would automatically assume the worst of a person solely on her continual need to be combative with Adam.

She leaned over, strained to snag her purse, then dug for her phone. She needed to get a grip. It wasn't really a date. More like a welcome to the city. Yes, that was it. She was just helping the guy get more familiar with the place.

The phone rang four times before someone answered. "You survived another family gathering."

"Barely. Adam brought a friend."

"The man never learns."

"This one was different. Not what you'd expect."

"Do tell."

"Even better, do you have some time tomorrow afternoon?"

"Sounds like I better make some."

With a game plan in action, AJ grabbed a book from the end table, took a sip of her tea, and immersed herself in the life of the Incan empire. But she couldn't quite drown out the penetrating gray eyes that haunted her from dinner.

4

The morning sun pierced the light clouds, temporarily holding off the predicted rain. AJ parked her car and gazed at the vacant old inn. Between climbs, AJ often visited the tidal pools nestled near the inn, her other refuge from the world. A far cry from the strenuous activity of the wall, the tidal pools substituted for comfort food, like a warm bowl of tomato soup wrapped in memories of days long ago.

As she stood on the path, the scent of roses mixed with sea salt floated around her and spurred memories of her father. Time spent together, where no one else could mingle, not her mother, and never Adam. With their morning outings, her father chipped away at the secrets of the sea with his explanations of starfish, anemones, and how the tides worked with the pull of the moon.

Though he had been dead well over a year now, AJ still ventured to their old haunts. Now vacant, neglected with time and the ever-changing hands of ownership, the inn sat haunted by the laughter of guests who had come and gone. Stirred by the echoes of stolen kisses and warm embraces, lovers perched on the back veranda, forever watching the setting of the sun.

AJ stared at the front porch and the long, wide veranda that wrapped itself around the building. Rather than head straight for the pools as usual, she turned to the porch. Amazement struck her when she grabbed the handrail. The wood was smooth, as if freshly sanded and stained. The stairs appeared recently swept. In fact, the whole veranda shone—no leaves, no dirt. Images of Adirondack chairs scattered around, the large patio swing swaying in the gentle breeze, the scent of freshly baked cinnamon rolls her father brought with them to share, all swirled through her mind. More memories flooded in. Sitting on the front porch, just returned from the pools, her father weaving stories of pirates, their ships, and their gathering of booty.

A melancholy smile touched AJ's face. She ran her hand along the old paint, surprised it had neither cracked nor weathered. She couldn't remember seeing a For Sale sign, so she didn't think there were new owners. Perhaps the current owners had maintained it through the years, and she never noticed in her hurry to get to the pools. She laughed. Always in a rush to get someplace just to slow down and relax.

AJ trailed to the end of the building where it turned toward the ocean. The sun warmed her skin in the morning light, dissolving the goose bumps raised by the shadowed front porch. The maintenance of the place seemed thorough. Freshly scrubbed windows caught the reflection of the ocean, and even the small yard had been landscaped with native plants and a few partially tended roses. Breaking away from the tranquil scene, AJ sighed. The inn wouldn't sit empty forever. She needed to enjoy her retreats before the place changed.

She headed back, now feverish to explore the pools, but as she reached the path that forked to the left, a noise made her pause. She tilted her head to the side and heard it again. A low creaking sound came from her right, where the path led down to a dock floating in a small bay. When the inn had been open, guests had used the dock to enjoy a good meal or splurge on the comforts of land for a night or two. But it now lay abandoned, lost to time and the elements.

Curiosity pulled her to the right. Leaving the tidal pools behind, she wove her way down to the dock. Fog nestled into the bay and swirled around, the warming sun unable to dissipate it. By the time she had traveled halfway down the path, the dock all but disappeared, nothing left but a vague outline, false images from her hundreds of visits over the years. Her skin crawled. It reminded her of the fog from her last climb, how quickly it had moved in, how the temperature hadn't dropped with the fog, and, as dense as it was, the lack of moisture.

Focused on the faded skeleton of the dock, AJ waited for the next sound. Instead, something materialized out of the fog. At first, she couldn't make sense of what she saw and stepped back, the object much larger than the dock. A low sound, different from before, urged her forward, her steps tentative, her arms pulled around her as if warding off a chill. She recognized the sound of slow, lazy waves slapping against the hull of a boat. She assumed a small boat, but what appeared, drifting in and out of the fog, wasn't any sailboat, at least not the size she would have expected.

The ghostly image of an immense ship emerged through the dense mist. A tall wooden mast rose high into the sky, its sails tucked neatly away. Dozens of ropes dangled from the mast, disappearing into the fog. The mast rocked back and forth, each small movement rolling in and out of focus. Then it vanished.

AJ rubbed her eyes and considered pinching herself. Her imagination was playing tricks on her, or maybe it was the stress from work. But no, she could still hear the faint creaking, the waves lapping against the hull. A stronger smell of the sea overtook her, and she tasted salt on her lips. She stared at the spot at which she had last seen the image, straining to force it back by sheer will, but the fog grew denser. Thick white tentacles of mist swirled around her, and the air grew quiet. She blinked. She strained to hear the sounds of the ship again, but she heard nothing. No waves, no birds, just silence.

Her interest piqued, a small shiver of apprehension tickled her. She crept toward the dock. The thickness of the mist wrapped itself around her, making the ground invisible. She called upon her rusty memory to stay on the path. Enveloped by a sense of disconnection, AJ's desire to see what was there overrode any sense of good judgment or concern for her safety. The soft lilt of the waves brushed the dock, and its worn old timbers came into view.

As if the fog itself had been a fabrication, the mist dissolved into the warm spring air, the sun once again taking ownership of the day. In mere seconds, the dock rematerialized and the sun sparkled on the water, casting bright reflections off the incoming waves. The sounds of squawking gulls returned. A slight breeze rustled her curls, cold against her skin as she stared at nothing. No ship. No masts. Just an empty dock.

AJ gazed at the dock and the open ocean for several long moments, then whipped around, expecting the ship to be behind her. Nothing.

She couldn't explain what had happened, but this ship looked just like the one she had seen on her climb. The day the fog had come from nowhere. Just like today. With no clear answer to her questions, the desire to explore the tidal pools vanished. AJ trudged back to her car, her attempt to restore herself shattered. A hysterical laugh bubbled up. Her quest for inspiration had turned her mad.

"The windows need cleaning."

Joseph's voice whispered in Helen's ear as she surveyed the backyard from the large picture window. A soft sigh escaped her. She would have to change the gardener's seasonal schedule. At times, the number of chores daunted her to the point of guilt. Perhaps she spent too much time with her friends. Quite capable of performing most of the household tasks, she should carve out time for them. But having promised Adam to lighten her chores, and to keep the peace, she hired others to perform the larger household duties Joseph and she had once tackled on their own.

She finished her tea and, as she she rinsed her cup, a melancholy smile appeared. Joseph's soft voice murmured in her memory, and his warm breath skimmed along her neck, laughing at her idea to make a list for spring cleaning. Each year, bit by bit, it didn't get any easier.

A knock sounded at the door as Helen marched to retrieve a pad of paper. A deep jolt pierced her, a sorrowful memory of the day he died. She hesitated, then slowly released her breath.

A familiar voice called out.

"Mom, it's me."

When Helen entered the living room, AJ stood in the foyer, bouncing on her toes and tucking curls behind her ears. Her daughter's eyes darted around the room, a habit of Adam's rarely seen in AJ.

"What are you doing here so early? Is everything all right?"

AJ's eyes flashed to her mother's, and she stopped bouncing. "I'm sorry. I should have called first."

Helen smiled and gazed into her daughter's soft brown eyes, the same color as her own. Joseph always spoke of their eyes. Warm and friendly, he said, except when they got a fire under them. Then small slivers of gold would flash, striking terror through him, and he would laugh.

"It's okay. It never seems to go away."

AJ removed her sweater, dropping it next to her bag. "I thought you were going to keep your doors locked during the day."

Helen relaxed with her daughter's admonishment. Everything was okay; no one was dead. "I never seem to remember. I'll start a pot of coffee. I could use a break." Helen turned back toward the kitchen, one hand fingering the pearls at her neck, the heels of her pumps clicking on the floor. "I was starting to make a list."

"A list? That's new." AJ followed her mother to the kitchen, finding her usual spot at the counter, moving the stool to face the yard now bursting to life with spring.

They fell into a natural silence. Helen finished the coffee and set out the accoutrements, keeping an eye on her daughter. AJ's shoulders seemed to relax from the tension that moments ago had wrapped around her, holding her like the casing of a moth trying to fly free. Helen poured the coffee and settled on a stool.

AJ poured the cream, turning the coffee a rich caramel color, and took a few sips of the concoction, drumming her fingers on her cup. "Have you been out to the old inn recently?"

Helen's eyes widened. AJ had often visited the place, a haven to calm her raging spirits, and she hoped something hadn't happened to change that. "It's been a few months since I've visited. The place never belonged to me, unlike you. I prefer the point by the lighthouse."

AJ looked out to the garden. "It was strange weather today. A dense fogbank settled in, then it just disappeared. I've never seen anything like it."

"I don't remember the weather report mentioning anything strange. I would have heard something on the coastal report." Helen stirred her coffee. Stiffness returned to AJ's shoulders.

"It was pretty quick. Maybe it didn't show up long enough for anyone to report it." AJ turned from the window. "Why are you making a list?"

Helen grinned. "It seems I took for granted all the work Joseph did around the house." Pensive, she added cream to her coffee and continued to stir. "All I can remember are the road trips, the hunt for antiques, or your father burying himself in his study, exploring some new book he found."

"I thought it was Adam who didn't enjoy the road trips."

"Oh, it was. But it's what comes to mind when I think of your father. The best of times. He loved sharing his passion with you. He was so delighted when it became your own. The road trips were mine. I loved seeking out new places, just for a different reason than your father's. It's too bad Adam never found any interest in it."

"Well, Adam always had you." AJ slid a glance to her mother, an apology ready.

"He was a geek, wasn't he?" Helen shook her head. "Mothers and sons."

AJ laughed. "I didn't think you knew what a geek was." She turned her attention back to the yard, letting the silence blanket them. "Have you ever seen things through the fog that you knew were there but weren't?"

Helen's face lit up with a small chuckle. "I used to always see things and point them out to your father. He would laugh and shake his head at me. No, he'd say, that's not it at all, look closer. He was always right, of course. If I studied the spot a little longer, the shape would turn into something entirely different." She took her first sip of coffee. "After a few years, your father stopped saying no and would let me ramble, describing in detail what I thought I was seeing. I believe he enjoyed listening to my little fantasies."

AJ pushed back in her chair. "He had a way of making everyone feel like the most important person in the room. I remember how patient he was, letting me follow him around the dusty old antique shops, asking a million questions. He always listened to the childish stories I'd make up about some object I found. What I remember most is how his eyes twinkled when he found some treasure in a stack of moldy books."

Both women smiled, comfortable with each other, lost in their own memories.

Breaking the moment, AJ took her cup to the sink. "I need to get to the office." AJ gave her mother a quick hug and strode out to the living room.

Helen followed. "Are you okay, honey?"

AJ kept her back to Helen as she put on her sweater. "Sure. Thanks for the coffee." Pausing, she picked up her bag and turned back, a small grin on her face. "We should do this more often."

Helen watched AJ drive away. Deciding her daughter had worked through her problem, she turned back to the kitchen to start her list.

———

DRIVING AWAY, AJ let the tears flow, allowing them to run their course. It had been right to go home. She meant what she said about stopping by more frequently, repeating her resolve to be a better daughter. But when the tears dried, other thoughts crept in —a foggy vision materializing into a large sailing vessel before dissipating into the mist.

5

The rain pounded after AJ as she ran from her car to the newspaper office. She treasured the bustle of mornings, the busiest time for the small staff. But her continuing drought of inspiration made walking through the door each morning a struggle. The decibel level of the office assaulted her senses, and she longed for the balm it had provided her just a few short weeks ago. Even the smell of the printing presses, leaking through the walls from the back room, couldn't raise her spirits. These were rare days when AJ longed for a quieter atmosphere and a drab gray cubicle to hide in.

AJ greeted her fellow staffers with a perfunctory smile and squirreled herself away at her desk, sighing when she saw the bright green sticky note next to the keyboard. She refused to admit relief at the list of tasks given to her for the day, even though it meant she wouldn't have to find her own.

Newspapers in large urban areas dwindled across the country, whereas many small-town papers still ran strong. The success of the *Baywood Herald* lay at the feet of its owner and editor, Samuel Taylor, who had a flair for blending national and local news with colorful feature articles. His favorite stories, and one of the attractions that brought AJ to the paper, were the in-depth historical accounts of the town and local communities.

AJ barely lived on the salary, but she couldn't have found a better place to work. Most days. Being the feature editor of the historical column gave her a large scope to research, which, until recently, seemed to be fertile ground. But these days, everything became rote, and she couldn't see a way to spark life into her choice of articles.

"I wish you'd tell me what you're working on."

AJ groaned when Samuel peered over her shoulder. "I thought you were gone." AJ pointed to the sticky note. "I see I have my list of activities."

"I was. Forgot something. Just wanted to see what you have on your story. You've been mysterious."

"Oh, this one will be worth it." AJ turned to her computer. If only he would take the hint.

"Well, they always have been. I'll leave you to it." Samuel scratched at the thin white hair that trailed over his balding head like gossamer webs. After a few seconds, he patted AJ on her shoulder. "But I really need those other items done too."

"Okay." AJ read the note Samuel left for her. His list of tasks left little time for her own assignments. Samuel knew how to run the business, but he disappeared frequently these days, leaving AJ long lists of his own stories for her to research. Blowing out her breath, she scooted up to the keyboard. She should consider these tasks a blessing—they might spark some overdue inspiration.

At the noon hour, AJ settled back into her chair and propped her feet on a neighboring chair, giving her neck a break from the computer. Her fingers drummed against a cup of freshly brewed tea as she mentally checked off her small list of accomplishments. She rubbed her temple. There had been no spark to motivate her next story. Her inventory of filler pieces would dry up if she didn't find an angle soon.

She sipped her tea, then inwardly cringed. Staying busy allowed her to ignore her looming appointment with Adam's mysterious friend. She lowered her cup and leaned her head back. "Appointment" seemed the wrong word, but "date" seemed worse. AJ banished Ethan to a small corner of her mind, compartmentalizing him to a blip in her day.

Five minutes later, she jerked awake to find the last of her tea dribbled on her jeans. Cursing, she sneaked a peek to catch any witnesses, but the office was empty. Damn it. Clara and Robert never seemed to run out of stories, as they were lucky enough to cover current events. She rolled her shoulders and slid the green sticky note under the keypad. AJ abandoned Samuel's list in favor of reviewing some of her more recent articles, a last-ditch effort to find a spark for the dry tinder she called a brain, her afternoon appointment easily forgotten.

THE COFFEEHOUSE OCCUPIED a small corner of an old, three-story brick building and shared space with a local bank. Customers of the neighboring businesses and local residents kept the small café hopping with social activity. This afternoon didn't seem any different to AJ when she entered the café from a small side door.

The din of chattering people and the humming espresso machines confirmed AJ's suspicions that finding a seat would be difficult. Entering by the side door kept most of the café hidden from view, allowing her to observe the patrons without being spotted herself.

She'd forced herself from the office to keep this appointment. But she had reached a stalemate staring at her computer, and she desired a change of scenery, even this one. The heady aroma of fresh coffee pierced her senses and cleared the fog settling over her. She should carry a purse-sized baggie of freshly roasted coffee beans—one quick sniff every hour would do the trick.

She turned the corner and searched the main room. Books, newspapers, and computers occupied most of the tables. A few couches held small groups of people who preferred the personal connection of talking with others, albeit with the help of hand-held devices.

Her smile turned to a grimace when she spotted Ethan watching her. He sat at one of the high tables next to the window, his dark hair immaculately in place, augmenting the severity of his face. The tallness of the table emphasized his height, accentuating his almost princely appearance. His gaze seared her, just like their first meeting, but his small smile offset the intensity. Something interesting hid beneath that smile, and AJ forced herself to pick her way through the crowd to the grinning Ethan.

AJ dropped her handbag on the table. "Sorry I'm late. The place is busier than normal. I'm surprised you were able to find a table. I don't remember it being this busy so late in the day." *Good grief! Stop blabbering.*

Ethan's smile widened. He held a large cup of coffee, most of it already gone. "I've been here for a while." His voice, deep and rich, held a trace of what AJ now recognized as an English accent. "I had an early day and decided to walk around town. It's given me time to watch people, something I do a great deal of in my line of work."

Ah yes, the security business. She relaxed against her chair, her fatigue dissipating. "Of course, that makes sense. When most of us people-watch, we think of what they could be planning for their day. Shopping, going to an appointment, plans for dinner. Are they going to meet a clandestine lover? You're wondering if they're planning on robbing a bank." AJ meant it as a joke, but the statement fell flat.

Ethan didn't seem bothered. "You'd be amazed at the devious nature of most people. Smiling at you, while all the time wanting to slit your neck from ear to ear." He studied her reaction, his response calm.

31

AJ stared back. "I guess you security types do see a monster behind every face. I suppose it makes us safer, but I wouldn't think it does much for your willingness to trust anyone." She removed her sweater and prepared herself for the next volley of words.

Instead, he surprised her by standing. "How do you like your coffee?"

"Black, a touch of cream."

He glided among the patrons to the counter to order their drinks. Even with his height, he seemed to meld with the crowd. But it had to be an illusion, an act for him, a practiced style he could turn off and on.

Ethan returned with their coffee, and his gaze swept the room. "So tell me about your favorite era."

Her eyes widened, and a flush of adrenaline seized her. "I have to admit it's the Renaissance of Europe, but I'm also intrigued by the turn of the century and the Industrial Revolution."

She leaned in, swept up by the hands of a master. He questioned her about the time periods she chose, extracting the information like a practiced investigator.

AJ shook her head and smiled. "You seem to know your history. Do you have a favorite era?"

"Not really. It all fascinates me, but I'm strongest with eighteenth-century Europe."

AJ's tiredness vanished as the two of them fell into a comfortable discussion about history, amazed to discover their shared knowledge and interests. She grew animated when they discussed the French Revolution, and the continual political intrigue and war that shaped events impacting millions of people.

AJ found Ethan's comments precise and clinical, but she didn't believe he was capable of falling into the past as she so often did. There was only one way to find out. AJ steered the conversation to the folly of the French, who allowed the return of the autocracy with Bonaparte after such a bloody rebellion.

"You would think they would have remembered what perils they were allowing to happen again." AJ understood the naivety of her statement and the complexities of those times, but she delighted in their discussion. She hadn't shared a deep foray into history with anyone since her father. With Ethan's keen insights, she decided to rattle him, see if any emotions lay under that haughty exterior. She smiled when she discovered his weak point.

"You don't believe the people had a choice in this." Ethan sparked at AJ's whimsical statement, his words sharp and heated. "There was no right to vote. No ability for the people to make their own decisions in these matters. It was a time for one more group of power-seeking men to take over from another. Their only thoughts were to their own comfort and welfare disguised as a savior to the people."

So there was something a little dangerous behind his wall. AJ could be fanatical about history, but her obsession didn't hold a candle to Ethan's. She hid her grin and sipped her cold coffee.

Ethan stopped. He sat back with a new appraising look. He laughed. "I guess your aim hit its mark."

"I was curious to see which of us was more over-the-top than the other." AJ laughed in return. "You win."

"Win what?" Stella stepped up to the table, dropped her purse, and dragged an empty chair from another table. "The traffic was a bear. I was across town showing a house, and I swear, the tourists seem to arrive earlier each year." She unwrapped her scarf and removed her sweater, making herself at home, seemingly oblivious to having interrupted anything.

AJ shot Ethan a quick glance of apology, but found him entertained by watching her friend create her own environment among them. She couldn't decide if she should be happy or annoyed by Stella's presence. She leaned back, tugged at a curl, and watched Stella take over. It was AJ's own fault. She had been the one to ask Stella to stop by, afraid to be stuck babysitting

Ethan. She'd had no idea how enjoyable their conversation would be and had forgotten all about Stella.

If Stella gleaned her disruptive presence, she didn't show it. She gave Ethan a slow smile, then stared at AJ. After a short silence, she sighed. "Well, I guess I'll introduce myself. I'm Stella, AJ's long-time favorite friend. Sometimes I think her only friend." Stella embraced Ethan's hand when he reached out for a handshake, and held on a little too long. His smile charmed in return as he squeezed her hand.

AJ groaned. Ethan was either enchanted or enjoyed participating in other people's games.

"I completely forgot I asked you to drop by if you had time." AJ folded her arms and turned to Ethan. "I think my mother mentioned I had a friend in real estate. This is her."

"Well, isn't that a great testimony to my talents." Stella pouted.

"Sorry, you're right. Stella is one of the best Realtors in town."

"Ah yes, I do remember Helen mentioning it. I could use the help. I'm getting tired of the hotel life." Ethan's manner cooled. The earlier excitement of history faded with the return of the security expert.

A barista swooped by and dropped a cup of coffee with a mound of whipped cream in front of Stella.

"Stella has everyone in Baywood pretty much working for her." AJ didn't bother hiding her awe at Stella's ability to get direct table service, one of the few in town afforded the honor.

"I do favors for people, and I reap small rewards. Nothing wrong with that." Stella blended the whipped cream into the coffee, savoring each movement.

Ethan seemed to hang on Stella's every word. He studied her, watchful and aware. There was no doubt he must be good at his job.

"I'm sorry to have to leave after you just arrived." Ethan stood. "But I have another appointment."

"Really? That doesn't seem fair." Stella looked to AJ for help.

AJ shrugged. She gave Ethan another look, trying to see him from Stella's perspective. Taken as a whole, he was attractive and shared her fascination with history. But the eyes gave her pause. Those gray eyes, one moment dark and scrutinizing, the next sparked with an inner light, bright and alive with animation.

Could anyone truly know or trust him? She would like to have time to learn more. But now wasn't the time. "I thought I was supposed to guide you around town?"

"I'm quite well-versed on your town. I've spent hours getting familiar with it." Ethan smiled and handed Stella a business card. "I suppose I should have mentioned that at dinner."

AJ's mouth dropped open. She lifted her cup to her lips. Empty. *He's a sly one.*

Ethan turned to AJ and his words held a note of challenge. "We'll need to return to our discussion of history. When you have the time."

He moved effortlessly through the crowd, and in a moment, he was gone.

"Well, that was interesting. You never mentioned he was tall, dark, and mysterious. What do you think he's all about?" Stella continued to watch the door after Ethan left.

AJ stared at her empty cup. "That's a very good question."

THE VIEW from his office stretched along the rocky coast for miles in both directions, and Ethan could watch the sea roll in or, as with this late afternoon, witness the sun's quiet stroll to the horizon. It was a sight that captured him in a trance. The vision reminded him of home, and a yearning for those times burned deep inside him. Dangerous days, a reckless youth, brash and headstrong, fighting those around him through insolence—his way of dealing with abandonment and isolation. He understood it all now, but not then, when forced to carve his own way in an inhospitable world at such an early age.

His rage at his parents, at the life handed to him, all worked to his advantage now. He sometimes wished he'd known this at the time, but he'd traveled too far on his current path to bemoan his past. He wasn't the first boy to face hardship before discovering his path, his journey guided him in directions he would never have chosen for himself. His days of worrying about where the next meal would come from, and whether he'd have to fight for it, fell far behind him. Fate—or was it destiny—interceded in the days he'd spent proving himself. His tale remained too far from complete to answer that question.

A soft buzz signaled someone entering the offices. He gave one last look to the setting sun, then glanced at the clock. He had no appointments scheduled this late. Ethan packed a few of his files into a small attaché and waited for the sound of footsteps. He tensed. Years of training prepared him for the unknown, even in this office, in this small town. Adam stuck his head into the open door.

"Ethan, I was hoping to catch you." Adam moved into the room and gave it a slow once-over. "Fabulous view. I always wanted a view like this. Not sure I'd ever get anything done."

"I admit it can be a distraction, but it's still worth it." Ethan finished assembling his files and closed the case. "What brings you this way?"

Adam stood in front of the floor-to-ceiling windows, gazing out to sea. He rocked back and forth, like a Weeble toy set in motion. "I could make something up about business before getting to the point." Adam slipped Ethan a sheepish look. "But I'm pretty sure you'd see right through my subterfuge."

He stared out the window, hands fumbling at something in the pockets of his suit, his usual take-charge attitude held in check.

Ethan laughed, realizing Adam's intent. "Do brothers still

watch after their younger sisters, especially when they're both adults?"

Adam laughed in return, although it seemed half-hearted. "See, that's why I made sure the firm hired you. You're a smart one, can't pull one over on you." He took a hesitant step toward an abstract print and studied it. He glanced at Ethan and then back at the print before taking another small step to another print.

"You're the one who introduced us. Are you having second thoughts now?"

"No, no." Adam stopped in front of a large wood-framed map displaying Baywood and the surrounding region. "I wanted to make sure everything was going okay. My sister can be a hard one to get to know."

Adam moved on to an ornate bookcase, taking in the wide selection of books, some related to the security business, a few legal books, a great many books on Oregon, and several on current events. "You have a sweet variety of books here."

"It keeps me up-to-date in my work." Ethan studied him.

Adam perused the office, getting his swagger back, taking control of the meeting. By the way his body relaxed, seemingly unafraid of the silence, he was no doubt planning his next move. He belonged in front of a jury.

"So you two got along okay?"

"We've only had one coffee together." Ethan held his smile in place. "And even then we were interrupted."

Adam's slow stroll around the office halted. Finding himself in front of another bookshelf, he randomly pulled out a book and flipped through it, paying no attention to the subject.

"Oh? Who was that?" Adam asked.

"A woman by the name of Stella. Apparently my new Realtor. Are you interested in history?" Ethan sat on the corner of his desk and folded his arms, waiting to see which topic Adam would land on.

"Oh, not really." Adam sounded disappointed. "Seems you can't get one without the other following close behind these days."

He shoved the book back on the shelf, his gaze lingering on the title. The case held a collection of history books for the last couple hundred years, many of them on the wars of the world from Napoleon to the World Wars, Korea, and the Vietnam conflict.

"Your tastes are pretty wide-ranging." Adam shoved his hands in his pockets. "Guess I'm jumping the gun checking up on her."

Ethan, tired of Adam's musings, collected his attaché and turned Adam to the door. "Let me walk you out. I can give you complete assurance I will be a perfect gentleman with AJ. But, based on our two brief meetings, your sister appears to be able to handle herself."

"Yes, yes, no question there." Adam allowed himself to be guided out the door. "You won't say anything to her, about me stopping by?" His gaze appeared earnest. "I wouldn't want her to know I was watching out for her."

"Your secret is safe." Ethan didn't believe Adam's concern for his sister's welfare. He'd witnessed the friction between the two at their family dinner. "Do you have anything for me yet?"

"No, but soon. I haven't forgotten."

Ethan walked him out, all the way to the street. "I appreciate you coming over, Adam, and thank you again for inviting me to your family gathering. You didn't need to do that."

"No problem. Thanks for keeping it between us."

If Adam had something to share, Ethan couldn't see it. "Sorry to be rude, but I have an appointment. I'll wait for your report." He turned and walked away. He had his own agenda, and, unless Adam's issues conflicted with his own, he didn't care what the man was up to.

ADAM WAITED until Ethan was a good block away before turning into an alley and, falling against the hard brick of a building, calmed his breathing. A small drizzle started to fall, and he leaned his head back to let the water wash away his troubles.

"What were you thinking?" he said aloud. He drew in a ragged breath and waited for the anxiety to pass. He hoped Ethan could be the one to help him out, but he was already too close to his sister. And now Stella was involved. He'd have to find another way.

"Mr. Moore."

Adam spun around at the sound of his name. He paled. He hadn't heard the man approach, surprising for the size of him. "Jeb."

"You're overdue on a payment." Even in early spring, Jeb's bare arms bulged with tanned muscles. His full beard hung well below his chin. A patch on his worn denim vest confirmed his name. A matching patch labeled him "enforcer."

"No." Adam's voice squeaked, and he tried to pull away from Jeb's hot breath, foul from afternoon drink, but the wall prevented escape. Jeb stepped back, and Adam gulped in fresh air. "I still have a couple of days."

"Victor didn't say anything about that."

"It was arranged. Just yesterday. I swear."

Jeb chuckled, a low, cold sound. "I know. I just wanted to make sure you knew how serious we were." His filmy blue eyes pinned Adam in place for a few seconds. Then he turned and disappeared around the corner.

Adam didn't take another breath until he heard the sound of Jeb's chopper start and the loud engine fade into the evening traffic.

The mist turned to a light shower. Adam pushed away from the building, glanced down the street to make sure no one was there, and hurried back the way he had come.

No choice now, he had to follow through on his original plan.

6

"Are you sure? We've barely looked at anything." Stella yelled above the wind, her hair whipping about her face, hands clasped around the steering wheel like an Indy driver. The forecast promised a dry spring day, so she took a chance with putting the top down.

She sneaked a quick glance at the man who filled the space next to her. Thinner than she preferred, his aquiline nose accented the sharp features of his face. His tailored suit and coiffed hair complemented the controlled intensity of his eyes. He sprawled across the front seat, legs tucked into the small space of Stella's sports car, arms dangling, head swiveling to take in the sights. Her question seemed superfluous. She doubted Ethan had any problem making a decision.

"I don't need much to be comfortable." Ethan turned away, his voice barely heard above the wind. "It reminds me of my childhood." Sitting straighter in his seat, he pulled at the cuffs of his shirt. "It meets my needs. No reason to spend time on useless pursuits."

On no more than a whim, Stella had stopped by the old eyesore after touring three other places. Ethan had mentioned he might like something on the coast, though she envisioned him living closer to town. But she drove to the house that flanked the edge of an older neighborhood. It hovered on the point, cast off like someone's disapproving uncle. She planned more of a drive by, and was shocked when Ethan asked her to stop. The house proved to be as dreary inside as it appeared at first glance, which explained why it still sat empty, even with its spectacular ocean view. The well-constructed house sported too many small rooms, and the dark wood paneling imbued a bleak atmosphere. Ethan didn't seem to care.

"I wish all my clients were as easy as you. I swear, some of them look at the same house twenty times before settling on a completely different house they've only seen once." Stella laughed. "It would drive me crazy if it wasn't exactly something I'd do."

Ethan returned a smile. "I met AJ's family the other night."

"I heard Adam brought you."

"My company just signed with his firm. Being new to town, he was kind enough to invite me."

"I thought you knew Adam." Stella raised an eyebrow and shot him a quick glance. "You recently came to town and already signed a contract. My, you are a fast worker."

"It was a little more involved than that. We wanted to ensure we had the business before making the move."

"Oh, I guess that makes sense."

"So what's your take on Adam?"

Stella contemplated the question. She didn't want to squirrel whatever deal he had with Adam, and had no desire to create a problem that could fall back on AJ. "He's an okay guy, a good family man."

"Oh, it's like that, is it?"

"No," Stella sputtered. "He's a nice guy. Good with his family, does a lot of stuff in the community."

"It sounds like a lot of fluff, not the true nature of the man. I'm sorry. It wasn't meant to put you on the spot."

"Look. I don't want to cause any problems for Adam. He's a nice enough guy, just not someone I'd spend a lot of time with."

"I was curious if you thought he was trustworthy. Does he toe the line in business?"

Stella released her death grip on the wheel. "Do you think he's doing something illegal?"

Ethan shook his head and laughed off her concern. "No. Nothing like that. I like to get a sense of a man through his friends. In this case, his family's friends are all I know, and I don't know anyone very well. I have my first impressions, and being in security, I'm a careful man."

"It just threw me off. Thinking you had known Adam awhile." Stella kept her eyes on the road as she drove through downtown, dying to sneak a peek at him. But with the warm spring day, early tourists flooded the streets, forcing her attention elsewhere.

"Why don't we stop for lunch and you can tell me more about your town?" he said.

"I know the perfect place." Stella pasted on a smile, but deep down, a large yellow caution flag waved. She tried to reconcile the successful, engaging businessman beside her with the man who asked uncomfortable questions. He might be trying to get acclimated, but she would bet her next commission check he wasn't telling the whole story. She just needed time to work her charms.

WHILE STELLA DROVE Ethan around town, AJ found the newspaper office bustling with activity. An accident involving one of the city councilmen blocked a main intersection for more than an hour. Envious that Clara or Robert had something to write about, AJ spent another morning shifting paper from one side of her desk to another, unable to concentrate on her own article.

"You have anything for me to read yet?"

AJ shook her head, tired of Samuel's frequent visits. "You'll like it better if you wait for the finished draft."

"Great. Fantastic. Can't wait to read it." He gave her a long troubled look before heading back to his office.

She could never lie well, and of course he had seen right through her. Not only had she not started on the weekend story —she had failed to produce any inspiration. AJ stared at the blank computer screen, the blinking pointer mocking her inability to focus, her mind as foggy as the pier. The talk with her mother had calmed her after the weird experience at the inn, but now the uneasiness returned. Something had happened she couldn't explain. She shuffled the investigative reports, old newsprint and scraps of notes around on her desk, hoping one of them might ignite her muse.

By midafternoon, AJ tired of rearranging her desk, and she once again faced her menacing computer. Instead of working on her article, she opened her internet browser, the search jumping from old sailing ships to strange appearances at the coast to the fog and weather forecasts. The results were as disconnected as her experience had been—a great deal of information, but nothing to relate the bits together. She found stories of old ships that sailors claimed to have seen magically appear and disappear from the horizon. All of them tall tales of ghost ships going back hundreds of years, the most popular being the *Flying Dutchman*. The more current accounts carried scientific reasoning behind them, such as superior mirages or a fata morgana.

AJ lost interest, turning her attention back to her elusive topic for the weekend edition when footsteps approached. Her routine reply to Samuel rested on her lips until she saw the figure stop. She sat back. "Adam? Is everything okay? Mom? Madelyn, the kids?"

Adam passed her a perplexed glance. "Yes, yes, everything is fine. Didn't mean to scare you." His last words turned into a laugh that fell flat. "I guess I've never been to your office before." Adam's eyes shifted around the room, never quite reaching hers.

AJ settled into her chair. Her alarm evaporated as she recognized his nervous tics. She couldn't remember the last time he seemed out of his element, but as strange as it was to her, he seemed to be on the defensive, trying to figure out how to ask her something.

"No. I don't think you have. It's a definite surprise." Let him squirm. She went back to moving papers. Adam wouldn't know she spent the entire day doing the same menial task, resulting in nothing but slow and painful time consumption.

Adam scanned the office. "I heard you went out with Ethan."

"I didn't *go out* with him." Too defensive, but she couldn't stop being the petulant little sister.

"Oh, I thought that's what he said." Adam turned his attention back to AJ, his trial maneuvers taking over. "Didn't you go to some coffeehouse?"

"It wasn't a date. It was coffee. A quick get-together before playing tour guide." Although it had annoyed her at the time, now it seemed like a saving grace. "And Stella was there."

"Of course she was," Adam said, just loud enough for her to hear. "Well, I wanted to stop by and make sure it all went okay." His eyes darted around the room again. "You know, since I introduced you two, I was having some misgivings about it."

AJ sat up. "What do you mean? You just signed a contract with his firm."

Adam leaned back against a neighboring desk. "And we're still happy with our arrangement, but that's with his company, not specifically with him." He picked up a photo from the desk, gave it a quick glance, and set it back down. "And, I don't know, the more time I'm around him, I'm not sure he's entirely who he says he is. Wait, that didn't really come out right. It's more that he may not have divulged everything during the discovery portion of our negotiations."

"Why would you think that?"

Adam shrugged. "He doesn't talk about himself. Always asks questions, never opens up about himself. Was he like that with you?"

Her brother's concern for her was unusual, and AJ didn't trust it. Ethan was mysterious, but she'd only had one date—one *meeting*—with him. A meeting cut short by Stella's entrance.

"We didn't talk about ourselves, at least not much." AJ laughed. "We talked about history."

"History? Really? That seems a little odd."

AJ shook her head. "He asked about my interests, and when I said antiquing and history, the talk just flowed. Nothing strange about it. He's well-read on the topic."

"Come to think of it, I did see several history books in his office. Wasn't he interested in your antiquing?"

AJ considered the question, fiddling with a pen on her desk. "I guess we never talked about it once we discovered our mutual passion for history. He doesn't seem like the type to shop for antiques."

"So, have you been out on one of your treasure hunts lately?"

Adam's change of direction made her look up, and she pictured herself in a courtroom, answering questions from the witness box. "Not since my trip down toward Coos Bay a few weeks ago. I haven't had the time."

"Did you find anything interesting? I mean, you usually find something on your trips, even the smallest of things."

Initially surprised by Adam's curiosity, she shrugged it off. Someone always asked her the same question. Whether Stella or her coworkers, they all knew how much she enjoyed her antique hunts. "I did find one small piece of jewelry, so it was worth the trip. Some old estate sale. Those can be the best places to find stuff if you can get their early. I was lucky to discover it. I only found the place after going down the wrong street and getting myself turned around."

Adam's eyes lit up as he leaned forward. "So what did you find?"

Before she could answer, Samuel hustled down the aisle. "Adam. Great to see you, it's been ages. Everything okay with the family, I hope?"

Adam glared at Samuel's intrusion but covered it with a quick smile. "Hi, Samuel. Family's great. I wanted to drop in and say hi to my sis since I was in the neighborhood." Adam shook Samuel's proffered hand.

AJ had caught Adam's glare, but that wasn't anything new; he didn't like any of her friends. Even though she had ducked Samuel for most of the day, she savored the rescue, relieving her from the uncomfortable discussion with her brother. Adam stood and patted his pockets. "Well, I guess I should be getting back to work myself. It was good to see you, sis. We'll have to catch up on your antique trip later. I'd love to hear more." He nodded toward Samuel and showed himself out.

Samuel returned to his same old concern. "You're not having trouble with this weekend's story, are you?"

AJ watched the door, Adam now gone. "No, Samuel, the story is on track. Nothing to worry about."

Ignoring another worried glance from Samuel before he lumbered back to his office, AJ pondered Adam's visit. He had showed up for a reason. But what? He had been curious about Ethan, then dropped the subject altogether to talk about an antique trip. She couldn't piece together what Adam was digging for, but one thing was for sure—he hadn't stopped by just to say hello.

AJ pushed away the disruption of her brother to refocus on her nonexistent story. She only got five minutes in before the office clerk buzzed. She had a caller. AJ answered, hopeful that maybe a story was calling.

"This is AJ. What can I do for you?"

"Always the cheerful one, aren't you?" The warm voice tinged with a light English accent.

She straightened, her mind clearer than it had been all day. She pushed back from the computer, trying to come up with a response, but her brain let her down. "Ethan?"

He chuckled. "Well, at least you remember me. I wasn't sure I made a strong enough impression."

AJ relaxed back into her seat. "It was barely a day ago. I'd like to think I can remember that far back."

"And I was hoping it might have been the stimulating conversation and my charm." His voice held a playful tone.

Tinkering with a pen, AJ jotted down words, never having been good at doodling. "So those security skills of yours tracked me to the paper. Dare I hope you're calling to give me a story I could use?"

Nothing but crickets. Perhaps she had overstepped.

"I might have something for you," he said. "Why don't we have dinner, and we can talk about it?"

Startled, AJ's mind raced. It was bait, but, desperate for a story, she didn't have anything left to lose. She had to break her writing block—her climbing hadn't produced anything.

"Did I put you off?" Ethan's voice sounded like a little boy afraid he wouldn't get supper.

AJ smiled at the image. "No. I got distracted. Dinner would be okay, and I could use some input for a story."

"I'll stop by your office at five tomorrow. I'll try to solve your distraction issue." And with that, Ethan was gone.

At first, the warmth of a blush threatened, but as she stared at the phone, a small twinge of righteous anger flared. He hadn't even waited for a response. She could be busy tomorrow, for all he knew. But the lure of a story softened the discourtesy.

The ping of her cell phone made her jump: a text message from Stella.

"See you at Joe's in five."

AJ laughed and typed back, "Okay." No one cared to ask if her schedule fit theirs. The day had been a complete bust anyway. She'd been scattered again, nothing but birds flying around in the dusty old barn of her brain.

She left the building, her day behind her, yet each step she took tugged at a string, leaving a sense of disquiet. Yesterday's visit to the dock crept in, dogging her, moving in and out of her subconscious like the ship floating in and out of the fog.

By the time she got to the Subaru, the intensity of the moment forced a sharp breath. Every brain cell told her it was nothing but a trick of light and mist.

But her instincts refused to let go of the vision.

7

R aucous laughter greeted AJ as she entered Joe's. A boisterous group of young businessmen had taken over a small section of the bar, beers in hand, recalling their business successes of the day and telling tall tales of the one that got away. Fishing stories or sales stories, they all pretty much sounded the same to her, the next person's bigger and better than the last.

Joe's, a favorite with the locals, provided a homey atmosphere. A tourist or two would occasionally find their way here, revealed to them by some local business. But its off the beaten path location evaded most of the infrequent travelers to Baywood. The restaurant was small, the bar area larger, which seemed fitting for the usual crowd. The pub-style food claimed notoriety for miles around with its fish and chips and to-die-for crab po'boys. The aroma of fish and grease clung all day.

The place geared itself toward the afternoon and happy hour crowds, Joe's main source of income. But the dinner crowd remained steady. Joe sold the place years ago to his dedicated bartender, who had been with him for more than fifteen years. If AJ recalled the story correctly, Joe settled in Arizona, escaping the dampness of the Pacific Northwest to live in permanent sunshine and warmth.

Although Joe had been gone for close to a decade, Tony, the new owner, hadn't changed a thing. The old but much-loved building's décor mirrored any diner in a coastal town, all fish and sea related, with wood-paneled walls adorned with remnants of fishing nets and old buoys. Pictures hung throughout the place of long-ago fishing trips and "catch of the day" remembrances, all from Joe's faithful customers and fishing buddies.

The bar area was filled with wooden tables and chairs, buffed to a fine sheen through the years by the backsides of hundreds of customers. Booths filled the restaurant area, and the old dark blue Naugahyde, softened over the years, never showed it's age, the fabric replaced as quickly as it was torn. The place might be old and the furnishings outdated, but Tony never let the place get shabby.

Another burst of laughter erupted from the bar. AJ turned to the other side of the restaurant, encouraged to see only a handful of booths occupied by early happy hour customers, also driven away from the boisterous bar. AJ seized the opportunity to grab a booth as far from the businessmen as possible. Although she preferred the bar area, today she longed for a quieter setting. Thankfully, Stella hadn't arrived first, or they would have been sitting in the middle of the mayhem, each word shouted in order to be heard.

AJ's first beer arrived moments before Stella fell into the booth, carrying her oversized purse and several bags of nearby purchases. She ordered a martini before the waiter left.

"Another rough day?" AJ took a long slow drink from her pint, licking the suds from her upper lip.

"Nope. This is more celebratory." Stella rearranged her packages, trying, without success, to reduce the footprint surrounding her.

"What did you sell?"

"Not sell, rented on a year lease."

"So we're celebrating with martinis for a rental now." AJ laughed. Stella loved to celebrate the big sales. Now it appeared she was willing to toast to almost anything.

"Not just a rental." Stella seemed pleased with herself. "The McDowell place."

Now AJ understood Stella's excitement. The large, partially furnished McDowell place had sat vacant for almost two years, despite its location near the beach. The house itself was a monstrosity, built decades ago, and difficult to maintain.

"Someone wants to rent the McDowell place? Wasn't it for sale?"

"At this point, the owners will do anything if they can cover the taxes and maintenance. The place is a relic. I don't know what ran through my mind when I agreed to represent it."

"Who would bother to rent it?" AJ's reporter's instinct was piqued.

Stella waited for the first taste of her martini to slide down her throat, folding her napkin into origami-like shapes. She sat back in her seat, smiled like she had eaten two canaries, and lingered for another minute before dropping her bombshell.

"Ethan Hughes."

"Ethan? Of all places to rent, it doesn't seem to fit him." The McDowell house sat on the cliff where she climbed. She would have to be more careful when she made it to the top. She wasn't ready to give up her climbing spot.

"I know, right? I did my usual first tour with him yesterday. I took him to the best place first. It's perfect for him. But you know people don't know what's best for them, so I have to show it to them first, then drag them around forever looking at all the other crap they'll never be happy with."

This was Stella's usual selling routine, and she was tops in her game, one of the most sought-after Realtors in town. She had a knack for sensing people the first time she met them, a sort of second sight into their style, if not the actual person. Unlike Stella, many Realtors never listened to their clients. Most people didn't believe Stella did either, with the amount of talking she did. But it was all a facade, a way of pulling information out of her clients other Realtors never bothered with.

"So right after I took him to the lovely studio over on Wilson Street, the one with those windows and huge rooms, I decided to flip over to something dreary, just to get my point across. So I dragged him over to the McDowell place. The place is dark and the rooms are small. The only redeeming quality are the large bay windows that look out over the ocean. Well, there's also one of those in the master bedroom. But the rest of the place isn't worth those windows. There are other places with great views."

"So how many did you look at today? There couldn't have been many if you're already here celebrating."

"That's just it." Stella leaned over the table to whisper to AJ like she was about to reveal a conspiracy. "I only showed him four. As soon as he stepped in front of the bay window, he stood and stared at the ocean. He didn't even look at the rest of the place. After about five minutes of the staring, he said he'd take it."

"You're kidding." AJ hunched over the table to catch every word.

"I told him the place needed some repairs, and I wasn't sure I could get the owners to fix them. He said he'd take care of it. You could have picked my jaw up off the floor." Stella sat back and laughed. "I tried all day to talk him out of it. We'd only been looking for a couple of hours, and he immediately decides on the worst place? I can't believe I kept trying to undo the deal. Even through our lunch, I kept at it, but he wouldn't budge or tell me why he wanted the crummy old place."

AJ sat back, nodding her head in agreement. "Maybe he'll tell me at dinner tomorrow."

"You have a date with him?"

"He called this afternoon. He mentioned he might have a story for me, so I'm not sure I'd categorize it as a date."

Stella slurped her drink. Waiting.

"He has an enormous knowledge of history." AJ tried to make her response seem reasonable, wishing Stella would stop staring at her. "Maybe he's found something about the town I could use. I'm drawing a blank for this week's edition."

"Hmm. I didn't take him for a history buff, but hard to tell behind all the armor." Stella finished off her martini and ordered a second. "We had lunch for over an hour, and all we talked about was the town and real estate. I couldn't get anything out of him about himself. He's extremely sly."

"You know the same thing happened with me. I'm not sure I asked anything specific, but he didn't divulge any insights."

Stella sipped her water, seeming to mull over her next statement. "He did ask about one thing I thought was strange." Stella played with her paper napkin, opening it and folding it, making triangles, refolding it back to its original shape, her mind deep in thought.

Finished with the napkin already tearing at the creases, Stella looked straight at AJ. "He asked about Adam."

AJ blinked. "Adam."

"Yep. Out of the blue, he asked what I thought of him. I mean, doesn't he already know? He signed a deal with Adam's company. But he said they only investigate the company itself. I don't know. Maybe get to know the president or a partner, but no one else."

Tilting her head, AJ pursed her lips. "That's weird. When I met Ethan at Mom's, Adam made it sound like they were friends." AJ ran the evening over in her head, but she hadn't paid attention when Adam introduced him. She had been on the defensive once again, which blotted out anything Adam said. "Maybe I'm not remembering it exactly right."

"Well, it doesn't sound like they're friends to me." Stella

snatched her phone that vibrated across the table. She took a quick peek and sipped more water. "It might be his nature or his job in security, but he sounded like he was investigating."

"Adam dropped by the paper this afternoon."

Stella sloshed her martini and used one of her origami napkins to dab at the drops that fell on the table. "What did he want?"

AJ sat back. "He was all over the place with his questions." She sprang forward again. "Oh my God. He was digging for some- thing." AJ stared at Stella, her awareness morphing from dawning apprehension to her usual anger at her brother. "I can't believe it —he was trolling for something. He caught me off guard coming to the office, and I never caught on."

"So, what was he asking about? You're killing me here."

Her words came slowly. "He was asking about Ethan. He said he was having second thoughts about introducing us." AJ let out a short, bitter laugh. "As if he was worried about me."

Stella grunted in support. "Yeah, right. But this sounds strange, even for me. What could either of them possibly be doing that would create all this intrigue? Other than giving us fodder for discussion."

AJ stared at her beer. "Not sure."

Stella's phone vibrated again. Without looking at it, she picked it up, dropped it into her purse, and collected her other bags. "I need to run. Can you catch this one?"

AJ waved her hand, her mind already shifting into reporter mode.

"Looks like you have some digging to do at dinner."

Stella's parting words hung in the air long after she left the table. Then something snapped in the back of AJ's mind. She had been so wrapped up in this latest twist of events, she'd forgotten about her episode with the ghost ship. She had hoped Stella could provide a logical explanation. Now it seemed it was hers to either worry over or forget.

8

The next morning, AJ sat in her car, staring at the scene before her. The fog hung low over the sea and surrounding woods, but it was starting to clear. Light from the masked sun fought to break through the last remnants of persistent mist. The fog had already departed from the old inn, framed by a small group of wind-bent trees dripping with the remaining dampness, the dew visible on the grassy areas.

AJ wasn't sure why she came back, and it seemed silly now that she was sitting here. She should have called Stella last night after forgetting to mention the mystery ship while at Joe's. She had been distracted by their discussion about Ethan and Adam, which had resulted in more questions with no answers. Her foray to the inn had receded to the background. Her mom had almost convinced her that her mind had been playing tricks. A result of too little sleep, too much worry over her writing block, and too many distractions. She'd never had an overly active imagination, at least not the type to conjure ghost ships. Her world consisted of facts and historical documentation, whether it was at the paper or with her antiquing.

Yet here she was again, when she should be climbing, forcing her creative juices to flow. Over her morning coffee, she convinced herself that this visit would confirm that the fog had been playing tricks on her. She could put this all to rest, eliminate one distraction. The weather was cooperating, the fog ready to reveal any mystery it might hold—but not with her sitting in the car.

She made her way to the old inn. Adam's visit to the paper popped into her head, and she recalled his questions about her antique hunting. Surely it was meant to distract her about Ethan. Adam abhorred antiquing, hated the road trips he was forced to endure with the family. But figuring out Adam's motives was as elusive as her weekend story or her mystery ship. In only one day, AJ had been surrounded by ambiguities. If only one of them could prove useful for a story.

At the split in the path, she hesitated, unsure whether to take the turn that led to the tidal pools or the one that dropped down to the dock. The sun broke through, but wisps of white haze hung over the bay. For the first time since coming to the inn, she felt trepidation at being out here alone. Perhaps she should turn back and chalk this up to folly. But if she didn't go down and prove it was nothing, she would never get any work done.

She pulled at her lip and stared at nothing for what seemed like hours. This was silly—there was nothing there. AJ stood taller and turned down the path, her strides fueled by a revised interest. As the dock grew close, fog again enveloped her, not as dense as before, but that same fog. No dampness. No cooling from the mist.

The blades of grass had no dew on them, unlike the grass at the top of the hill. The wooden dock, partially visible in the fog, remained dry. Through the fading mist, back in the direction from which she'd just come, rays of light touched the trees, and the sparkle of the dew still clung to the needles.

Her chest tightened and her stomach somersaulted.

AJ searched the path to find the line of demarcation separating the dew-drenched landscape from the dry. She found a fuzzy line where the mist still remained a few short feet away from where she stood at the edge of the dock.

Then she heard it—the sound of lazy waves slapping against something more substantial than the dock, and a second sound she couldn't place. AJ swung around and took a step backward, one hand covering her mouth to stifle a small cry.

The ship was neither as large as she had first imagined nor as small. It blended in and out of the fog, rolling with the tide against the dock, almost hypnotizing her where she stood. She couldn't seem to pull herself away from the sight of the wooden hull, forming just before it disappeared again into the dewless fog.

She found a small rock and tossed it underhand at the ship. It disappeared into the fog but made a small splash in the water, and her relieved laugh sounded mildly hysterical. The ship wasn't real. Her mind was snapping.

Then the fog dissipated, leaving behind the weather-beaten surface of the ship.

This time, AJ selected a larger rock, and, fully expecting the ship to disappear again, she overhanded the throw. The rock landed with a loud thud against the wood. She took a quick step back. The fog folded back on itself, and the first rays of sun poked through the receding mist, revealing more of the ship.

AJ sensed the lightening of the sky around her, but she seemed frozen in place, trying to wrap her mind around the image before her. The ship resolved into greater depth, as if she could reach out and touch it. Breaking free of its spell, she crept closer to the edge of the dock, the mesmerizing movement of the ship reclaiming its hold on her. She stepped closer and leaned over, stretching her fingers toward the ship.

AJ took one final step. The fingers of her right hand wavered, reaching...and touched the hard surface of the hull.

She pulled her arm back. It was real. She waited for the fog to come back, but instead, the sun breached the last defenses of the mist, and she could hear the gulls.

She stepped closer and extended both hands out to touch the side of the ship. Her fingers tapped the wood, surprisingly smoother than she would expect, not that she had any experience with wooden ships.

"Hello." The rich sounding voice floated to her from above.

AJ jumped, pulling her arms back, the unexpected voice making her stumble.

A deep laugh followed. "Watch yourself there. I didn't mean to scare you."

AJ pulled her sweater around her and stepped back to take a better look at the ship. She raised her hand to block the sun, now bright against the azure sky. She couldn't see anyone at the railing, where the voice had come from. All she could see was the tall mast and the sails stowed in tight folds. She scanned the ship but could see no one there—just deck and wood, railing and ropes.

"Are you Mr. Jackson's agent?" The voice came from beside her, making AJ jump again. She hadn't heard anyone approach.

She turned and tried not to stare. A tall, broad-shouldered man stood beside her, dressed in black cargo pants and a white shirt. His laughing eyes and warm, inviting smile made him appear harmless, but with the ship in the background and a lock of hair falling over one eye, AJ could almost imagine a patch.

The man watched her, his gaze inquisitive, as if sizing her up, trying to make a decision. "So are you?"

AJ detected an accent, either Irish or Scottish—she couldn't tell. She shook her head. "Sorry, what?"

"You are a curious one. Did I startle the words out of you?"

AJ blushed. She *had* been staring, dammit. Right into those amazing forest-green eyes. "I didn't know there was a ship here."

He watched her for a second or two longer. "So, I guess you're not the agent?"

AJ finally caught up with the question. "Whose agent?"

"Mr. Jackson's," he said in a weary voice. "He said he'd send somebody." The man turned and swaggered down the dock.

AJ followed behind him. "Who's Mr. Jackson? I don't think I know him."

"Do you know everyone around here?" He stopped at a cleat and retied the rope, testing it to make sure it was secure.

A puzzle piece snapped into place. The cleat. That was the other sound she had heard in the fog—the rope rubbing against it. Then the man's comment registered, sounding slightly rude. "I grew up around here. I don't know the whole town, but I know enough."

"Well, I didn't mean to upset you, lass. I was curious."

Lass. AJ couldn't stop from rolling her eyes. He didn't seem much older than her, yet he talked to her like a child. Her anger flared. "Sorry to have bothered you. As I said, I hadn't heard there was anyone here at the old inn. I wanted to check it out." She didn't want to lie, but she didn't want to try to explain the truth. He'd think she was nuts.

"You didn't know anyone was here, but you wanted to check it out? How did you know there was anything to check out?" That smile was back, but AJ found it annoying instead of pleasant.

"I'm a reporter." The words rushed out, sounding offended. "We investigate things." She sounded like an imbecile, but she couldn't get her brain to work. Too much had happened in the space of a few minutes.

"I see. Well, it's been nice to meet you, Miss Reporter. I have a few things to do yet to settle the ship." He walked up a small gangplank she hadn't noticed before. Once on deck, the man peered at her. Her chest fluttered, but with her simmering anger, she found it easy to ignore.

He leaned over and rested his arms on the railing, a lopsided smile appearing. "I'm sure we'll meet again, lass." He paused a moment and took another full measure of her. "I have no doubt you'll want to investigate further." He turned and disappeared from sight.

AJ stared at the empty railing, shunned and a little humiliated. She walked back up the path, reviewing what had happened. He had been so rude. But she had just appeared, as the boat had, and didn't announce herself. Then she stood there, like some dimwit unable to get a sentence strung together. No wonder he'd dismissed her so readily.

It wasn't until AJ drove away that she remembered, not thirty minutes before, she hadn't even known the ship was there, that it seemed to magically appear. It had to have been the fog playing tricks on her. But the arrogance of the man overshadowed the mystery. *"I have no doubt you'll want to investigate further."* She repeated it in a mocking Irish tone, with a slice of sass. Well, that was one thing he was right about.

9

A J was still fuming when she turned into the small parking lot, delicately shaded by large oak and fir trees. She sat in her Subaru, staring at the old colonial style house, painted a dark sandy tan with red, cream and white trimming. It was a handsome house, with a small flower bed, where spring-blooming irises and peonies announced their show for the year, and a small dogwood tree morphed from flowers to leaves. The wraparound porch matched the dark tan of the house, trimmed by a white-and-cream open railing. Rattan chairs and a table sat empty just off the front door, waiting for their afternoon occupants to enjoy the solitude of the setting.

The house sat on one of the busiest thoroughfares in Baywood, but rarely did anyone hear the bustle of the town tucked a mere fifty feet away from the street. The sign, posted at the edge of the property, reflected the nature of the business and was conservative for the owner of the property.

As much as she wanted to retain her incensed state, she couldn't when surrounded by such beauty. AJ gave in to it, allowing her shoulders to drop, whispering her count to ten, and another ten, the tension breaking its hold and flowing away.

With her head relaxed against the seat, her mind wandered, remembering one of her recent climbs. She remembered the wetness of the ocean spray on her face as she swung for the next hold. She could hear the waves crash in with the tide, then wash away from the churn they created. Her mind jumped to see herself as a small child, racing through the tidal pools to catch what treasures the waves left behind before the next one returned. The sun tanned her face as she ran up the trail from the pools, racing along the cement path before it turned to dirt once more and led her down the other side. She recalled running along the dirt path with tall seagrass waving in the light breeze, the smell of salt in the air, the riotous laughter of the seabirds blending with her own. Her small feet carried her all the way to the dock rolling up and down with the tide, in rhythm with the large sailing ship now tied to the dock. The big-ass ship that had come out of nowhere.

AJ's eyes popped open, her irritation returning. So much for meditation and the power of Zen. The quiet solitude of the shaded lot could no longer hold in her frustration. She spotted the red sports car in the far side of the lot and hoped Stella and a large pot of coffee would bring the salvation she sought.

AJ stepped to the front door and buzzed the bell, providing Stella with a warning of her presence. Not bothering to wait for a reply, she walked into the small entryway, decorated with chairs adorned in bright floral prints and tables dressed with selections of magazines to entertain an array of client interests, from home décor and fashion to financial advice and muscle cars.

Stella's audacious style was apparent in the wide assortment of colors and ornamentation. Reds, oranges, greens, and bright yellows played against walls of pale blue. Flowers filled the air with their lush aroma. Today's scent was lilac. The purple, pink, and white sprays would no doubt appear in every room of the building, changed out every two days to ensure a fresh floral scent. Peeking into the room on the right, AJ confirmed there were no early clients. The over-sized sofa and chairs sat alone, like the chairs on the porch, waiting for clients to lounge, view listings, or peruse contracts.

On the other side of the lobby, AJ walked into Stella's office, as comfortable as it was efficient. Another large floral-covered sofa with matching armchairs sat facing the window to allow a view of the shaded lot. Fresh sprays of lilacs arrayed in a huge crystal vase comprised the only ornamentation on the polished wood coffee table. Two smaller bookcases stood against either side of the walls, framing the room with their cherry finish. None of this décor, however, could compete with the desk with its dark mahogany finish and impressively carved legs. The desk, one AJ had found for her, sat in the middle of the room. Three small drawers ran along one side, leaving the rest of the space open and airy to balance the heaviness of the wood. Another smaller vase of lilacs sat on one corner of the desk. The only items to distract from the pleasant array of vintage furnishings, were the large LCD flat-screen monitor and laptop encroaching on the desk. While Stella surrounded herself in style and comfort, even she required technology to keep the place running.

Grabbing a side chair from the wall, AJ dragged it around to the desk and waited for Stella's appearance. She would know someone was here from the bell, but Stella liked her grand entrances. Right on cue, Stella swept in from the hall bearing a tray, complete with coffee urn, mugs, and accoutrements.

"Morning." Stella, bright and cheerful, didn't seem surprised by AJ's visit.

"How did you know it was me?"

"Only a handful of people would visit this time of morning, and each of you have your own way of announcing your presence. Believe it or not, you're the only one that uses the buzzer before entering."

AJ laughed. "As long as the reward is coffee, I don't care how you do it."

Stella laughed with her, pouring two mugs of steaming coffee, one heavy with cream and sugar. She passed the other caramel-colored brew to AJ, who sipped and almost disappeared into the chair.

"This is heavenly stuff you make, my dear," AJ said. "I should stop by more frequently."

"So what's up? I didn't think I'd hear from you until after your dinner with Ethan tonight."

AJ cringed. After this morning's events, she had forgotten about dinner. "Seems we have another mystery on our hands."

Stella perked up, always ready for new gossip. "Do tell." Stella took a closer look at her friend. "You seem a little off this morning. Are you okay?"

AJ sighed. "I'm not sure where to start exactly." Then the story of her first trip to the dock rolled from her tongue, spilling out all the confusion and doubt she'd held since yesterday morning. "I still can't get the image of the ship, floating in and out of the fog, out of my head."

Stella took a minute to digest everything, then shook her head. "Your mind was playing tricks on you. You know how it is with fog—now you see it, now you don't. I wouldn't worry about it."

"That's what Mom said. And I was planning to ignore it. At least I was, until I went back this morning." AJ took another sip of coffee. The cup jostled when she put it back on the table.

Stella's brows narrowed. "It wasn't foggy this morning."

"It wasn't foggy until I got to the inn. By then it was pretty dense. I walked down to the dock." AJ shook her head, still trying to put the pieces together. "I wanted to confirm in my own mind it was a trick of the weather. That nothing I saw, or thought I saw, was real."

"You're giving me goose bumps here. What did you see?" Stella leaned forward in her chair, both hands grasping her coffee mug.

"The weather was clear at the inn itself, but you could tell there had been fog earlier—everything was dripping. But as I approached the dock, the fog was thick, almost palpable, and you couldn't hear a thing. Which is unusual, right?"

"Sounds can usually be heard better in the fog, but you can't always pinpoint the direction of them."

"Right." AJ couldn't remember any sounds. "I don't remember hearing anything strange until the fog started to clear. Once it did, it seemed almost instantaneous. Then I heard the waves hitting the side of the boat."

"What boat?" Stella almost whispered it.

"Well, when the fog cleared, there was this huge sailing ship sitting at the dock."

"No way. Where do you think it came from?" Stella leaned in even closer.

AJ stared at her friend.

"What?" Stella said.

"Is that all you can ask? Where did it come from? What about how did it appear out of nowhere? Why did it come and go in the fog? Aren't those better questions?"

Stella sat back and gave AJ a long look. "We just said fog can make things disappear. That's not unusual, honey. I'm sure it was there yesterday too, and maybe the fog was too thick for you to see it. Things don't magically appear. You're letting the fog play tricks on you."

AJ wasn't convinced as she sat back, hugging her mug.

"Things have been nuts the last couple days with Adam, and now Ethan," Stella said. "You've been having problems coming up with stories. Now you're letting the fog take you for a ride."

"You're right." Her mom had said almost as much. "Guess I'm not thinking clearly." She laughed, her voice shaky. "And I still need a story for this weekend. Maybe I'm creating one in my head."

"See. You needed to talk it out." Stella pried the mug out of

AJ's hands and refilled it, administering the cream to the perfect color. "You said the ship was huge?"

"It seemed pretty big to me. But that wasn't the strangest thing. It's an old ship, wood and tall masts, ropes hanging from the masts."

"So it's a junky old ship."

"No, not junky at all. I don't mean old like built in the last few decades. I mean old like built a couple of hundred years ago. But it was clean, almost looked new." She wasn't explaining it right. She put her hand up before Stella could speak. "I know, it's old but it looks new. You'll have to see it for yourself. I can't really explain it other than to say it looks like a vintage ship."

"Well then, it's right up your alley. Leave it to you to stumble over an antique boat."

AJ smiled. "I do have a knack for finding odd rarities." She took a long sip of coffee, holding the mug close again, comforted by Stella's reasoning. "I guess the guy on the ship unsettled me after everything else."

Stella nearly spit out her coffee, dropping the mug to the table with a loud bang. "What guy? You go on and on about the fog and some mystery ship, and you're just now mentioning a guy. Like no big thing."

"I guess I should have mentioned him before, but it was the way I discovered the ship that had my mind twisted."

"I agree your mind is not at its peak right now. You're talking to Stella here. You *always* mention the guy first."

The last tidbits of confusion melted away with Stella's simplistic view of the situation. This time, AJ's sigh was long and audible. She leaned her head back. "You're such a good friend Stella. You do see right to the heart of the matter."

"Enough. Tell me about this guy. What did he look like? Was he good-looking? How old?"

AJ raised her hand again. "Whoa, calm down. You'd think you

hadn't been out on a date for months, and I know that isn't even close to the truth."

"Fair enough, but none have been keepers, so I'm always keeping my options open."

"Well, you won't like this one either. He was incredibly rude and condescending."

"You're right, sounds more your type." Stella laughed.

AJ gave Stella a withering look. "He came out of nowhere and half scared me to death. I'm not sure I can put my finger on it. Something seemed off. Maybe it was his overbearing nature. He kept calling me lass."

"Oh Lord, sounds like you dug someone up from the archives. What is he, ninety?"

AJ could only remember the lean muscular frame, the lock of sunlit hair hanging down across his forehead and the piercing, judgmental gaze. A slight tremor ran through her at the memory. AJ turned away from Stella and dug through her purse until she pulled out a small notebook and pen. "Why would he dock at the inn, why not the marina? There are more services there."

Stella pursed her lips. "Maybe he's on a longer trip and stopped there before heading on to his destination. No fees there."

"Maybe." Something nagged her about what he said. She finished the last dregs of her coffee. "Oh, I forgot. He mentioned a Mr. Jackson. He thought I was someone working for him."

"Mr. Jackson? I don't think I know him." Stella turned to her computer, working the keys. "Maybe the guy expected the inn to be open for business. It's been years but maybe he had old information."

"It's possible, I guess. Now that you mention it, the place looked like someone was maintaining it. But still, it's obvious no one lives there."

"Maybe we can find something out about the owner of the inn, then see if it leads us to Mr. Jackson."

AJ's reporter's instincts told her they'd stumbled onto a mystery, one she was suddenly keen on unraveling. A good story could always use a mystery to draw the reader in. She stood to look over Stella's shoulder.

Stella's fingers flew across the keyboard. She moved around the internet, jumping from one site to another, screens flashing faster than AJ could keep up.

"How can you find anything if you're not stopping to read it?" The screen hopping gave AJ a headache. She preferred a more methodical approach when reviewing search sites.

"Just getting warmed up. I need to find a site with information on the old inns. Unless we know the address, I can't bring up any current ownership of the place." A few moments later, Stella stopped searching. "Here we go." Stella showed her the screen.

"This is the site of a company that used to market inns, kind of a co-op for advertising. Some people still advertise this way, the smaller places and stuff. I'm not seeing anything." Stella's search slowed, then she looked at AJ. "Do you know the address of the place?"

AJ tried to picture a mailbox or numbers on the front door or porch. "No. I'm not sure I ever knew it."

Unconcerned, Stella brought up another page. "Let's find it on a map and see if we can figure out the address." After a few more keystrokes, the women waited for the results.

"Well, I can see the street name, but there's no address. This may take a while to figure out. Let's try a search on a Mr. Jackson in the Baywood area."

"Great idea. Search engines seem to have something on all of us these days. That's how I find most of my contacts for stories." AJ edged closer.

Several listings popped onto the screen. Many of the names appeared duplicated. Stella scrolled down the page, opening some of the links to see more details. "I'm still not seeing anything to help us out."

AJ slumped back in her chair. Nothing seemed to go her way these days. Even the internet conspired against her.

Stella slid a glance at her. "Hey, maybe we should try this from a different angle."

"What do you mean?" AJ sprang up.

"Mr. Jackson. Do you think you could dig something up on him? Something from the paper archives."

"Maybe. But, as you just proved, Jackson is a fairly common name, even in a city the size of Baywood. It's not going to be easy." She perked up, reinvigorated. "But I could try to find something on the inn."

"Excellent idea." Stella checked her watch. "I need to get ready for an appointment. Yet another trip back to the same house we've seen three times already."

AJ collected her purse. Stella followed her to the door and surprised AJ by giving her a huge squeeze. "I know this is bothering you. I'm not sure why yet, but we'll figure this out. I have some time this afternoon, so I'll do some digging."

Tears welled up, and AJ squashed them, not knowing where they came from. She forced a smile. "Maybe it's my way of trying to make a softy out of you."

Stella turned back to her office, waving to AJ. "That'll be the day."

10

Several messages awaited AJ when she arrived at the office, most of them from Samuel. The pressure of needing a story within the next couple of days was starting to take a toll on both of them. AJ peered at Samuel's glass-walled office, relieved to see he wasn't there.

"The boss was looking for you again." The sudden appearance of Robert's tall, gangly frame made AJ flinch. At least it wasn't Samuel.

AJ nodded toward his office. "It looks like he left."

Robert looked behind him. "Yeah, the coatrack is empty."

"Samuel and his raincoat." Samuel always kept his raincoat with him, right up to the first of July. At least she wouldn't have to lie about the story.

"Now that Tuesday's paper is out, I'm going to need to know how much space your article will need. Same as usual or you have something bigger?"

Robert's innocent question made her cringe. AJ wouldn't need more space, but she wasn't ready to admit she might not need as much as usual. She decided on the non-committal approach. "Give me another day if you can."

"Sure. Samuel has something big in the works, so he may need more space." Robert shuffled back to his own desk.

AJ could have hugged him. He probably knew that she didn't have even a single word drafted for her story. She turned to her blog, but after an hour of responding to subscriber comments, she was no closer to a story than when she started and found herself glum as well as bored.

Distractedly hitting the keys, AJ gazed around the office and spied Clara at her desk. With the Tuesday edition out, Clara would be updating the latest edition into the paper's database. No better time than now. Relieved to find a distraction, AJ sat up and pulled her keyboard closer.

She typed "Jackson" into the paper's database search field, not surprised to see how many hits filled the screen. AJ scrolled through the listings, clicking anywhere the topic of the article wasn't clearly identified. She searched back ten years, finding only wedding announcements, new business openings, and obituaries. Nothing seemed to tie in with the old inn.

Even though Stella had tried a few hours ago, AJ gave up on the paper's database and tried the name Jackson on the web, adding the name Baywood, hoping to localize the search. She found the same references to the more recent wedding and obituary results, and little else. A few listings appeared to include addresses, but without knowing if it was the right Mr. Jackson, the articles were useless. She assumed he lived close to the inn, so the addresses themselves could prove useful. Might as well send them to the printer. It gave her a place to start.

AJ sat back and stretched, then looked up at the huge clock hanging on the far wall, surprised to see it was lunchtime. She hurried to catch up with Clara, who was leaving her desk. "Are you going to lunch?"

Clara slowed. A harried expression sharpened her thin face, and her bobbed hair, cut at an angle, did nothing to soften her features. With her quick wit and bluntness, she could have been an East coast transplant, but Clara was homegrown and would live here forever, someday running the paper. "Just down to the café. I'm buried."

"Yeah, me too. Mind if I follow?" AJ never understood what kept Clara so busy playing part-time office administrator, but having no clue about all it entailed, she probably shouldn't judge.

The paper shared space in the building with a small neighborhood diner, the Hill Street café. Only open during the weekdays, Hill Street had a tiny seating area, catering more to the carryout clientele. AJ usually brought her own lunch from home, but her current inability to handle the smallest of tasks had taken a toll on her normal routines.

Gazing at the menu reminded AJ of her dinner plans with Ethan. She wished she could find a way out, as her moods hadn't been social lately, but she knew she had to go. Maybe he really did have a story idea for her. Thinking about the evening dampened her appetite, and she decided on an apple and a bag of chips.

On the way back to the office, Clara turned back to AJ, a step behind her. "What were your searching for this morning?"

The question caught AJ off guard, and she hurried to catch up. "What do you mean?"

"You were searching the database. Did you find what you needed?"

"How do you know I was searching for something?"

Clara raised her hands in surrender. "I can't see what you're searching for, just that you're accessing the search command. I was in the system uploading the latest edition."

"Oh, right." AJ was embarrassed by her outburst. "No, I didn't. I was looking for a person, but the name didn't bring up anything more interesting than weddings or funerals."

"That's right. Searching on a single name, especially if it's a common name, could bring up too many possibilities, so the searches are limited."

"I assumed the search would bring up everything."

"We're not Google. Our system is only so big, so we have to give it parameters. You might try combining more related elements to get a different output. Something more than the name or, in our case, the city. You know, are they related to any business, or something more specific to the person?"

AJ stopped walking. Clara took a few more steps before turning back, her response terse. "Wait till you're in the office to have a brain fart. I need to get back." Clara walked on, and AJ, still not sure she'd heard the term "brain fart" come out of Clara's pristine mouth, jogged to catch up with her.

Plopping down at her desk, AJ tried Clara's idea. The only other term she could add was the name of the inn, the Westcliffe. This search proved less productive than her earlier attempts. Frustrated, she gave up and soon lost herself in reviewing old articles, searching for inspiration, even turning to articles in papers from across the country. Nothing resonated with her. She became so engrossed in reading that she didn't hear the approaching footsteps until they stopped next to her desk. She glanced up, expecting Robert or Clara, or worse, Samuel.

"Am I too early?" Ethan's question was casual, as if he didn't care one way or another but wanted to be polite.

AJ was struck again by how tall he was, how handsome. With his dark looks, he seemed broody most of the time, but today a half smile lightened his face.

She stared at him, and visions of wavy brown hair and laughing eyes on an old wooden ship blurred her vision. AJ shook her head to clear the cobwebs. She had started to stray, and saw no reason to compare them. The glance at the wall clock was instinctual—she had lost track of time again.

"No." AJ banished the crazy boat man from her mind. "You're right on time. Let me shut things down."

"Take your time." Ethan took a slow turn around the office, quiet and stealthy. He had a way of blending into his surroundings, a useful skill for his security work, and was just as interesting to watch. He stopped in front of a collection of pictures that, over time, had come to be known as the "wall of history," a wall of old front-page pictures considered the best of their time.

"We haven't added any pictures for a few years now," AJ said. "I guess Baywood has gotten a little boring over the years."

"You're looking at it the wrong way, then." Ethan's scrutiny shifted to her.

"What way is that?"

He returned to surveying the prints in front of him. "I don't see a collection of big, exciting stories. I see a story of the town. How it grew and where it's been. Maybe you've forgotten the point of the wall."

As soon as he said it, she knew he was right. She should have seen it herself, but it had become part of the décor, and everyone had lost sight of it.

Before she knew it, he was standing next to her. "Shall we go?"

AJ stared at Ethan, suddenly interested in what other insights she could garner from this man, who looked at everything from a different perspective. So far, he hadn't been dull.

Ethan selected Serrano's, one of AJ's favorite restaurants, famous for its pasta, fish, and intimate setting. The place was tucked away, down a side street in the heart of town, and she didn't know who could have told him about it. Maybe Adam. The host guided them to a small table overlooking a lush enclosed patio where, in warmer months, customers waited in line for a table. Ethan ordered a bottle of wine, set the menu aside, and gave AJ his full attention.

"So how was your day?"

AJ exploded with laughter. She covered her mouth to contain the unexpected display, thoroughly amused by what sounded like such a routine question, as if they were an old married couple. Then Ethan joined in. They both quieted, containing their mirth around the other diners, as the waiter decanted the wine and received Ethan's approval.

AJ continued to giggle after the waiter left and picked up her glass. "I guess I needed that." The merriment had been the right thing to drain away the strain, and with the first sip of wine, the worries over the past several days evaporated.

"It's good to see you laugh. I've only known you a little while, and you're so focused, I wasn't sure you ever gave yourself time for pleasure."

AJ took a moment to consider his words. "I have my lighter moments, but I think this week can be laid at the feet of a reporter's deadline." She decided not to admit that his entrance into her life, and the mystery ship at the dock, added to her perplexing week.

"Let's see if we can avoid the topic for a while. I enjoyed our brief discussion of history the other day. I'd like to hear how you came to love it so much."

AJ pinched her napkin, losing focus. "There's not much of a story, at least not on my part. My father was passionate about history. His library was always filled with books, mostly about the European continent, but he had a few on Asia, the Silk Road, feudal Japan, and other stuff." She paused a moment to reminisce, and a warm smile lit her face.

"I would always find him sitting in his big leather chair, reading some musty old book before dinner. When I was little, before I could read, I remember climbing onto his lap to watch him. Sometimes he'd have a book with pictures, and he'd tell me stories of faraway places, tales of pirates, unlucky queens, or mysteries of the Far East. Each evening would be a new story, a new piece of history to make my own." She quieted, blinking away the emotions the memories rekindled.

"Were the stories true?"

She tried to remember some of the stories, but it was too long ago, and so many had been told. "I think so. My father wasn't one to tell tall tales, but he may have embellished them for the listener."

Ethan smiled. "That's the thing about history. You can only learn from what was written, a single person's recollection of the events. If there is enough written, and the stories are similar, you would expect that to be the truth of it."

"And if one had read enough stories on a subject, then one person's embellishment could be closer to the truth than you might think."

"An interesting perspective, but in my experience, most embellished stories are just that."

AJ bristled at his comment and what it implied about her father. "I guess your experiences far outweigh mine in those areas, with your job and all."

"I didn't mean to ruffle feathers. I'm speaking in generalities. I'm sure your father spoke as close to the truth as he knew it. Perhaps he wasn't embellishing at all but sharing his perception of what he read."

AJ relaxed. "Sorry. You're right. I guess we get protective of our family, especially when they're not around anymore."

"Your brother mentioned that he died two years ago."

"Almost two. A heart attack, out of the blue. It was rough on my mother for the first year, but Adam's children helped her bounce back. She keeps busy anyway."

"So, after sitting on his lap and hearing about history, you started reading it yourself."

"It was the antiquing. My father loved to get as close to history as possible, being able to pick up or touch some relic. So in his forays, he would look for old children's books I could read. Then he quickly moved me to other books, and I learned to love the musty old smell."

It had been a long time since she spoke to anyone about her father, but Ethan seemed to dislodge her reticence.

"And you traveled a lot?"

Still wrapped in her memories, AJ turned her wine glass, the flame from the table's candle catching her gaze. "Yeah. Small towns known for their antique shops, big cities for their museums. Always a family vacation and, as we got older, small weekend trips." Then AJ snapped out of her reverie. "What about you?"

Ethan seemed thrown off-balance by her question. "Not much to tell."

"Oh no you don't. I showed mine, now it's your turn." AJ couldn't be sure, but he seemed to falter, piquing her interest at what he wouldn't share. "It's going to be a quiet dinner, because I'm not going to talk anymore unless you share something about yourself." She paused, a smile hovering. "Unless this was meant to be more of an interrogation than dinner."

Ethan sipped his wine. "My story isn't much different from your own. I too learned to love books at an early age and became fascinated by the stories. You know how boys are about wars and civil unrest."

AJ smirked. "Boys and their wars. Pretty easy to see why history would be of interest when told from that perspective."

Their conversation remained with history, taking turns discussing their favorite time periods. Ethan seemed well-versed with war and battle strategies, as most men were with an interest in history. Considering how interested he was in nineteenth-century conflicts, she found it odd he seemed to have little interest in the Civil War, or the World Wars. But to each their own. There was usually no specific reason as to what drew people to history.

AJ enjoyed herself over dinner, but she didn't know what to make of Ethan. He had melted into his chair, focused on everything she said, yet he cast furtive glances around the room, his eyes performing a quick study of each new diner. She didn't know how he could do that and assumed the skill had developed over time. He never allowed a glimpse behind the wall he'd erected.

Instead of dessert, Ethan ordered them both cappuccinos, and AJ eased back in her chair to broach a more personal subject. "Stella tells me you rented the McDowell place." Her eyes met his over the rim of her cup.

"It's a marvelous old building and sits on prime real estate. You can see for miles when the weather is clear."

"The key word is old. It hasn't been kept up very well, from what I've heard."

"It's in desperate need of repair, but I'm willing to assist. It will offset the rental fee. But the bones of the place are solid."

"Do you do construction as well?"

"I tinker here and there, but I'll hire most of it. I prefer the finishing work."

AJ was impressed. "You enjoy the detail work. Why doesn't that surprise me?"

Ethan laughed. "See, you've learned enough about me to know I live by the details."

"I'm not sure I've dug enough. So why rent instead of purchase? I thought you were staying for a while." AJ inwardly winced. It seemed too personal.

"I may eventually." Ethan moved back in his seat, taking a quick sweep of the room. "It seemed right to rent for now. And you've touched on the subject I wanted to discuss with you. Seems you took me off topic with stories of the past."

"Which wasn't all my doing."

"I'll concede to my small part." Ethan moved his cup away and leaned in. "The McDowell place. Do you know how old it is?"

AJ shook her head, moving her own cup closer. "No. I hadn't given it much thought."

"It was built in the early 1900s, before the First World War. It was built by a ship's captain. There's a fascinating story about why it was built and what happened to its first owner."

AJ perked up. "I had no idea. It's always been just the old McDowell place to me."

"With your love of history and all the old timeworn pieces dragged out of people's attics, has the age of the buildings never drawn your interest? Didn't your father ever discuss their history?"

Ethan's words touched her, like opening a door that had always been there, but she had never walked through. "My father didn't ignore the buildings, but for some reason, I never paid attention. I've looked at older homes, but mostly at what people have accomplished in their attempts to restore them, whether they've hit the mark on the original design. I've never been too interested in the houses themselves."

Her mind traveled to all the old places in town, some of them dating back more than a hundred years. Ethan disappeared. Time stopped. All she could see were the houses, the lighthouse, the old museum building, the Cramwell estate house—and so many more.

Finally, Ethan spoke. "I think you've found your next story."

Another moment or two passed before AJ realized what Ethan had said. She ran it over in her mind, sketching the idea. "Not just a story, a whole series. I can't believe I've never thought about it before."

"All this time and you've never written about a building?"

AJ shook her head. "Not as the focus of the piece. I've mentioned buildings as part of other stories, bits and pieces of their history written as background, but never as the subject matter. This is huge." She moved her cappuccino out of her way, fully engaged, laughing as if a huge stone had been lifted from her shoulders. "You have no idea how wonderful this is."

"I can see it's lightened your mood." Ethan smiled.

"I won't have to worry about my next story for weeks, possibly months. There will be other stories in between, of course, but the old buildings will be the main focus. The first two or three weeks should be all about the buildings anyway, a good start to the series."

"Excellent. Then why don't we get started tomorrow?"

Ethan's question pulled AJ out of her planning. "Get what started?"

"The McDowell place. What better place to begin? You have permission from the current occupant to visit the house, and I have discovered some information in the house you might find of interest."

AJ sat back and regarded him, but he gave nothing away. He appeared earnest and eager. "You've thought of everything. Why?"

Ethan leaned closer. "I was curious myself as to the origins of the home. The craftsmanship, the amazing detail in the wood, it all looked hand done. Finished with love, if you will. It intrigued me, and I knew there must be a story behind it all."

"And I mentioned I was in search of my next article."

Ethan shrugged, his earlier excitement abated. "It seemed interesting to share, and I was longing for an evening out with a beautiful woman."

This caught AJ short, and she turned wary. "Here it comes."

Ethan's hands came up in a defensive manner. A smile played at his lips. "For conversational purposes only. I wanted a nice meal and pleasant conversation that wasn't centered around my business."

AJ relaxed. "All right. I believe you. Besides, you did come through for me on the story, so I shouldn't look a gift horse in the mouth."

"Well said. And not to give you any more ideas, let's get you back to the office. I've lost the battle for conversation now anyway. I can see the wheels turning about in your head." Ethan rose, laid cash on the table, and gestured for her to leave first.

True to his word, Ethan dropped her off at the office and, being a perfect gentleman, or the instinctual security man, he waited for her to get to her car. He stayed until she waved and pulled out of the parking lot.

Once home, AJ poured herself a small glass of wine and grabbed her laptop, notepad, and pen, everything she usually needed to work on a project. She sat in her big comfy chair, her favorite place to work. Her small library of books was close at hand if she needed guidance.

Ready to search the internet, AJ was typing in "McDowell" when another idea struck. Instead she typed "Westcliffe Inn." Like Stella's and her own earlier search, not much came up. Her search for Mr. Jackson had gone nowhere, but the inn was the only place she could begin. She had hoped she would be able to find more than Stella. But she was just scratching the surface on this research. There were other ways to get what she needed.

After a half hour of going nowhere with the research, her wine pretty much gone, AJ turned back to her more immediate need—her article. She spent the rest of the evening outlining her story on the McDowell house.

AJ climbed into bed, her mood the lightest it had been in weeks. Her story had finally come together. It always did in the end, but sometimes the stress was unbearable before a topic would finally break through. She snuggled into the comforter, her mind quieting, thankful that Ethan wasn't anything like her brother. Adam would never have brought her the treasure she was sure to discover in the old buildings.

Something else nagged. She sat up. The inn wasn't always called the Westcliffe. It hovered, just out of reach. She'd remember eventually. But she wasn't sure if it would help solve her mystery.

11

The morning air was crisp. The sun, obscured by a thin layer of clouds, held no promise of warming, unable to disperse the tenacious fingers of gray that refused to release their hold on the coast. The lightest touch of a breeze caressed the ship, the gentle waves creating a soft, rolling motion, indiscernible to the man leaning against the railing, his long lean fingers plying the ropes in his hands.

Finn had been up before the sun, going over every inch of the sloop, ensuring it was ready to go on a moment's notice. He didn't like to be caught by surprise. Never again, he had promised himself. He checked each rope to confirm that nothing was fraying, nothing needed repair. Anything he found, he fixed then and there before moving on.

He had not grown up to be such a meticulous man. The early days of Finn's youth were carefree, wasting most of it like any other young man whose family had some influence. His father was a lenient man, wanting only the best for his family, and they'd had enough money to hire help for many of the chores, leaving Finn to run wild with the neighbor boys on more occasions than his father would have wished. Finn's only interest in those days were ships, horses, and girls, in that order. Today though, he could give no traction to his youthful days. He kept his mind on the task at hand, the maintenance of his ship.

Finn completed his work on the standing rigging and moved toward the bow along the starboard side, when the faint rumble of a truck sounded from above. Without looking up, he ran his hands over a brace, watching and feeling for fraying, releasing it only when footsteps sounded on the dock.

"Mr. Murphy? Are you there, boy?" The voice was old and gruff.

Finn smiled. It had been some time since anyone had called him "boy." He wiped his hands on a rag, walked to the port side, and looked down at the man.

The old man stared at the ship, unsure of Finn's location, and his eyes squinted against the glare of the bright morning light. The African-American man was tall, with a slight stoop, his skin as smooth as polished glass, which surprised Finn. From the gray in his thinly cropped hair, Finn guessed the man to be at least sixty, but he didn't see a wrinkle on him. The man scanned the ship, and Finn could tell he wasn't looking for him anymore. He was lost in the ship, observing her details, marveling at her lines. The admiration in the man's reflective gaze added to Finn's respect for him.

Finn leaned against the rail and called out to the man. "Mr. Jackson. I suspect you're right on time this morning." Finn kept his manner light, his smile warm.

Mr. Jackson laughed low and deep. "That I am, Mr. Murphy, and I guess it's high time I get you to town so you can buy yourself a new watch. If you're waiting for me to tell you the time, you'll be late to your own funeral."

Finn laughed with him and met Jackson on the dock. He allowed more of a lilt to enter his voice. "And that would be a shame, because I would expect it to be the grand affair." Finn patted the old man on the back, and they moved up the hill. "I appreciate what you're doing for me. I know you think it would have been better if I had tied up at the marina."

Jackson shook his head. "You don't have to explain wanting to have some privacy. I don't go into town every day, but I can get my boy Anthony to come by and check on you, see if you need to go anywhere."

"That would be grand. Would you have time today to give me a tour of the town so I can get my bearings? I was in a hurry last time."

"I can give you one quick drive around. I have an appointment, might keep me busy for an hour or so. The truck is yours if you want to do more."

When they arrived at Jackson's truck, Finn hesitated. "It doesn't seem right to use your truck."

Most of the old truck's paint had faded with time and weather, making it difficult to tell what the original color had been. This morning it was a muted gray-black with undertones of brown, which could have been left over from red paint or, more likely, rust, from being so close to the ocean.

Jackson chuckled. "What, you don't think this old thing will get you where you're going? Nonsense. She's got years left on her. Purrs like a kitten." Jackson climbed in the driver's side, and Finn settled himself next to him. "Besides, you're paying me enough to buy this truck ten times over."

Finn grinned, unable to argue the point. The truck started up on the first try and crept out of the lot. The speed never increased on their way to town. Finn thought a horse would have gotten him there faster. After a while, though, he settled back, stretched out his legs as much as he could in the cramped cab, watched the scenery pass by, and listened to the old man tell him about the town.

"The Meiners were the original town barons. Funny name in that they didn't own mines." Jackson snorted. "They were in timber. That there is their old mill." Jackson pointed out an old wooden structure, much larger than a barn, smaller than an airplane hangar. It looked like it could collapse in the slightest of breezes. "Not much now, but the town stores stuff in there."

Finn eyed the building and raised his eyebrows. "They're not afraid of it falling?"

"Oh sure, it doesn't look like much, but the beams are solid inside." The old man veered to the right when the road split. "Roof is passable."

As they drove through the edge of town and deeper into its center, Finn paid close attention to street names, trying to get his bearings.

As if reading his mind, Jackson glanced over at Finn. "The town looks bigger than it is. The newer sections are more wide open. When we get to the main part of the city, you'll see how easy it is to get around."

Rather than drive directly to the heart of the city, Jackson crept up on it, starting in a large circle and then moving closer, street by street, letting Finn get a good look at the area. Finally they closed in on what Finn assumed was the center of town.

"Do you mind going around a couple of blocks, just one more time?" Finn asked before Jackson could park.

Jackson checked his watch. "Sure, I've got a minute or two."

Finn grimaced. Knowing Jackson's driving speed, even a couple of blocks would take a great deal longer. Jackson circled again, and Finn determined the downtown area was centered within a few blocks, everything within walking distance.

Getting out of the truck, Jackson stretched his back and pointed west. "The marina is only a few blocks over there if you need to pick up anything." He hitched up his pants and met Finn in front of the truck. "Now, I have two appointments. Take about an hour or so. There's a pharmacy around the corner. It should have a decent selection of watches. I suggest that be your first stop. There's a small diner in the building next door, sandwiches and such, so you can find me in there."

"Thank you again, Mr. Jackson," Finn said. "I'll be on time."

"Yeah, yeah." Jackson waved him off, made his way to a brick building, and disappeared inside.

Finn turned away from the building, assessing the scene around him. Sleek, flashy cars, loud noises, myriad signs and tall, tightly spaced buildings all combined to overwhelm his senses, leaving him a touch claustrophobic. He longed for the open sea and would even welcome the roughest storm over this sprawl of urbanization. At least the storm was something he knew how to conquer. Honing his bearings, he followed Jackson's instructions and headed for the pharmacy, but instead of purchasing a watch, he bought a prepaid cell phone.

Back outside, Finn changed directions. He kept a casual pace, his long strides making good time without appearing to be in a hurry. He glanced in each window that he passed as if window shopping, but always remaining aware of his surroundings, occasionally turning his head to take in the sights, using the glass window fronts as mirrors. He didn't think he was being followed, but Finn hadn't gotten where he was by being careless.

Even with the onslaught to his senses, Finn had to admit he needed to get out and stretch his legs on solid land. He had tired of walking the deck. As much as he loved the ocean and the feel of the waves beneath him, he longed for the day he could settle down and focus on his other passion, his horses. But that life seemed so far away. At times, it seemed his memories were merely dreams, his home having never existed, except as wild fantasies that crept into his mind in the wee hours of the morning.

Stopping at his final destination, Finn took a casual look around, and, not seeing anyone appearing interested in him, he stopped in front of a bookstore. After one last look down the street, he ducked inside. The thick smell of books and coffee reminded Finn of home. The building was older but well-kept, the original wood floors well maintained through the years. Row upon row of tall wooden bookcases ran deep through the store. What he could see of the walls above the cases appeared to be brick painted a rich russet brown. The few windows provided enough light, and with the incandescent lighting, the room emitted a warm, inviting atmosphere. The place reminded Finn of his own library, although the store had a grander smell, the aroma of coffee mingling with the mixed combination of new and old books.

"Welcome. Can I help you find anything?"

Finn spun around to find a young woman, more of a child, peering up at him through rimmed glasses. She took a small step back, then her smile widened.

Finn smiled in return. "I'm just looking, but I'll tell you if I need anything."

The girl nodded, still smiling. "I'll be close by. Don't hesitate to ask."

When she didn't move, Finn bowed his head and turned back to the aisles laid out in front of him. He could sense her still watching him, but he ignored her, used to the stares of others.

He meandered through the aisles, glancing at the spines of the books, and found the source of the coffee. A small counter occupied a section of wall midway through the building. Several tables were positioned around the counter, half of them occupied, people either chatting with friends or reading. The aroma was so enticing, he couldn't pass it by, so he bought a cup of brew. Carrying it deeper into the store, he noticed the books got older and the musty smell stronger. Finn stopped to read a few titles, recognizing some of the literary novels. Others appeared to be historical reference books. He assumed the used books weren't as popular, which explained why they were shelved in the back, but he spied a couple of individuals perusing the shelves.

At the back of the shop, a small area opened up, revealing three small sitting areas. Smaller bookshelves and a plastic plant separated each section, providing customers with a more private setting. Two gentlemen lounged in the outer sections, leaving the middle section empty. Finn studied the men, trying to discern if one of them was the man he sought.

The man to the left had three stacks of old books in front of him. He picked books one by one, turning each over in his hands to read the cover before opening it and flipping through, stopping occasionally to read something, then moving on. When finished, the man set the book onto one of two small piles, then picked up another book, working through it, repeating the process. This was a buyer, not the man he was looking for.

The second man sat in the seating area farthest from where Finn stood. He partially faced the wall, making it difficult for Finn to get a good look at him. He appeared well-dressed, judging from his tailored coat. A small briefcase of high-quality leather sat on the floor next to his chair. The man held no book and none rested on the table in front of him. He stared at the wall, and except for one glance at his watch, sat still as a statue. This was the man he was seeking. Finn edged around the surrounding bookshelves to get a better look at him.

He moved to the opposite side of the room, allowing him a clear line of sight to the man. Average height, easy to see even from a seated position. His pale face indicated someone who spent a great deal of time indoors. Although this far north, it could be the effects of the gray weather that created the pallor—a sharp contrast to his dark hair, cut short to match his manicured appearance.

As Finn approached the seating area, the man stared at Finn with a sharp intensity. He looked Finn over with a distasteful grimace, then hid it behind a more congenial face.

"Mr. Murphy, I'm guessing." His intuitive statement held an assertive command, though he kept his voice low. Finn could see the lawyer in him but, for a reason he couldn't explain, he sensed this man didn't spend much time in a courtroom. He'd bet his talents came with finding the loopholes.

"Aye, it is." Finn let the brogue slip out, hoping the lawyer would consider him a ruffian. He might have made a deal with him, but he preferred to keep the lawyer on a tight lead. Finn didn't often use fear to garner results, but he'd become impatient with the length of his mission. He took a seat across from the man, diminishing his height advantage and allowing a more even playing field. Finn relaxed, stretching out his legs, trying to appear casual next to this carefully controlled man.

The lawyer sat motionless, on the edge of his seat, ready to escape if necessary. He appeared bored, as if this is was all beneath him. Finn was paying him a large sum for his work, and he had been told the man was desperate for money. But the lawyer displayed a cool disinterest in Finn, as if he could take or leave the work. Perhaps Finn had misjudged him. He might excel in the courtroom after all.

He tightened his lips as he waited for Finn, a sign of nerves. Was he bluffing?

"Have you found the stone?" Finn said.

"No." The answer was simple and definitive. "But I have found its last known location. I should know more in a couple days."

"You've had several days already."

"And I've worked a small miracle in tracing it so quickly." The lawyer's response carried some bite.

Finn smiled. So there was some shark behind the clothes and smooth demeanor. "Agreed, you have. But you must admit, I did give you a fair amount to start with."

"Yes, but the original name you gave me is no longer around. It's all with the woman's granddaughter. I need a couple more days to wrap it up."

Finn didn't like this new information. It seemed it was always something. Nothing was ever straightforward. "Is this going to be a problem?"

"No, no. I don't think so," the lawyer hesitated, his eyes shifting to a spot over Finn's left shoulder. A small movement of his feet the only other visible indication of nerves. "I could use the next part of the retainer."

Finn leaned forward, leering. "I see. You wouldn't be trying to drag this out."

For the first time, the lawyer's eyes showed fear, and he responded with a raised voice. "It's not my fault someone died." He finished with a hoarse whisper. "I have no control over these things." He pulled himself together, finding his spine to sit straighter.

Finn let him stew before standing. He pulled a folded envelope from his back pocket and tossed it on the table in front of them. "This should be enough until our next appointment. Don't take my friendly demeanor as a sign of someone who doesn't expect results."

Finn marched through the bookstore, never looking back, knowing the envelope had been snatched by the lawyer before Finn had walked five paces. He retained a smile so anyone looking at him would only see an engaging man, but inside, pangs of dread flooded him. This was taking too long, and there was so much at stake. Each time he got so close, and then, when it was within his grasp, it vanished. Every failed attempt pushed him farther from home, and at times, the anguish threatened to overtake him.

He pushed through the door and leaned against the building, letting the sun warm his face. He caught the scent of the ocean. Though he was a few blocks away, he had time to clear his head before meeting with Jackson, so he turned west, heading for the marina.

12

AJ was in high spirits when she ordered her lunch at the Hill Street café, splurging on a toasted sandwich, a peanut butter cookie, and an iced latte. She grinned, realizing that Stella would cry with shame if she saw how she was celebrating her new series of articles. AJ had to agree it was not quite a martini. That was okay—she had her first story on old historical buildings almost in the bag. She'd accomplished most of her research on the McDowell place, some through the internet, some through old county records, and, finally, a call to one of the city historians. AJ had been able to sketch out a general outline on the ill-fated story of the builder and his wife.

The story intrigued her. A sailor by trade, James McDowell spent months at sea as captain of his own vessel before making Baywood his home. He built the house for his new bride, Mary, the love of his life. When he was at sea, transporting cargo along the western coast, she lived alone in the house with their young son. They seemed happy until complications from Mary's second pregnancy ended in her death and that of McDowell's second child. Lost in grief, McDowell became a recluse, leaving his son in the care of his in-laws. Then one day, he sailed away in his ship, never to return.

The horrific tale dampened AJ's mood. Such pain and suffering, waiting all those years for a home and family, and then it ends with such tragedy and sorrow. She couldn't imagine being in that type of situation, a love so deep that a person loses themselves entirely, with no reason to live after the other person was gone. She didn't see it, and she couldn't feel it, but she could try to write it. All she needed were the old pictures of the house Ethan had discovered, which she hoped to collect that afternoon.

With the McDowell story pretty well completed, AJ shifted her focus to the next piece, the Westcliffe Inn. Her calls to Stella had been a bust, resulting only in voice mails. She knew Stella would call when she could, but AJ was growing restless.

She finished her sandwich and studied the cookie, trying to decide whether to eat it now or save it for later. It was just sitting there staring at her. She sipped her iced latte, deferring her first decision of the day, and glanced up as someone walked into the diner. Stunned, she dribbled iced latte down the front of her shirt, and AJ dabbed pointlessly at the spot. Her eyes darted back to the door.

It was him. She couldn't believe it. There he was. She had been thinking about the inn, then he popped through the door. Well, not exactly popped—more like swaggered in.

The man on the ship.

Grateful for snagging a table in the back, she doubted he'd see her unless he actively searched the place. She hunched over the table, trying to make herself small as she ducked her head. He scanned the room. After a moment, her head snapped up, and she squared her shoulders, admonishing herself for hiding. She had every right to be here; she simply didn't want to speak to him. She wasn't spying on him, she was researching the inn.

Her face reddened. Okay, she'd investigated Mr. Jackson. She *was* spying on him, and she couldn't face him without her guilt showing.

Berating herself for being foolish, AJ packed up her trash, the decision about the cookie resolved as she folded it in a napkin. She casually lifted her head to see if the man had seen her, and found him sitting at a table with another man, an older man with a thin gray layer of fuzz over his head. She couldn't stop staring. His brown waves repeatedly fell over one brow, only to be pushed back. His eyes crinkled at the edges when he laughed, fully engaged with the older man, who seemed to be keeping them both ensnared in conversation, hand gestures and all.

AJ kept moving back to the younger, brown-haired man, who she gauged to be in his early thirties. His long legs stretched out in front of him, and AJ recalled him standing on the dock in front of her, tall and lean, shirt opened to reveal light brown hair on his chest. Warmth raced through her. She cleaned her table, watching them. They got up to leave.

Shoving the cookie into her bag, AJ grabbed her trash and latte, ready to follow them out. It wasn't her best idea, but she was a reporter with a story to investigate, and she might never find him away from his ship again. Besides, Stella would want all the details. Her resolve in check, AJ raced to the door.

She peeked through the window. The men walked toward the street, deep in conversation. AJ followed, trying to stay out of sight. She stopped at the edge of the building, waiting for them to get farther ahead before following, but the men had stopped to climb into an old beat-up truck, the older man at the wheel. She couldn't make out the license plate, but the truck looked like an old Ford, the faded paint color impossible to discern. AJ turned as the truck passed her, blending into traffic. While there was no way AJ could possibly know for sure, she would lay odds they were headed for the inn.

AJ had found Mr. Jackson.

AJ WAS PUMPED when she returned to the office, her investigative juices buzzing. Things were falling into place. She'd almost put this week's story behind her, had stories sketched out for the next month, and, after her close encounter at lunch, the electricity shooting through her toes told her she was on to something with Jackson and the mystery man.

She picked up her cell and checked the time. *Damn, I'll be late for my meeting with Ethan.* But she needed to talk to Stella, frustrated again with reaching her voice mail. AJ left a cryptic message, then raced out the door for the McDowell place. Her focus should be on completing the McDowell piece, but she couldn't get Jackson out of her mind. She needed a way to find him. He couldn't live too far from the inn.

AJ groaned. She should have searched county records on the Westcliffe when she researched the McDowell house. She shouldn't be surprised. She got a blind spot when she hooked a story, shoving everything else to the back burner until she was done. With the McDowell story almost complete, her attention shifted to the inn. She needed to speak with Jackson, and the Westcliffe story would lead straight back to the captain of the mystery ship.

AJ found the McDowell house enchanting. Shades of green everywhere, and the spring flowers, planted years ago, were in full bloom. The landscape was no longer manicured, and a natural wildness had taken over, which seemed appropriate. Knowing its history with the tragic love story demystified the legend. AJ no longer saw doom and gloom when she looked at the aged structure, just a building that had once seen happiness before a terrible tragedy struck. She snapped a great shot of the front of the house.

Ethan stepped out to greet her dressed in pressed slacks and a tailored black shirt, the sleeves rolled up, the look more casual without his usual jacket. She had a fleeting image of a different man, another side of him he never showed. It wasn't anything she could put into words, and the vision disappeared as she remembered her reason for being there.

"Sorry I'm late." AJ took a last picture before turning back to him.

Ethan guided her around to the side of the house. "Let's finish the outside before heading back in."

"Makes sense."

Ethan strode toward the back of the house, his silent movement graceful but with purpose, even in his own home. "The front of the house properly reflects the love that built the place. But it's the back that echoes the darkness and the tragedy."

AJ let Ethan move ahead of her. She wanted to get a good look at the house, seeing it for the first time. Even the moldings on the outside of the house looked hand carved. The number of windows astonished her. She doubted the look was typical for its day, but she was pretty sure the house was the original design.

"A great many windows." Ethan seemed to read her mind. "I checked the original plans. There have been a few upgrades through the years, but the design was all McDowell." Ethan turned to the house. "He wanted to catch as much light as possible."

"To keep the inside of the place as light as possible through the northwest winters."

"Or to keep as much sky and open sea available to him while he was trapped ashore." Ethan walked out toward the ocean. "This should be a good spot to capture the back of the house." Ethan stopped at a point off-center from the house.

"Why did you put it that way? Trapped." AJ had walked out to where he stood and turned, pulling the camera up to frame a shot.

"He was a sea captain. The sea was his first love. Its open air, open skies. He would have felt a bit trapped, I would think, living in a house on land. The windows would have eased some of his sense of confinement." Ethan moved closer to the shore, looking out to sea.

AJ stopped taking pictures. "But he was in love with Mary. Surely that would have changed things."

Ethan stared at some unknown point, rock solid against the breeze tugging at his shirt and ruffling his short hair. "Nothing mitigates the love of a captain for his ship and the sea." Ethan turned back to AJ, nodding back to the house. "McDowell built this place to show his love for Mary, but it was also to give her a place to love as he loved the sea."

Ethan turned toward the house, leaving AJ to stare after him, set against the raw power of the house, with its wood and glass structure. Her perception of the house changed as she looked at it from McDowell's perspective, then again from Mary's. "Mary would have loved this place, the home her captain had built for her," she said. "But they would have been away from town back then, too far away for Mary to reach town for supplies or see family. McDowell had built this place to ensure his proximity to the sea. His gift of this house, he said, was a tribute of love. But, if he truly loved her, wouldn't he have built something closer to town to preserve her happiness?"

"Now you see it as I do. If she had lived closer to town, to her parents, perhaps she wouldn't have died."

AJ studied the house before turning back to the sea. A shiver ran through her. "She must have been lonely, maybe even terrified out here. After his wife's death, perhaps McDowell finally saw the house for what it was, a glass cage where he kept his possessions, belongings he had long neglected. And in that neglect, he discovered the guilt that lay at his feet."

"Very insightful. Perhaps the reason why he abandoned his son and sailed away."

"Never to be seen again."

"And it seemed the sadness never left their son when he

finally returned to the place. A legacy of tragedy." Ethan walked to the back door and waited for AJ.

She ran to catch up with Ethan, eager to see what he had discovered in the house, but she already knew she needed to change her story. This was still a tragic love story. The tragedy, however, was not what fate had handed the captain, but in the heartbreak of his own making. In the end, she realized everything rested with the decisions people make.

The house proved difficult to find, which surprised Adam since it could be seen from the coastal highway, bits and pieces peering through the dense forest. Yet there seemed to be no direct route to it. He'd told his office he'd only be gone a couple of hours, but he should have blocked out the entire afternoon.

The weather wasn't cooperating either. The skies had been a light gray when he left Baywood, but the rain started a few miles out of town, and its intensity increased the farther south he drove. He would be fighting the weather all the way home.

The GPS guided him off the coastal road and down a tree-thickened street, small but passable with oncoming traffic, the warm voice from the navigational system first turning him right, then right, then left and right again. The road finally led him to the small town of Kalapuya—if it could be called a town, it was so tiny. The simple post office told him it had to be a town, although in all the years he lived here, he had never heard of this place, never knew it was tucked away among the firs, hidden from plain sight. Along with the post office, the town boasted a small diner that appeared closed but not vacant, a machine repair shop of some sort—maybe farm equipment, maybe auto—and a general store with a couple of cars parked in front. As quickly as he arrived, the GPS guided him away from the small hamlet and back onto another tree-encased street, made darker by the clouds and rain.

Adam sighed for the hundredth time and reflected on how he got himself into these situations, each time a little deeper, each time requiring more effort to extricate himself. He could never leave well enough alone, and here he was, digging his way out again. At what point would he learn his lesson? He had worked hard to achieve his position as partner at the firm, not to be a hireling sneaking out of the office, working leads like some dime-novel private eye. His self-recrimination came to an end when the trees gave way to another small clearing, and the robotic voice told him he had reached his destination.

Three houses sat on the dead-end street, like forgotten sentinels in the rain, no longer remembering what they guarded. Yet they all appeared well maintained, two of the houses of newer design, perhaps built within the last couple of decades. The third, an old turn-of-the century farmhouse, had either been recently restored, or the owners had provided meticulous care over the decades. The back portion of the building looked like an addition, but it too appeared to have been completed some time ago. This was the house.

Relieved to see a car in the drive, Adam hoped someone would be home. He had taken a chance coming in the middle of the day, but his options were limited if he didn't want to make excuses with Madelyn. He parked the car and stared at the house, deciding the best approach, when he caught a glimpse of someone coming out the back. A small figure, a young woman or teenager wearing a rain jacket and hood, carried a basket and scurried, head down, toward the back. Perfect.

Pulling up the collar of his Burberry raincoat, Adam raced across the street, sidestepping puddles. He stopped by the short wooden fence framing the small yard to wait for the woman. She bent over what must have been a vegetable garden and pulled out something that looked like lettuce. After she placed it carefully in the basket, leaves from some other plant joined the head of lettuce. Thankfully, being early spring, there wouldn't be much in the garden for her to pluck.

As she turned from the garden, her pace quickened, trying to escape the rain that followed her up the path.

"Excuse me." Adam tried not to shout, didn't want to scare her.

She stopped and turned. Her head became visible under the hood, and Adam confirmed his guess that it was a young woman. She looked startled but not worried. "Hello. I didn't see you drive up."

One thing Adam loved about small towns—everyone was friendly and eager to help. Although small towns had their share of domestic violence and drugs, it hadn't yet impacted the warmth of small-town hospitality, at least not in Baywood. This always worked in Adam's favor, even when they discovered he was a lawyer.

"I don't mean to bother you. This should only take a minute," Adam said. "Are you Mrs. Mayfield's daughter?"

"Her granddaughter, Sarah." The young woman stepped under the porch roof, set down the basket, and stripped off her wet gloves.

"Oh, good, good. I was wondering if you could help me. I'm looking for something I believe belonged to your grandmother. I'm afraid I wasn't able to make it for your estate sale."

Sarah nodded. "Then you'd better come in and get dry. There are still a few pieces left. I haven't decided yet whether to sell them through a dealer." She grabbed her basket, left the gloves, and headed through the back door.

Adam slid through the gate, not believing his good fortune. Finally, luck was on his side. He smiled and almost whistled as he followed Sarah into the house.

14

AJ dropped into her chair. With dinner and dishes done for the evening, she finally had time to relax. She picked up her book from the side table—*Marie Antoinette: The Portrait of an Average Woman* by Stefan Zweig. Her discussion with Ethan about the French Revolution sparked an interest to revisit the subject, reminding her of how her father could entice her onto a topic. Turning to find her place in the book, she performed a quick mental cleansing of her day.

After returning to the office from Ethan's, AJ spent the rest of the afternoon and early evening finishing the McDowell story. The old photos Ethan had discovered hidden away in some cabinet completed the article. When she restructured the story, she found herself writing toward Ethan's interpretation of the house and Captain McDowell. She had no reason to believe his version was more accurate than a historian's, yet everything he said rang true.

After skimming the same page several times, AJ closed the book. The last few days whirled through her head. She picked up her notepad and jotted down words: ship captain. Historical center. Old buildings. Town history. The inn. Ship captains. Mr. Jackson. Brown wavy hair.

AJ's pen froze. Ship captains. That was it. The connection between stories wasn't just old buildings like the McDowell house and the inn. There was an additional link between the two —the ship captains. One was long dead, somewhere across the seas, wherever he met his fate. The other, a living modern-day ship captain, who might be tied to the inn. He had a reason to dock there. It could be a coincidence, yet she might find a connection if she dug a little. She couldn't see a reason not to try.

Assessing her options, AJ kept returning to the same conclusion: She needed to interview the captain. Deep in thought, she was scribbling notes and interview questions when the phone rang. She answered without checking the caller ID.

"Sorry I haven't gotten back to you. I had a very long closing yesterday, and I've been in Mapleton all day. But I want to hear about your dinner with Ethan." Stella's chatter couldn't hide how tired she sounded.

"Why Mapleton?" AJ scratched through one of her notes and wrote something else.

"New clients looking for a place in town, but they need to sell their old place. Asked if I could take a look."

"And?"

"Oh, it was a nice place. Acreage, farmland, if you're into that kind of thing. Nothing I could do for them, so it was a waste of a long day. But hey, I'm all about client happiness, so what could I do?" Stella's normal sparkle returned. "In the end, I turned them over to a friend. I'll just get them their new place, which we found, a great little place over in the Meadows Estates. Cute little two bedroom. They want to scale back so they can travel. That's my plan when I retire." Stella had regained her energy and was throttling back up to full drive.

"Hmm. That's nice."

"You're on a story and didn't hear a word I said."

"New client. Farm. Nice two bedroom. And there's no way in the world you would ever retire to travel. Does that pretty much sum it up?"

Stella laughed. "That's why I love ya. The true multitasker. And I could travel. So you found a story? Well, forget the story. Let's start with Ethan."

"Funny you should ask, since they both connect." AJ laid down the notepad, updating Stella on her dinner with Ethan and his idea about old buildings as the subject of a new series, starting with the McDowell house.

"And I'm sure you put my name in there somewhere. I was the one who took Ethan to the creepy old house in the first place."

"Yeah, I haven't found a spot yet."

"So what else about Ethan?"

"There's nothing else to tell. It was a dinner and small talk about the buildings, then it moved to history."

"So is he a nice guy? What about his background?"

"Ethan seems to find ways to talk about anything but himself, then ends up questioning me."

"Maybe he was some sort of cop before he got into security."

"I don't know. He would fit the type, I guess, but there's something about him I can't figure out."

They both fell silent. AJ thumbed the pages of her notebook. "So I have an idea on finding out more about the inn without looking nosy."

"Oh God." AJ could almost hear Stella slap her forehead. "I was supposed to be doing research for you. I'm so sorry, AJ. These last two days. But my calendar is almost non-existent the next couple of days. I can get on it in the morning."

"I understand. It's great you can help. But listen to this. I think I found Mr. Jackson. I was having lunch today at the café, and guess who walked in?"

"Sorry again, you left a message about him. How do you know it was him?"

"It wasn't Mr. Jackson that walked in, it was the ship's captain."

"The guy on the boat?"

"Yep. And he was meeting an elderly man, someone I didn't recognize. They talked for a few minutes and then the captain left with the guy. They got in the older guy's truck. That has to be Mr. Jackson."

"How do you know what truck they got into? There's no parking lot."

"I followed them."

Stella's voice turned conspiratorial. "My, my, you are on the hunt. So now you're Miss Marple?"

"It was maybe half a block. I didn't track them around town. Besides, I knew where they were going." Sometimes Stella exasperated her.

"True enough."

"So anyway, seeing them and working on the McDowell piece, this is my opening to research the inn as my next story. And interview our mysterious ship's captain." AJ's excitement grew.

"Oh my God, it's perfect." Stella sounded earnest. "I forgot how old the inn is. Unlike the McDowell place, the inn has been well maintained over the years, but it couldn't have been built much later than McDowell."

"But I need an actual date. Then I'll have my next story."

Stella laughed. "You mean you now have a good reason to stalk and spy?"

AJ feigned hurt. "I investigate. Big difference."

"And it's different how?"

AJ attempted a cool, sophisticated air. "What I do is for the good of our readers, who have a need to know."

They both laughed. "I'll work on the county records in the morning. Good hunting." Stella was gone.

AJ fell back into her notes, spurred on by her friend's call.

Stella's agreement to help validated her course of action, assuming Stella wasn't in it just for the gossip. Always a strong possibility. Eager to begin, she smiled and pictured the captain's emerald-green eyes. She didn't think she'd see that smug grin of his once he became the subject of her story.

15

The stars declined to give way, foretelling of a glorious day if AJ could depend on what the clear skies and the warmer morning air told her. A gentle breeze kissed her cheeks as she grabbed for the next hold in the cliff. Her muscles were singing, and she was only halfway. She knew better. She hadn't climbed in a few days, and her body punished her for the lack of physical exercise. The admonishment was gentle. She wasn't tired, and although her muscles strained, AJ knew she'd make the top without any problem, her arms and legs falling into their natural rhythm.

AJ had woken refreshed, mental clarity revitalized after days of cloudy darkness. When pressed for a story, she lived in a tunnel, her brain as gray and dismal as a Pacific Northwest winter. Over the last year, she had developed methods to work past her dry spells, typically through climbing or, strangely enough, poring through history books. She suspected staying away from her story freed her subconscious to work behind the scenes.

The interruptions over the last few days had not proved useful in giving her subconscious free range. Her mind had been too busy, all these new people. Her natural mental rhythm had been steered off course.

AJ grabbed the lip of the cliff, and with one quick swing, she landed and rolled onto her back to stare up at the dawning sky, stars still refusing to retreat from the rosy edges of the horizon. She gazed at the sky and sucked in air, ignoring the pain in her muscles, letting them melt into the ground next to her.

Once her breathing evened out, AJ peeked around her. She was trespassing now, but she didn't want to find another spot to climb. She didn't see anyone but noticed a light in one of the rooms of the house. With it still dark enough to provide some cover, she inched her way to a four-foot conifer, its shape perpetually bent, contorted by the constant winds.

She gazed out to sea, allowing the conifer to act as a shield from the house. The tide had begun its early return, the shallow waves mesmerizing, the calmness of the ocean a soothing balm.

"Good morning." The man's deep, rich voice made her jump but displayed no hint of any surprise on his part.

AJ spun around. Ethan stood a few short feet away from her. He sipped from a coffee cup, then lifted it toward her. "I'd have brought a cup for you had I known you were coming."

AJ flushed, grateful there wasn't enough light for Ethan to see it. She never considered herself trespassing when no one lived here. There was no one to bother or even notice her. She was about to apologize when Ethan stepped near her, extremely close to the edge. She remained silent as he gazed out toward the same calm ocean she had been viewing.

"There's no better way to wake than to smell the freshness of the salt air and watch the morning light reflect off the waves." Ethan took another sip of coffee and peered over the cliff's edge to the shore below. "Especially after such a strenuous climb." He turned to her, and AJ was relieved to see he wasn't mad—more mildly curious, if she could read him from their few short meetings.

She looked out to sea. "This is one of my favorite climbs. The house was abandoned for such a long time, I figured no one would care. This point is a perfect spot, close to town but secluded enough to leave nothing but the sea."

"And do you always climb so early?"

AJ ran a hand through her curls, then tugged on an end. "It's the best time. I know the cliff well enough I don't need much light, but I carry a headlamp if I need it. Being able to catch the first glimpse of the day, it's like a fresh start, a reset. No matter what happened yesterday, today is a new day." AJ played with the metal loops on her belt, a touch of pink on her cheeks.

Ethan studied her. "A philosopher. Well, I don't see any reason why you can't keep climbing here if it's your favorite spot. As long as you don't mind occasionally discovering me out here as well, welcoming in the new day."

"I'm sorry. I forgot where the climb was taking me."

Ethan barked a short laugh. "I seriously doubt you forget anything. The invitation still stands." The light was probably now sufficient for Ethan to see AJ's small blush at being caught. "Do you want to come in for some coffee?"

"No." AJ's response was more abrupt than she intended. "I need to get to work." Her tone softened. "Thank you for letting me climb here. It means a lot."

"If not coffee, why don't you come down the shore with me? I heard there were some antique shops in some town called Chilton, not far from here."

AJ couldn't help but be surprised. "You want to go antiquing? There are better places than Chilton."

"I'm not expecting to find a treasure, but I could use your expertise in what you look for. Better still, how you know something is not what it appears."

AJ pulled at a curl. Her mind raced through her limited options, but an excuse refused to show itself.

"Perhaps your friend Stella would like to come along," he said.

"Stella would enjoy some time away from work." AJ refused to concede more, but Stella would love the adventure and wouldn't mind seeing Ethan again.

"Saturday, then?"

"Saturday it is. We'll meet you here at eight."

AJ stood and grabbed her rope, cinched in, and pushed off for her descent. A few feet down, she looked up to the edge and saw Ethan watching her, his face shadowed against the blue sky. Yet, for an instant, she caught something in his regard. She was almost to the bottom of the cliff when it came to her.

What she had seen in his gaze was admiration.

THE ALARM HADN'T BEEN SET. Stella's languid body, curled against her pillow, jerked in reflex to the sun hitting her face. She had overslept. This was not her favorite way of waking up, preferring about six slaps of the snooze button before prying her eyes open. Stella's feet hit the cold wood floor, jolting her senses. This day was going to go awry, she just knew it.

Making an effort to shuffle into the kitchen to hit the button on the coffee machine, Stella trudged back to the bathroom. She was half-alive by the time she brushed her teeth, but it was the first long slurp of her steaming morning brew that woke Stella's brain. She sat at the breakfast nook, allowing the sight outside her window to complete her morning ritual: the flowers, alive in kaleidoscope colors, contrasted with the darker shades of foliage, her own private Eden.

Stella smiled with pride as she turned back to her kitchen. She remembered the first time she had pulled up in front of the place, a small cottage styled house bearing up under neglect. Purchased a couple of years earlier, it had been a dump. Keeping the bones of the place, Stella refashioned the house into a showplace, combining modern with traditional, her rustic kitchen filled with granite counters and top-of-the line appliances. The focus of her open living room was a large sitting area with plush, comfortable couches and chairs, framed by artwork, and along one wall, a state-of-the art entertainment center. Replicating her office, several ornate vases overflowing with floral bouquets dominated the rooms, filling the whole house with spring.

Sipping her coffee until it cooled enough to take larger gulps, Stella considered the day before her. She could have slept in more than she already had. Stella wasn't prepared for the idleness of her next two days. It wasn't that Stella never took time off. She enjoyed taking a couple of days of retreat to recharge her batteries, pampering herself, spending long days shopping, or attending events at the town's small art center. Underneath all the flash, the chaos of hectic schedules, and demanding mercurial clients, she was self-aware enough to know it was her own homebody nature that she witnessed in her clients, and she embraced it. She usually had to carve out time for herself, because it didn't typically fall at her doorstep.

Over breakfast, she recalled her late conversation with AJ and her obsession with the Westcliffe. Stella understood AJ's passion for her stories, it matched Stella's own enthusiasm for work, but something seemed different. AJ's fixation seemed more about the captain and his mysterious ship than the inn. They lived in a coastal town—it wasn't like there weren't a ton of boats out at the marina. AJ hadn't said much about the man, other than his obnoxious behavior, and Stella found it odd that AJ would have been bothered by it.

There was only one way to see what all the excitement was about. She needed to jump into the fray, and her best angle was to put her own skills to use. If AJ thought this mystery man and the inn were tied together, she was probably right. Her instincts rarely led her astray when she was hot on a story. Let AJ work on the captain and Mr. Jackson. Stella would dig from the other end.

When Stella finally emerged from the house, the sun was well on its way toward midday. Even with her mission in front of her, Stella had succumbed to a bath, indulging before pulling herself together for town.

Stella loved the city. She loved how the ocean air clung to it, the exhaust from the cars, the faint drift of roses, and, if it was Wednesday, the encapsulating aroma of the barbecue special from the diner that sat across from the city and county building. Baywood lacked the glamour of the big cities, but it was hers just the same.

Living in the heart of the city, Stella could easily walk to most of the city and county offices, but she lived by the adage, "Why walk if you can do anything else?" Today, she had let the hour grow too late and ended up parking at a meter two blocks away from the old historical building.

The county records office was located next to the office of permits, allowing Stella to tap both offices for the information she sought. Armed with the address of the old inn AJ had provided, Stella entered the building and was assailed by shiny marble floors, freshly polished wood furniture, and an underlying hint of mustiness a century-old building couldn't escape. She understood the attraction this old building held for the city. AJ was enthralled by the architecture, the old paintings, and the sensation some people got just walking into a slice of history. For Stella, it was just a building she frequented for her business, and if it had held charm for her once, it had long worn off.

She checked her watch. Stella had timed it perfectly. The county workers would hustle more when kept from their lunch hour, and she hoped she would find a halfway competent person to help her before the break. She stopped to admire a fresh bouquet of spring flowers. Turning to enter the title office, she ran into a man making a quick escape out the door.

The bump was jarring, and though his head was turned away from her, Stella recognized the man's voice from his hurried apology.

"Adam," Stella said.

He stopped short, hesitated, then dropped his shoulders. He turned and managed a small smile. "Stella. I'm so sorry. I didn't see you."

As usual, Adam's smile seemed forced. Neither one of them liked the other. They both happened to be connected to AJ, dooming them to see each other at the occasional family gathering, to which AJ sometimes dragged Stella. She assumed as some form of punishment, though she never quite knew who AJ was punishing at the time.

"That happens. I'm usually in a hurry to get out of government offices as well." Stella kept her expression friendly. "Working on a case?"

"Huh?" Adam searched the lobby, looking like he wanted to melt into a wall. "Yes, yes, that's it. A case. It's a real strange one." Adam gave Stella a quick glance and seemed to snicker. "Well, I must run." He turned and dashed off before Stella could respond.

"Good seeing you too," Stella said to the retreating figure. She stared after him for a minute, then turned back to the office. It didn't make sense, but Adam had acted guilty about something. She was still sorting it out when she stepped up and plopped her bag onto the empty counter.

The clerk, a woman in her fifties or so, was picking up a stack of folders and, seeing Stella arrive, set them back down. "Can I help you?"

Her voice was perky, and Stella felt a little ashamed of her earlier misgivings about government workers. "Yes, sorry, I need to get myself together. A man nearly knocked me down leaving here." Stella pulled a notebook from her bag and riffled through the torn, overused pages to find the address of the Westcliffe.

"Oh yes, he was pretty brusque, wasn't he? But we're always the last place people want to be, and sometimes the searches take a while when we have to dig through old files. I'll be so happy when we get the old ones on the computer. We never seem to have enough budget to get it all done."

Stella paused in her organizing. The chatty clerk was well-dressed, her softly graying hair cut short in a modern style. Her makeup was perfect for an office setting, and her eyes twinkled in response to her smile. Stella caught a whiff of a powdery floral scent she couldn't imagine wearing herself, but it seemed to suit this woman. Stella instantly liked her.

She returned the clerk's smile. "Money is always the problem, isn't it? Well, I'm not in a hurry myself, and I'm afraid I may have another one you'll have to dig for."

"Well, that's my job, so tell me what you need."

Relieved she wouldn't have to beg for such an old file, she wrote the address on a small slip of paper and slid the note across to the clerk. "I'd like to get the titles for this address since the house was built. It might go back a hundred years."

"It shouldn't be a problem." The clerk took the paper and had taken a few steps when she looked at the address, then stopped, turning back to Stella. "Are you sure this is the right address on Shoreline Drive?"

The question caught Stella off guard and, though she knew she had written the correct address, she checked her notebook again. "Yes, 453 Shoreline. Isn't that what I wrote?"

"Yes, that's what you've written. It's just, well, I pulled the title on this property a few minutes ago, for the man you ran into." The clerk walked to the stack of folders she had set down when Stella arrived and picked up the top file.

Stella stared at the clerk and then at the thin old file the woman placed in front of her. She was at a loss for words.

"Must be a hot property, with it being on the coast and all. I was wondering if the old inn would ever open back up." The clerk went back to other tasks, leaving the folder with Stella.

Stella stared at the folder, afraid to open it, as if a dozen snakes might be coiled under the first page. Adam had asked for the same information. Her hand hovered over the folder until she mentally kicked herself for being foolish. Opening it, she flipped through the pages.

She didn't see anything that might require an attorney. Maybe it was like the clerk said and the property was being sold. She returned the pages to their original order before going over each page, snapping photos of them with her phone. Wait until AJ heard who she had run into.

16

After her morning climb and the surprise welcome from Ethan, AJ second-guessed a trip to visit the ship's captain. She felt silly about that. She was investigating a story and there was no harm in it. Yet something troubled her about the captain. The way she discovered the ghostly ship still left her a little on edge.

Her morning tasks completed, AJ checked the clock on the wall. There was nothing holding her to the office, and a drive to the inn couldn't be avoided, as she would need pictures for the article. It was simple. She would get the shots and only then decide whether to walk down to the dock.

It didn't occur to her until she parked in front of the inn that the captain might not be there. Her stomach tightened, and she convinced herself it was only because she might miss out on a good story. The sun warmed her face as she approached the Westcliffe, and she wished she had left her sweater behind. But in the next moment, a shiver ran through her, a combination of the salty breeze brushing her skin and the remnants of ghosts lingering on the front porch. She pulled her sweater close.

At the split in the path, she hesitated. Her plan was to get the pictures, but she could do that anytime. She wanted to see if the captain and ship were still here. Emboldened by the good weather, her investigative curiosity returning, AJ turned left and headed to the dock.

The ship impressed her each time she saw it. On this trip, she could see it wasn't as large as she remembered. The main mast, devoid of full sails, still made the ship appear larger than it was— or perhaps it was just that it was a centuries-old ship. The wooden hull wasn't as sleek and shiny as the refined wood of some sailboats or the fiberglass of others. As she got closer, she could see the wear in the ship, though it did not have an old, worn-out look, nor an appearance of having been moored at some marina or dry docked for months on end. The deck was scrubbed. Bits of brass sparkled in the sunlight. This was a well cared for, well-used ship, not some museum piece.

This time AJ walked the entire length of the ship, taking in what she could see of the deck. The sails were tied tight to long wooden beams that, if she remembered correctly, were called yards, but her knowledge of sailing was limited. She wasn't sure how the rigging really worked, but she assumed some form of pulley system, as the canvas of the sails had to be heavy.

She strolled, taking her time as she looked over every piece of the ship. When she arrived at the stern, she pulled out her phone to take a picture and saw the name *Daphne Marie* carved in soft bronze stretching across the transom. What type of woman could make a man name a ship after her?

For the second time, the voice made her jump.

"It's you again. The reporter."

She turned to face him, caught by the amusement that crinkled the corners of his eyes, accompanied by a crooked grin. How many women had fallen for his looks—perhaps someone named Daphne? He wore work jeans and a sweatshirt. A hammer perched in a bucket he carried by his side. His face held the tanned color people got from working all day in the sun, and he wiped at a trickle of sweat that rolled from his brow.

The captain looked at his hammer. "Sorry, I've been doing some repairs. There's always something to do on board a ship." The captain set down the tools, his hands moving to his hips. "Is there something I can help you with?"

The breeze picked up and, not wanting to shout, AJ took a step closer. "Yes, my name is AJ Moore, and I'm a reporter for the *Baywood Herald*. I'm doing a story on old historical buildings and was interested in the inn."

"I see. And so tell me, Miss AJ Moore, what makes this inn so interesting?"

His question seemed sincere, but his penetrating stare weakened her resolve. AJ pulled away from the inspection to take a long look at the dock and then toward the main house. "I thought it might have a story to tell."

He took his own time to look around, matching AJ's tempo. "I'm new here, so I'm afraid I can't tell you one way or the other. Mr. Jackson might be able to help you. From what I understand, he's cared for this place for some time."

"Mr. Jackson. Isn't that the man you mentioned the first time I was here?"

"Yes it was. You have a good memory. It must be those reporter skills."

"Have you known Mr. Jackson long?"

"I believe I mentioned I was new here so, no, I haven't known him long."

"How did you come to dock here instead of the marina?" The questions rolled out of her, refusing to stop. She matched his glare, refusing to waver.

The captain's gaze hardened, the smile no longer reaching his eyes. "Didn't you say your story was on the inn?"

AJ detected the change before seeing it on his face. She had felt some pull from this man, as if a thin, unseen string connected them. Then, just as quickly, it broke. He didn't like being questioned. AJ wanted to push forward, dozens of questions unanswered, but the captain had folded his arms in front of him. She tried a different tactic.

"Sorry. I guess this old ship intrigued me. I've never seen anything like her. She seemed like a nice addition to the story on the inn." AJ walked toward him, focusing on the ship, her admiration sincere.

He joined her as she strolled by. "She's a true ship to be sure. She's never disappointed." His natural pride for the ship couldn't be hidden.

AJ found herself leaning in to hear the last sentence. The captain's change in demeanor made her want to place a hand on his arm before being caught by an urgent need to pull it back, although she hadn't actually reached out. "And does she have a story to tell?"

His smile returned, his body visibly relaxing. He patted the side of the ship. "She's seen many a storm and has pulled me out of each, delivering me to sunny shores."

They stood at the end of the dock and the path leading back to the inn. AJ struggled with how to get the discussion back to her story, surprised when the captain helped her out.

"Mr. Jackson should be here later this afternoon."

"I guess my timing's off. I could use an interview with him." His green eyes snared her, and she couldn't stop the blush from reddening her cheeks, forcing her to look away.

"He was to meet with me to look over the repairs for the inn."

"Repairs. Is there going to be construction on the place?"

"Nothing that dramatic. Enough to make it livable again."

"Are you moving in? Do you own it?" The questions piled up in AJ's head and rushed from her mouth.

The captain's laugh was loud and spontaneous, and for a moment, the mystery of the man seemed to fall away.

The questions begging to be released vanished when AJ heard

his deep, joyful laugh. It made her laugh in return. "I know." She turned back to look at the ship. "I can't seem to help myself. It's almost as if I've dropped into a different time, and I just don't know where to begin."

The captain's smile faded, and he turned away. After a long pause, he glanced toward AJ. "Maybe I could give you a small tour of the ship."

AJ whirled back. "That would be fantastic." Her own smile faded. She didn't know this man, and now, out in the middle of nowhere, she had second thoughts about boarding.

The captain sensed her hesitation. "Of course, we should probably wait until Mr. Jackson arrives. He's been wanting a tour himself."

She tugged at her lower lip. She didn't know Mr. Jackson any better than the captain. "What time did you say Mr. Jackson would be here?"

"He tends to run on his ·own schedule, but I believe I remember him saying something about two." The captain walked her partway up the path. "Will you be returning?"

AJ wasn't sure what to make of this man. A few short minutes ago, he was disturbed by her persistent questions, but now it appeared he didn't mind if she came back. She couldn't read his face; he didn't divulge anything one way or another.

"I don't think you told me your name."

The captain's slow grin returned, his look mischievous. "No. I don't believe I did."

AJ sighed, trying to look put out, but unable to hold back her own grin. "May I ask your name, sir?"

He gave a small bow with his right arm outstretched and increased his brogue. "Aye, it's Finnian Murphy, but most call me Finn."

"All right, Finn. I'll be back at two o'clock to meet your Mr. Jackson." AJ refused to look back as she hiked up, but she was dying to know if he still watched her. She swore she could feel those blazing green eyes on her backside. She was almost to the top of the path when she heard him call out.

"It's been a pleasure seeing you again."

AJ blushed to her roots, lifting her hand in response, refusing to look back, and the sound of a soft chuckle could be heard just above the wind.

FINN WATCHED AJ WALK AWAY, so full of confidence, though she must know he followed her movements. She was tall, athletic, and a bit too thin, but it seemed to suit her height and natural grace. He had put her off guard with his comments, and he found her charming, especially when she spit back.

But her last name made him curious as to why she was here. He couldn't be sure, and he didn't like coincidences.

When she was gone, he searched his pocket for the prepaid phone he had purchased at the pharmacy. He dialed and waited patiently for several rings. He was about to hang up when the craggy old voice finally answered.

"Can you meet me at two?" Finn said.

"I got nothing better to do," Jackson said and hung up.

Finn smiled. Something not enough people treasured—a man of few words. He walked back to the ship, but before boarding, another thought came to mind. He reached into another pocket for a slip of paper with several names and numbers. After finding the one he wanted, he made one more call.

Time dragged, reminding AJ of a few days before when she couldn't come up with a story. Each minute stretched into ten. After the first hour, she took off her watch and slipped it into the pocket of her jeans so she wouldn't keep looking at it. The phone was the next distraction, AJ waking it to find the time creeping just as slowly there. At noon, she stopped at the first small store she could find and bought a tolerable lunch. She called Stella, who was distracted and didn't want to talk, but she agreed to meet AJ for happy hour. She could have driven back to the office, but, after calling in, nothing demanded her attention.

With the remnants of lunch scattered across the passenger seat of her car, a full stomach, and the sun warming the car, AJ found the stress that had built up from the morning oozing out of her. She leaned her head back and prepared questions for her meeting. If she wrote them down, it would help her stay focused —she had been too scattered that morning. Instead, she drifted off, unsure if it was the distraction of Finn or being unprepared for the interview that made her feel like a novice.

The chime of her phone dragged her out of her daze. Finally, someone to talk to. It took her a minute to find it, and she answered without checking the caller ID. She was surprised to hear Ethan's voice.

"Have I caught you at a bad time?"

It took a minute for AJ's head to clear. "No. This is fine."

"You sound like I woke you. Not sleeping at your desk, are you?"

"I'm not at my desk. But I may have been...quietly reviewing my day...and got lost in my thoughts."

A small chuckle escaped through the phone. "So you're napping someplace other than your office."

"You should be a detective instead of in security."

"There is some intuition in security work. It's not all brawn."

"My mistake." AJ laughed, fully awake now. She opened the window to let a breeze rustle through the car.

"I wanted to confirm our visit to the antique shops. Are we still on for Saturday?"

She had already forgotten and tried to remember why she agreed to a day of antiquing. Her focus should be on her new story, but in truth, she needed to step away and let her subconscious work through it. And she would need some distance from Finn Murphy, who seemed to keep her off-balance. But she also found Ethan to be a good sounding board, and he might have some insights to the inn. "I haven't had a chance to ask Stella yet, but I'm sure Saturday is still okay."

"Great. I'll let you get back to your nap."

"Funny."

She disconnected the call and dialed Stella, but again got her voice mail. She left a quick message about Ethan's invitation and checked the time. Less than an hour to go.

Recovered from her nap, AJ walked around a small park not far from the inn. The crisp ocean air, the chirping birds, and the sounds of the waves coming on shore woke her senses. The nap had been the perfect antidote to revive her. She ran through her questions. How old was the ship? Where did this captain sail from? Dozens more, assuming she'd get that far. Either way, Finn Murphy would not control her interview.

WHEN AJ PULLED into the lot of the Westcliffe, the two men stood at the top of the path. Finn stood tall over the other man, who appeared bent rather than shorter, like the small firs surrounding the inn, worn down by the winds. She hadn't paid attention to the second man when she spotted them in the diner. Her focus had been on the captain.

As she left her car, AJ's nerves tingled, and she swore, irritated at what was becoming her typical response on seeing Finn. Squaring her shoulders, she increased her pace, forcing the questions she had rehearsed to come back to her.

Both men turned from their discussion, and their greeting surprised her. Mr. Jackson's smile was warm and inviting, his chestnut eyes sharp with intelligence. The finest of lines in his face betrayed his age, as did the light gray hair, and the physical bearing of one who had spent many years working a farm or construction. Perhaps both. He wore overalls and a plaid shirt. His rough hands and scraped, dirty nails reflected those of a man acquainted with hard work.

Finn's sharp gaze also held a broad smile, but there was something else, as if he were assessing her again, not sure what to make of her. AJ silently cursed. Without even saying a word, he had already taken control of this meeting.

Before AJ reached them, Mr. Jackson stepped forward with his hand outstretched to take hers. Despite the older man's calluses, his hand was gentle and his grip firm.

"I'm Jackson, the caretaker of this old place." His voice was a deep, rich baritone, like a voice-over for a commercial advertising an exotic liqueur. AJ smiled and took his offered arm. He turned her toward the inn. "Mr. Murphy tells me you have some interest in the old girl."

AJ let him guide her, their pace so quick, she wasn't sure if he was being direct or had some other place he needed to be. Before they reached the porch, AJ extricated herself from Jackson's grasp, stopped short, and raised her camera. Finn veered off to avoid running her over.

She kept her voice light. "I gather Mr. Murphy told you about my interest in doing a story on your 'old girl.' If you don't mind I'd like to get a couple of shots before we get closer." AJ stepped away from them and took her time to frame the shots of the building.

Jackson appeared impatient and Finn amused, but to their credit, neither man said a word when AJ returned to the path, climbing the stairs to the porch. She ran her hand over the side of the building as she had the first day she'd encountered Finn's ship. Like the ship, the wood here was also aged but well cared for. "How did you come to be the caretaker of the inn, Mr. Jackson?"

The old man gazed up to the porch's ceiling, his eyes unfocused, and he shook his head. "It's been such a long time, not sure how it originally came to pass. I take care of several homes around here. Most are vacant for the winter, and the owners or renters come for the summer. This is the only one sitting vacant for years."

"It seems someone would have bought it ages ago. Its prime real estate," AJ said.

"It is surprising that it hasn't reopened for business, but as for not being sold, that's not surprising at all."

"Why not?"

"Because it hasn't been for sale." Jackson turned and hurried along the long front porch, turning toward the back of the house.

AJ followed with Finn so close behind, she could have swung her arm back and touched him. The old man moved fast, and she increased her pace to keep up with him. "So what can you tell me about the people who own the inn?"

"Nothing." Jackson yelled his response over his shoulder and led them around the next turn in the deck to the back of the inn.

AJ spied a couple of abandoned chairs and a long bench, and for a moment, she caught a fleeting image of inn guests relaxing in the glow of a summer evening, waiting for the sun's last gasp as it receded from view.

Jackson stopped halfway to the sitting area, playing at a piece of wood that had pulled away from one of the windows. "Time to bring some tools," he muttered to himself as he dropped onto the bench and looked out to sea.

The view was breathtaking, wide open and unencumbered by anything other than the simply landscaped yard, giving way to natural grasses and the wind. Two fir trees hovered off the far deck, as bent as Mr. Jackson, trying to hold their ground against the gusts that often rocked the coast. Today, the sun shone bright against the sea, almost blinding.

Jackson interrupted the quiet. "Sit down and I'll tell you what I know about the building, but I won't speak about the current owners. None of my business."

AJ held her sigh and smiled, taking one of the deck chairs and pulling it around to face the man, her back to the sea. Finn positioned a deck chair between her and Jackson, facing it more toward her instead of the storyteller.

Everyone settled, AJ took out her notepad and directed her interview at Jackson. "Tell me what you know about the inn."

Jackson sat back, pulled out a pipe from the front of his overalls, and set it between his teeth. AJ could have sworn she saw a slight puffing although there was nothing in the pipe, and the piece looked as if it had never been used. After a minute, he rested the pipe against his knee.

"The inn was built in 1911, but it wasn't an inn at the time. It was built for the Ramseys, who were new to town and fairly well-off. They had a large family, so they needed a lot of rooms. They lived here until the old man died somewhere around the late thirties. Most of the kids had moved away, but the oldest son returned with his wife and children to help his mother. A few years later, the mother passed, and we were at war again. After the attack at Pearl, the young Ramsey joined Civil Defense and became an airplane spotter watching for the Japanese. He was too old to go to war, and the army refused to take him, so he did his duty by being a spotter, to the point that it became an obsession. At least it's what I've read down at the historical society."

Jackson stopped and looked pointedly at AJ. "They have some pictures and journals from some of the residents of these older buildings. Have you ever been over there?"

"Not yet." AJ mumbled the words, caught like an unprepared schoolgirl. "The first house I wrote about had a great deal of its history still in the house, old pictures and news clippings. I did make a few calls..." She trailed off, irritated she hadn't thought to call the society. She must have lost her touch during her dry spell. What else could be clouding her thoughts?

The old man nodded. "The McDowell place. Read the article. Decent job, got most of it right. There wasn't much more to say about the place."

AJ raised an eyebrow and slid a glance to Finn, who, to her dismay, seemed to be studying her. "So the older son became obsessed with spotting."

Jackson put the pipe between his lips again. The only thing missing was the rocking chair. She hid her smile. A quick glance at Finn revealed a conspiratorial smile.

"His wife got tired of it several years after the end of the war," Jackson said. "He never gave up waiting for an attack, sitting in one of the bedrooms, always watching the sea, sometimes late into the evenings. The upkeep of the place ended up falling to her, so she packed up the kids and left, moved into town. Ramsey stayed until he died in the early sixties, heart attack, stroke, can't remember. He wasn't old, but he was nuts. His wife sold it to a young couple. They remodeled it, added a couple of bathrooms, and made it into the inn."

The conversation grew silent. There wasn't much to say about the life of the Ramseys and the final self-destruction of the obsessive patriarch. AJ found disturbing similarities between Ramsey and McDowell. Both men were equally obsessed, one about the sea, and the other about an imaginary foe who could find its way to shore by the same route.

Finn surprised her by breaking the silence. "So what happened with the inn?"

Jackson, who had returned to sucking on his pipe and staring out to sea, turned his gaze to Finn. "It was a success for a while, from what I can remember. I was pretty young. But it changed hands a few times in the early years, and I lost track of it. Been closed longer than I can remember."

"So who owns it now?" AJ said.

Jackson looked at her, his expression stoic. "You'll need to discover that another way. It's not for me to talk about my employer."

"You can't even tell me who?" AJ said.

"Nope. Not my place."

AJ looked to Finn for help, but he shook his head. No help there. She let it go. She'd find out through county records. She joined the men in gazing out to sea, taking in the lazy warmth for a short time. Seeing that neither man seemed eager to move on, she tried a new tack.

"Maybe it's time for that tour of your ship." AJ hadn't decided how to tie the ship to the inn. Maybe it warranted its own article. The ship appeared to be older than either of the buildings she had researched. She wasn't sure Finn would be docked here long enough for her to put a story together.

"As good a time as any." Finn slapped Jackson on the knee.

"Come on, Mr. Jackson, I know you've been dying to get on board."

Jackson took longer to stand. "One boat's as good as the next." Jackson made it sound dismissive, but he showed a slight grin and tucked the pipe away. He made a beeline for the ship, back the way they had come, not waiting for either Finn or AJ to keep up.

18

The ship seemed to invite AJ as she drew near, ready to reveal her secrets. The deck was spotless and freshly washed, the sails tucked and tied sharply in place. The mast seemed to stretch forever into the sky, forcing AJ to lean back to find the small crow's nest perched on top.

She strolled along the deck, stopping to examine the rigging. An array of ropes wrapped themselves like snakes around aged wooden pins, holding them in place. Small pieces of brass, scattered here and there, sparkled in the sunlight, and she had to restrain herself from touching, afraid of leaving fingerprints on the shiny surfaces.

AJ focused so much on the details of the ship, she didn't notice the men had disappeared. She scanned the deck. Faint voices emerged through the light wind, somewhere below deck, and AJ turned toward the stern, searching for a passageway.

The dark and narrow steps opened to a room. A large table claimed most of the room. A lone tin mug shared space with a large brass lantern that cast a shadowy light through the room. The lit lantern indicated there was no electricity on board, unless it had been retrofitted, but as she reviewed the entire room, the ship appeared as rustic as the day it was built. She ran her hands over the table and along the wall, fingering the base of the lantern, warm from the flame. Why keep it this way? Didn't the ship have a communication center of some kind? Whether it was a museum piece making its way to another port or some man's obsessive hobby, AJ couldn't tell.

As AJ turned, another table on the far side of the room caught her attention. The navigation area. A chart lay open, spanning the entire surface of the table, carved glass paperweights holding the corners in place. Other charts were rolled and stacked to one side, and even more were kept in open storage cubes under the table. Several instruments lay on the chart. AJ stepped closer. The objects appeared new or well cared for, but if they had been in an antique store, she would have judged them to be a hundred years old, possibly older. AJ leaned over to get a look at the chart.

Finn's voice made her turn. He leaned in from a side room.

"Jackson said you might be interested in the galley and the hold."

AJ took a last glimpse at the chart, too far away to see it clearly, and silently cursed. Why did men think women always wanted to see the kitchen? She reluctantly turned from the table. "Have you been plundering the high seas and hold riches for us to see?"

Finn laughed. "So now you've found out my true nature and my pirate ways. It's good fortune Jackson is here with us to prevent me from sailing away with such a beautiful prize."

AJ snorted, but she hoped the light was too dim for Finn to see her blush. His face reflected amusement, but a flicker of something else too. She shivered as if it wasn't too far a stretch for him to whisk her away.

"My father always told me I was born under good fortune, so I guess it's paying off," AJ said and squeezed past him, picking up the scent of something akin to cedar and a combination of masculine scent, and the quick touch of fabric against fabric sent a different type of shiver through her. She quickened her pace toward Jackson's voice, not sure if the man knew he was talking to himself.

Jackson was past the galley, standing inside another room, which appeared to be one of the ship's storage areas, holding a can of food and eying a large bag of flour. AJ stepped next to him so she could see farther into the room. It didn't lead anywhere—it was an enormous pantry stacked with bags of flour, grain, and sugar, all sitting in high piles next to cans of fruits, vegetables, meats and other unknown items. Large, unmarked crates ran along one side of the room. When Finn joined them, they were both investigating the items like they were lost treasures.

"Looks like you're set for a long voyage." Jackson moved toward the door, still surveying the room.

"I like to be prepared," Finn said.

"I've never seen bags like these for food storage." AJ inspected each label, brands she'd never heard of. She picked up a can of food and turned it around in her hands, scanning the other items in the hold. "Quite a mixture of old and new."

"Let's move back to the galley." Finn turned, leaving no room for questions.

AJ sighed. Back to the kitchen. All the interesting stuff was in the pantry, but she had no choice but to follow.

They found Jackson standing in the middle of the galley, scratching his head. "It doesn't look like you need any more supplies," Jackson said. "But all you have to do is ask and we can make a run. You could do with a meal in town and get something a little more fresh if you're going to be here long. Nothing worse than eating out of a can too long."

"Aye." Finn slapped Jackson on the back. "I could do with some fresh fruits and vegetables. Maybe tomorrow would be a good time."

Jackson stood at the stairs leading to the deck and scratched his chin. "Not sure I can do it, but I'll send Caleb over with the truck. He can take you anywhere you want to go. I can give him some errands to do if you want to spend time on your own."

"Any time will do. I appreciate your help."

"So does that get me a tour of the gun deck?"

AJ didn't hear any more of the men's conversation. Her thoughts were miles away. What she had seen in the stores perplexed her. The packaging on some of the food and other items looked old but freshly packed. Other items had been purchased recently, based on the well-known brand names. She couldn't fathom the reasoning behind such historical rendering when it came to food and tack but supposed she had seen stranger things, although she couldn't remember when.

Ignoring the men, she wandered back down the short passageway. Her intention was to get a look at the chart table, but when she saw another door, she couldn't stop herself. When she opened the door, she knew she had intruded too far, but couldn't help taking a quick look around.

A huge bed dominated Finn's cabin, but plenty of space remained for trunks of various sizes, a small hand-carved bookcase filled with books, a side table adorned with a large bowl, a pitcher, and what might be personal grooming gear. On a smaller table, a mug lingered next to an open book. AJ found herself curious as to what Finn would be reading but didn't dare cross into his private chamber.

Several items could be valuable antiques, some less ornate than others, but all wonderful representations from several generations ago. They could be replicas, but AJ didn't think so. Too many other things she had seen and touched had been authentic, and she had no reason to believe all this wasn't as well. Again the dedication to history. Before she could come up with an explanation, soft footsteps approached. The warm, masculine scent of cedar filled the air.

Finn's body came close, almost touching her, warmth radiating from him. She didn't want to move forward into his private sanctuary, yet he allowed her no quarter to step back without running into him. He didn't say a word. So close. She imagined her hair gently moving from the touch of his breath. Panic took hold, and she fought the primordial instinct to take flight. She scanned the room to find another way out—none. She closed her eyes and tried to think of something to say, to explain the meddling, as innocent as it was.

The silence magnified his presence. She was positive he could hear the rapid pounding of her heartbeat. The ship creaked as it nestled against the undulating waves. The bed seemed to have doubled in size. Now would be a good time for someone to ask her to take another look at the galley.

She forced herself to turn and push past him. The warm hardness of his chest brushed her arm. "Sorry," she said. "I didn't mean to intrude." She fled back through the chart room and up the stairs. She broke through the door and gulped air, the bright sunshine dissolving her flight response. She rubbed her hands against her jeans, brushed her hair back, and looked around for Jackson, hoping he didn't witness her rush to the deck.

Jackson picked his way down the gangplank, his back to her. AJ raced to follow and was halfway down before Finn arrived back on deck.

He was right behind her by the time she stepped onto the dock. She wished Jackson had headed back to the parking lot so she could follow, but he had waited for them on the dock. She looked at her feet, out to sea, and then back toward the ship, any place other than in Finn's direction.

"I hope you both enjoyed the tour of my ship." Finn's voice was light, seeming nonplussed by the intrusion and subsequent flight.

"It's a fine boat. I just wish I could have seen the guns," Jackson said.

"Guns?" AJ's self-induced dilemma vanished. She turned to look at Jackson.

"Yes." Jackson pointed to the side of the ship. "See the gunports? She should be carrying cannons."

AJ stared at the small doors that ran along the side of the ship. She hadn't paid attention to them until now.

"As I told Mr. Jackson, the cannons were removed long ago. There was nothing to see on the gun deck except crew quarters and the cargo hold."

"And that's a shame. Hard to have a good replica without the guns. I see the gunports look usable."

"I keep everything working where I can," Finn said.

"Well, either way, she's in wonderful condition for her age," Jackson said. "It would be great to see her in full sail."

"Perhaps you'll soon have the opportunity." Finn gazed with pride at his ship.

AJ frowned. She might not get her story after all. "How difficult is it to sail her? By yourself, I mean. She looks like she could use a crew."

Finn turned a respectful glance toward her. "Aye, she's a handful by myself. But as long as I keep her close to shore she's manageable with one sail. I would need several more hands to take her out to sea."

Jackson chuckled. "We should find you a few hands so we could see what she's like."

Finn laughed in return. "I agree we'd need more than the two of you to put her in full sail."

AJ bristled at the comment, though she knew nothing about sailing. "And you don't think we're up to the task?"

"And how many times have you run a sail?"

AJ refused to back down. "I'm a quick study."

"Are you now?" Finn winked at Jackson.

Jackson laughed, then grimaced when AJ gave him a scathing look.

"Yes," AJ said, her response subdued. She had talked her way onto dangerous ground and didn't know how to get herself out of it.

"All right. Why don't you come back for a short sail? Sunday would work. If you're up to the challenge."

AJ had walked into that. Both men waited for her reply. The moments below deck forgotten, she stood in the daylight, facing the gauntlet thrown at her. She wanted to experience it, the ship plowing through the waves, and she couldn't imagine any of the sleeker, more modern ships able to compete with it. More importantly, this could be the break she needed. She could gain a great deal of information for another article with one quick sail.

"With one condition," AJ said, remaining resolute with her decision. "If you're willing to let me interview you about the ship for my article, then Sunday would be fine."

A slow smile appeared on Jackson's face. "Well, you two have a good time," he said. "Wish I could be with you, but Sunday is my day with the family. And to be honest, I'd prefer to keep my feet planted right here on shore. I was getting woozy just walking around her tied to the dock. Hate to see what a mess I'd make once she left the bay." Jackson chuckled, then headed toward the path. "I'll send Caleb out to take you to town." His last words were partially lost in the wind.

AJ didn't want to be left behind with Finn, didn't want to explain the intrusion into his private chambers, and wished she could take back her stupid challenge about sailing. "Wait, Mr. Jackson, I'll walk with you." Forcing herself to look at Finn, she discovered he was looking not at her, but at the retreating old man.

"Ten o'clock," Finn said.

"What?"

"Sunday, ten o'clock. No later. The tide will be perfect." Finn turned to her, warmth in his smile. She read no malice, no challenge, no other agenda in his emerald gaze.

"All right. I'll see you then." AJ hurried to catch up with Jackson. Finn didn't say anything else, and she refused to look back to see if he was still watching them.

Because, she realized, she would be disappointed if she turned and he was gone.

FINN WATCHED her move up the path until she was out of sight. He had been irritated by her intrusion into his private space, peering into his cabin, but he had been the one who offered them a tour.

She had given the room a thorough review but didn't intrude past the door. She was just curious. He had no idea what she had thought of it all, and hadn't meant to stand so close to her, but he couldn't help himself when he caught her soft scent of lavender. She was just there, her body so close, he could sense the warmth. He wasn't able to do anything more than stand there, glad Jackson was right up the stairs, the setting too intimate. He was relieved when she shoved past him, most likely embarrassed for being so nosy.

His plans for Sunday would keep them out in the light of day and busy working sails. He would be too busy dodging her questions, while trying to sneak in a few of his own, to give any thought to more familiar matters.

19

A dam couldn't sleep. After what seemed like hours of restless dreams, he stared at the ceiling, coming to the realization he was awake for the day, and silently cursed. Usually an army tank crashing through the front door would do little to disturb his sleep. His cases at work never bothered him. Most were mundane, and even if he took on a prickly one, it was never bad enough to interfere with a good night's sleep.

Madelyn was also a heavy sleeper, so she didn't move when Adam sat up and slid into his slippers. It amazed him that his children had survived through their infancy with both of their parents being such heavy sleepers. Madelyn had kept baby monitors on the nightstands, one for each of them, but the house could have burned down before either of them would have been woken by any squalling coming from the tiny units. Nothing ever happened, of course. Madelyn's maternal instincts seemed to wake her when she was needed, sometimes before hearing any crying. Having reached the toddler years, the children's occasional tantrums echoing down the hall still didn't faze either parent sleeping contentedly in their beds.

Times were different now, and Adam had no one to blame but himself. He had been distressed for weeks before a small respite came his way. He truly believed he had found a solution to his problem. He should have known better. He was finding it difficult to extricate himself from the mess he'd created. And now this. Someone he had no desire to be involved with was smack dab in the middle of preventing him from getting clear.

Sighing, Adam moved from the bed, grabbed his robe, and headed to the kitchen. He turned on one small light, not yet ready for the full brightness of the kitchen, everything white and stainless steel. He made instant coffee. If he made a pot, it would get old before Madelyn got up, and she liked a fresh cup in the morning. He took his coffee into the study and slumped into his recliner, the perfect spot for reading legal texts and strategizing cases.

Madelyn kept a small comforter close by in case Adam fell asleep, or if the house had a chill as it sometimes did in the dampness of winter. He didn't deserve someone like her, always ensuring his comfort. He wished he could talk to her about his problem. She was his sounding board, always able to see the forest. Adam was typically good at it himself, but with some cases, he got too buried in the legal meanderings and needed someone to remind him to look at the bigger picture. That was where Madelyn shone.

Not this time, though.

He took a sip of coffee, leaned back in the recliner, and pulled on the comforter, wrapping it around himself like a protective cocoon. He worked through his predicament as if Madelyn were there next to him, guiding each bullet point like a practiced legal assistant. He had needed money and he was too ashamed to tell anyone, even Madelyn—especially Madelyn. People would think him foolish and weak.

The last two days had focused on finding his way through the nightmare, but he seemed further than ever from his goal. He still questioned the wisdom of getting involved with a stranger who, if he had to admit it, deeply scared him. He drained the last of his coffee and set the cup on a stand before pulling the comforter tighter around him. He stretched out the recliner and shifted his focus to the ceiling. After a few minutes, he closed his eyes. His next steps remained shrouded, just a hair out of reach. He wished he could ask Madelyn what she thought.

MADELYN FOUND Adam asleep in his favorite chair. She frowned and tucked the comforter tighter around him. Something was worrying him, something he didn't think he could share with her. He never held anything back, whether it was about work or home, and the fact that he wouldn't talk to her was more than she could bear.

She knew in her heart it wasn't another woman. And he wasn't drinking too much—that would be obvious. He enjoyed his poker nights. Maybe the gambling had gotten away from him. Maybe he got into some trouble at work.

He was a proud man, but this wasn't like him—sleepless nights and closing her off. She brushed a light kiss on his forehead, the worry lines erased in easy slumber.

She wouldn't push for now. But if it went on much longer, she wouldn't have a choice. They were stronger when they dealt with problems together, and she had a limit to the amount of disruption she would allow in their lives.

20

Saturday morning brought AJ out of a groggy sleep. Why had she committed to such an early time for an antique trip? A quick look toward her window revealed the dismal grayness, and she fought the desire to roll over and go back to sleep. She had worked late into the night on her article on the inn, but it didn't seem complete. Something was missing. Maybe it was the Ramseys, or the first family that turned the Westcliffe into an inn, or maybe the continuing mystery of Finn. He seemed to have nothing to do with the inn, other than his close proximity to it, but sailing into the bay with a historical ship seemed to tie him to the place, in timing if nothing else.

Making her way to the kitchen, each step required AJ's full concentration, as if she had spent the night clubbing. Stress at work over the past few weeks, combined with her life being thrown off tilt the last few days, topped off with five hours of sleep, did not make for a fully functional brain.

Coffee.

If she could get to the machine, she could have her hands wrapped around a glorious mug of magic brew in less than five minutes. Five minutes more, after the caffeine hit, her world would rotate back to a level horizon.

With the coffee machine set to its chore, AJ shuffled to the window overlooking the building's garden and groaned at the light misting of rain. She had forgotten to check the forecast. Dragging herself back to the counter, she wrapped one hand around a steaming cup of blessed relief, grabbed a banana from a basket with the other, and let her mind drift to her article.

She had planned to meet with Stella on Friday, but her friend had been interrupted by an early closing over in Eugene, an all-day event.

Having the day to herself, AJ made a trip to the Historical Society Museum. Since AJ was unable to see the inside of the inn, the Historical Society had been instrumental in giving her the only view to what the building had looked like in the early years as a family home, then as an inn. The museum had the only documented pictures, and even they had not been able to get anything after the seventies.

The building itself was unremarkable from the early years, other than the number of bedrooms included as part of the original design. A bit unusual for a middle-class family and perhaps an omen for the obsessive nature running through the family.

The Historical Society had not been able to retrieve much in the way of journals, so the accounts of its morphing into the inn were from third-party recollections of events. The main story of the inn had been as Mr. Jackson said. The oldest son and his fixation on the war, what he thought might be an ultimate attack from Japan, and the eventual fall into general madness before a stroke took him.

Light broke through from the garden window, and AJ smiled. The clouds were lifting from the day as well as from her mind. Getting dressed for the trip, she finalized her next steps. She had to find out more about the inn. But Mr. Jackson wasn't going to be an easy nut to crack.

The key was the ship. Perhaps nothing sinister was going on, but Finn Murphy's reluctance to talk was enough to pique her interest. An old ship magically appears one day sitting at its dock —the whole mess just begged her to dig. She would get her next story and determine for herself if there was a connection between her ghost ship and the Westcliffe Inn.

She grabbed her sweater, then stopped to grab her rain jacket. There was no way around it. She would need to spend more time with Finn Murphy to learn about the ship. And while she no longer thought he knew anything about Westcliffe, he might be able to help loosen up Mr. Jackson. She dreaded having to deal with either man.

At first, she didn't want to be alone with a stranger in a remote setting, but as she rolled it around in her mind, she wasn't scared of Finn. Her anxiety seemed to be triggered by his brashness. She would not let the man continue to get the upper hand in her interviews. She was a professional. She blew out a long breath and, before leaving the room, tossed the sweater and rain jacket aside in favor of a light windbreaker.

She headed out the door, her course determined, when another idea popped into her head. Ethan had the right skills to help with the investigation, if he was willing to help. He might not be willing to be her covert agent, but there was only one way to find out.

AJ guessed Stella's mood when it took three separate blasts of the horn to encourage her friend to greet the day. She looked like the walking dead. Hands wrapped around a huge travel mug of coffee, her steps tentative, and her sunglasses shading her eyes though the clouds hadn't fully lifted.

"Good morning," AJ said, tempting fate with a perky greeting.

Stella grunted and threw her bag in the back. She reclined her seat back several inches, her mug of coffee held protectively on her lap.

"It's going to be a marvelous day."

"All right already." Stella's voice was hoarse. "You're lucky I made it this far. Who in God's name gets up this early on a Saturday?"

AJ took pity on her friend. Stella did look pretty worn. "Long drive back from Eugene?"

Stella leaned up to take a long gulp of coffee. AJ hoped it had cooled enough, or that Stella was awake enough to know if she was drinking scalding-hot coffee. It seemed to be working. Stella raised her seat an inch. "I don't know why they called us to close. The paperwork wasn't ready, which delayed everything by two hours. Should have waited until Monday."

"I couldn't do that."

"You get used to it. The other Realtor was amazing. He kept the conversation going, had us laughing over the funniest stories."

Stella still looked groggy.

AJ smirked. "Uh-huh."

"It's not like that." Stella raised her seat to face AJ.

"Sure. I understand."

"Please. You think I dragged him home to bed? You know I would have led with that." Not defensive, just matter-of-fact.

"You did seem to have a long day." AJ paused for effect. "And night."

"Yes, it was a long night. We went to dinner over in the Dell, that new restaurant. Can't remember the name, it opened last month." Stella's forehead wrinkled.

"Fishers Cove or Fishers Bay."

Stella nodded. "Fishers Cove, that's it. Great atmosphere, good food." Stella grabbed her bag from the back, fishing through it until she found her makeup bag, and dropped the visor to check herself in the mirror, touching up areas that didn't need it. "Anyway, I hadn't met Rick before, since he works out of Lincoln City. And before you ask, he's divorced, one kid. His wife moved over to the valley, but he sees his daughter once a week."

"Well, at least you know he's got a decent job."

"Yeah, maybe not the most respectable of jobs, but he's got one." Stella laughed, sounding more like herself. She nursed her coffee while rearranging her bag. "Oh, I forgot. We never got together to go over the county records."

"Anything of interest?"

Stella dug through her bag and pulled out her notepad. "I was able to see a clear chain of ownership from the Ramseys to a series of inn owners." She flipped through her notes. "Ownership moved from Tanner to Smith to McAllister and finally Owens before changing hands in the 1970s to a corporation."

"A corporation owns it?"

"It looks like it. And it's the same name as the inn. Westcliffe."

"Any specifics on the company?"

Stella turned a page in her notebook. "The corporation is privately held. The only name on record is a representative of Westcliffe by the name of Hensley. They have a post office box in London, of all places."

"It explains why no one has seen the owner."

"Maybe that's why Jackson won't talk about them. He's never met them."

"Maybe." AJ was disappointed. A corporation in London was of no help.

Stella stuffed her notepad back in her purse. Taking another gulp from her mug, Stella spotted the McDowell place. "You know, it looks less sinister when you know someone lives there, or maybe it's the "who" of who lives there."

AJ could see Stella's face brighten at the sight of the house. This was going to be an interesting day. She pulled next to a shiny black Escalade, the back hatch open. They had just stepped out of the car when Ethan walked out from a detached garage with an ice chest.

"Good morning, ladies. I have some water on ice for us." Ethan set the chest in the back of the Cadillac. He looked up at the thinning clouds. "I do believe we'll see some sun today." He brushed his hands against his jeans and smiled at them.

This was the first time AJ had seen him in jeans and a shirt with no accompanying jacket. His clothes almost fit his personality, but he didn't seem to have the easy nature of Finn. There remained an edge to him the change of clothes couldn't soften, as if he wanted to keep a fence between himself and others.

"I can't believe you're brave enough to take two women shopping." Stella staked out her place in the front seat. She dropped her shoulder bag on the floor and tried to fit her oversized mug in the drink holder.

Ethan raised an eyebrow, gave AJ a questioning glance, then moved toward Stella. "I was thinking more of an educational adventure rather than shopping. Here. Why don't you try the side holder?"

"What's educational about women shopping?" Stella smiled as her mug snuggled into the side holder.

"We're looking through antiques not with a mind for shopping but for a glimpse into history."

Stella rolled her eyes, sighed, and slid into the front seat. "Well, that doesn't sound nearly as interesting as shopping, but I'm willing to give it a whirl. AJ only took me antiquing once and for some reason never asked again." Stella sounded wounded but smiled as she shut her door.

AJ hopped into the back seat, dropping her small bag next to her, and Ethan climbed into the driver's seat. "This is going to be a test of patience for Stella today," AJ said.

"It's why I selected Chilton as the best option. Not only does it have several antique shops, but a good supply of art galleries, small cafés, and, I believe, two wine bars."

"Now that's a man who knows how to take care of a lady. I think you'll do nicely."

Ethan shot a look at AJ through the rearview mirror.

She grinned. "We're going to scare Ethan off before we make it out of town."

The drive to Chilton took an hour. The small town was south of Baywood and sat a mile or two inland, requiring the quiet hamlet to work hard to attract visitors, which they accomplished through an active antique and arts community. The shops ran east and west down the main street, with a few others scattered along narrow side streets. The salty air tickled the noses of tourists and locals alike, and shore birds could be heard squawking by the estuary bordering the town. The only thing missing was the shore.

Ethan parked on one of the small side streets, close to the middle of town. As they stretched their legs, streaks of sunlight pierced the remaining clouds, leaving their reflections in small puddles created by the morning rain.

They moved from shop to shop, Ethan always eager to explore the next shop. He peppered AJ with questions about various pieces, from small figurines to large armoires and everything in between. At first, the older artwork intrigued Stella, but her interest waned, and she often wandered away to be found at the next art gallery or a women's clothing shop.

While Ethan spent most of his time with AJ discussing odd

and ends of history, he shared time with Stella, discussing a piece of art or giving his opinion on a dress she picked up. His smooth transitions between the two women amazed AJ. It was as if he was spending a day with two sisters with opposite interests, needing to keep both happy so one wouldn't pout.

At one store, Ethan vigorously shook his head at a dress arrayed with bright colors. Stella held the dress against her, looking at herself in a mirror, explaining to Ethan why it was perfect. Ethan remained firm in his opinion to put it back, aggrieved to the point of selecting a different dress with an equal amount of diverse colors, a tone down on the color wheel. AJ smiled. It was a beautiful dress—a perfect dress—and AJ was surprised Ethan had picked it out. When Stella saw it, she tossed the dress she was holding over a rack, grabbed the one Ethan held, and draped it against herself, staring into the mirror. After a quiet moment, Stella checked the size before disappearing into a dressing room.

"That was amazing," AJ said.

"I have always found it difficult to understand why it takes so long to find a dress. The choice seems so obvious to me, but you spend hours pulling out items, unable to make a decision. It makes no sense." Ethan looked around the room. "See, this one would be perfect for you." Ethan pulled out a short summer dress with tiny forest-green flowers, several shades darker than the rest of the dress.

Immediately drawn to the colors, AJ couldn't help reaching for it. She let her fingers play over the soft fabric, imagining how fun it would be to wear. She pulled the dress to her and looked in the closest mirror, a silly smile meeting her gaze. Damn, he was good.

"Stella would love to see you try something on," he said. "It's a nice break from the antiquing, which doesn't seem to suit her."

He was playing her, but she didn't care. She liked the dress, so why let Stella have all the fun?

Ethan held back a smile as AJ followed Stella to the fitting room. After a few seconds, the women were chittering away. He turned to the sales lady. "Please let them know I'll be across the street, at the shop with the old watches in the window."

"I know the one," she said. "And thank you for the sales." The woman flashed a broad smile, seeming assured she had sold two dresses.

Leaving the shop, Ethan turned left instead of crossing the street, retracing his steps to a shop they had visited earlier. This was the first time he had been able to extricate himself from either woman, and he was eager to be back in his own element, away from the shopping, even for a little while. Ducking into the shop, Ethan kept a leisurely pace until he arrived at the back counter and nodded at the owner, who was helping a customer. The man gave Ethan a returning nod and asked his assistant to finish with the customer. He led Ethan to a small office and closed the door behind them.

Fifteen minutes later, newly purchased items in hand, AJ and Stella perused the shop with the watches across from the dress shop. AJ lost herself in the watches and old jewelry while Stella toyed with items—a touch here, a fondle there; no individual item received more than a second glance.

Stella sighed in relief when Ethan entered the shop. "Thank God. We didn't know where you went. I'm famished."

"Sorry, I was distracted by another shop." Ethan's response was clipped, and Stella's body stiffened.

"It's not a bother." Stella selected an old spice rack, giving it more attention than anything else she had seen all day.

With more enthusiasm, Ethan said, "You're right, it's way past lunchtime. It must be the company I'm keeping."

Stella brightened. "I know what you mean. I can shop and forget all about eating, but once the body says enough, I become such a grouch. The woman at the dress shop suggested a little outdoor café down the street. The weather has improved enough to sit outside, don't you think?"

"I'm sure it will be fine."

"Excellent." Stella dropped the spice rack. "AJ, let's go. You can come back if you have to."

AJ studied two items in her hand, an old watch and a bracelet, turning them over in her hands. "I found the most marvelous things. This watch must be close to a hundred years old, and it still works. I don't think they know what they have. This is a great price."

She handed it to Ethan, and when she finally looked at him, she sensed a reticence that hadn't been there earlier.

He took the watch and gave it a good once-over. "Yes, it's a marvelous find."

"We're going to lunch. Everyone is getting a little cranky from low blood sugar. I know I am." Stella took the bracelet AJ held and slipped it onto her wrist. "Where did you find it? This is marvelous. I can't believe I didn't see it."

AJ and Ethan laughed. Stella snickered but admired the bracelet, turning her arm this way and that. Ethan returned to his previous duties, giving the bracelet an appraising look, pausing over the odd-colored stone, rubbing it gently with his thumb, before turning toward the door.

"Don't you think it will go nicely with the piece I found last month?" AJ said.

"Oh yeah, I forgot about that." Stella inspected the stone and shook her head. "I'm not sure it's the same color, but hard to say."

"Let me just buy these. I'll meet you at the café." A quick glance at Ethan made her stop.

Ethan seemed frozen in place, his face a shade paler as he

stared at the bracelet.

"Are you all right?" AJ asked.

He stared at her, then seemed to recover from wherever he went. "I'll get us a table while you make your purchases."

"What's up with him?" AJ said after the door shut behind him.

"Oh, he's hungry. He's been like that since he came back. Can't say I blame him. I'm starving. Pay up, and I'll meet you outside."

AJ paid for her purchases, bothered by what had gotten into Ethan. Hunger alone wasn't enough to impact Ethan's mood, which had definitely changed since they had split up. Where had he gone when he left them at the dress shop? Maybe the sales lady misunderstood his intent. She placed her newfound treasures inside the bag with her new dress, the dress Ethan had selected. AJ refused to spoil the wonderful time she was having on some perceived change. Maybe it was just low blood sugar. She put the incident aside and stepped into the sunshine.

To Stella's delight, the café doubled as one of the wine bars in town, and Ethan secured a secluded table tucked away in the green foliage of the patio, amidst the perfume of peonies heavy in the warmth of the sun. A slight breeze rustled in from the coast, allowing sea air to wash over the town. AJ was so content, she could have curled up for a nap. These were the perfect Saturdays: hunting for lost treasures, the company of good friends, and the fresh aroma of baking bread.

"I can honestly say AJ is the only person who could be dropped in the middle of a huge pile of garbage and still find the one sole piece of treasure buried in it." Stella was regally ensconced in her chair, a glass of white wine held firmly in her hand. "I, on the other hand, could land in the middle of nothing but treasure and find the sole piece of garbage."

Ethan and AJ laughed. If nothing else, Stella had no misgivings as to who she was or what talents she did—or in this case did not—have.

"You weren't raised to see the treasures as I was. Dad schooled me from an early age on how to look at things and, over time, you learn a shorthand. I guess it's the best way I can describe it." AJ sipped her wine and glanced at Ethan.

He appeared to be the same charming host they'd begun the day with, but his edge returned. He smiled and continued to entertain them, while at the same time he monitored his surroundings, taking things in, apparently mulling them over, deciding if they had a hidden purpose or could be ignored. AJ wasn't sure she liked this side of him, always on guard, always suspicious of a situation or person. She wasn't sure how one lived like that.

Ethan locked eyes with her, and AJ recalled the first time she'd met him. His eyes peered into her depths, as if he were deciding if she could be trusted, if she were friend or foe. Then, as if the moment never happened, he smiled, the warmth spread over AJ, and her first impression disappeared. Almost.

Stella, seemingly oblivious, sighed in contentment and lay her head back against her chair, her eyes mere slits. With barely a chance to relax, her eyes popped open, and she bolted upright so quickly, she jostled wine onto her lap. "Well, drat, good thing it's white wine." Stella grabbed a napkin and, dipping it in a glass of water, dabbed at her lap. "I almost forgot to tell you about my trip to the county records office."

Ethan smiled. "Exactly the intent of the day. At least you had a small respite."

"I'm sure it will be a short diversion." AJ welcomed the conversation. Stella usually had a good tale. "So what's all the mystery? You gave me the names. What more is there?"

"When I went to look at the records for the inn, I ran smack into Adam coming out of the records office. He almost knocked me over."

AJ frowned and sat back. "It was such a perfect day and you had to spoil it. He's a lawyer, gathering information to sue some poor old lady out of her money."

Ethan grimaced. "Isn't that a little harsh?"

AJ had forgotten that Ethan had a working relationship with Adam, and as much as she disagreed with her brother on almost every level, she didn't want to cause his family harm. "You're right. I wasn't fair. I don't know why we have the history we do, but there it is. I don't think it will ever change. Sometimes you just don't like your own blood."

Ethan's expression softened. "You're right. Blood doesn't give them a free pass." He seemed lost in thought before allowing a small chuckle to escape. "I seem to have turned melancholy this afternoon."

Stella and AJ traded glances, then Stella circled back to the point of the story. "Well, it wasn't the fact he was coming out of the records office. When I went in to ask about Westcliffe, the clerk said she already had the file out. I have to tell you, I was surprised at how helpful and friendly the clerk was. You know most times the city and county workers don't seem to give you the time of day, and it's like you're asking for the moon when you try to get anything from them."

Irritation flickered on Ethan's face, but AJ was accustomed to Stella's tendency to wander off onto tangents. "So the clerk already had the file out," AJ said.

"Yes, I already said that. And it was a little weird she would have a file out on the same address I was looking for. But guess who asked for the file before me?"

"No clue," AJ replied, and sipped her drink, preparing herself for one of Stella's stories.

Ethan said nothing, appearing to politely follow the conversation.

Stella sighed and sat back. She sipped her wine and played with her napkin. "Adam. Your brother. That's why he was at the county office."

"*Adam?*" AJ looked back and forth between her lunch

companions. "I don't get it. Why would he be interested in Westcliffe?"

Ethan sipped his club soda. AJ, looking at just the right moment, caught a flicker of interest before his gaze went blank. She didn't want to play poker with him. She'd bet her best antique he would be good at it.

Stella gulped some wine and perched on her seat. "What could he be up to?"

"It doesn't mean he's up to anything." AJ shook her head. "It must be some case he's working. Maybe he's getting affairs in order for the owner. The owner has been the same for a while now, right?"

"Yes, since the seventies," Stella said. "Maybe they're planning on selling."

"Yes, I remember the dates now. Mr. Jackson didn't mention anything about it when I spoke to him the other day."

"But if he's the caretaker, he wouldn't necessarily know anything about it," Stella said.

"True." AJ sat back, turning her wineglass in her hand. She didn't know if this new discovery meant anything. It was an odd coincidence she couldn't completely ignore.

Ethan played at his sleeve where he had rolled up his cuffs, patient as the silence grew. "So what's the interest in the Westcliffe?"

"It's my next article after the McDowell story."

"I'm not familiar with it. What made you select this building? You said it was an inn?" Ethan shook his head after a brief moment. "I don't remember seeing it when I first arrived. I'm sure I reviewed all the possible hotels and inns."

"It's closed," Stella said. "Has been for years, almost as long as the current owners have owned it."

Ethan looked at AJ. "Whatever made you choose the inn for a story over all the other possibilities?"

AJ wished this line of discussion would go away. All of a

sudden, she had no desire to mention the ship or Mr. Jackson. And she certainly didn't want to discuss Finn Murphy. Not with Ethan. Perhaps it was best to keep him out of the puzzle. She hadn't even told Stella everything, including her agreement to go sailing with the man.

AJ was so busy pushing Finn to the dark recesses of her brain, she almost didn't hear Stella.

"AJ says it's all about the building, but I think it has more to do with the mystery—"

"It's the tidal pools." The words burst out of AJ, prompting surprised looks from both her lunch mates. She fidgeted in her chair. "My dad took me to the old inn for years when I was growing up." She didn't like talking about her time with her dad. It was private—at times still raw. But it was safer than treading into talks of mystery ships, at least until she sorted out the pieces. "The inn was a special place for us. And the place is almost as old as McDowell. It seemed like a nice fit with the series of articles."

Stella patted AJ's arm. "Sorry, AJ, I know how personal it is for you. I found it interesting after all these years that Adam would be looking into the place."

AJ's hands gripped the edges of her napkin like a white-knuckle ride. Releasing it, she grasped Stella's hand in return.

"I'm sorry for prying," Ethan said. "I didn't know it was a sensitive topic." If he thought there was more to the exchange, he had the good sense not to show it.

"It's not your fault. We brought it up." AJ smiled to lighten the mood. "I always thought Adam was jealous of the time my father and I shared, and, I don't know, I guess the Westcliffe always seemed to be the symbol of our bond. Now that he's looking into it for some reason, it seems strange after all these years."

Ethan's voice took on a measured tone. "I can see your point, but it's been a long time since then. I'm sure it's just business. He has his own family now. I doubt he remembers it's even the same place."

He made it sound so logical, AJ couldn't argue the point. Maybe Adam never considered the inn as the division between their father's love for them. Ethan was right, Adam probably didn't even know it was the inn with the tidal pools.

"An amazing coincidence is all," Stella said. "Fate. A few minutes one way or another and I would have missed Adam. No one would have been the wiser."

The statement, while harmless enough, silenced the group anew. Fate seemed to have played heavily in their lives over the past few days.

Ethan broke the stillness. "You mentioned a Mr. Jackson. Does he live there?"

The mention of Jackson snapped AJ out of her daze. Leave it to Ethan to find the fissures in her story. "I ran across him on one of my trips to take pictures of the inn." Not a *complete* lie. "He's the caretaker of the place. He happened to be there to check things over or fix something, I can't remember." She trailed off, afraid to travel too deeply into her deception.

"I see," Ethan said.

He knew there was more. AJ could see it in his face, and she was grateful when he decided not to push any further.

"Well, mystery solved all around. I think it's time I got you ladies back home." Ethan stood and dropped money on the table, and waited for the women.

Stella had been quiet during the last exchange, and as she passed AJ, she slid her a pointed stare. AJ knew she owed the piper. Her friend would require the whole truth once they were alone.

AJ walked in front of Ethan, and though he was a few steps behind her, she felt his eyes boring through her, trying to interpret what she wasn't sharing. Although she was busy with her own secrets, she hadn't forgotten the mood swing in Ethan, or his subtle curiosity about the inn. It was becoming difficult to interpret the men in her life.

22

The women drove away from the McDowell house in silence. Stella had kept the conversation going on the drive back from Chilton, sharing points of interest with Ethan and discussing market conditions. But the day had ended on a different note. The goodbyes were brief but friendly —smiles, kisses on cheeks, and promises to get together soon. AJ spied Ethan watching them through her rearview mirror, and his eyes seemed to follow her long after they made their first turn.

Stella finally let it burst. "Is there something you haven't been telling me?"

To AJ's relief, Stella's question wasn't accusatory—more frustrated than anything. AJ wasn't ready to divulge the secret of Finn Murphy, even to Stella, but her sailing trip would be risky. She needed someone to know she was meeting him. Her mother wouldn't be the appropriate person, nor Samuel. Her editor beamed over her idea for the articles and had given her carte blanche. But he might consider it unwise to do the interview alone and would want to send Robert or Clara with her. That wouldn't work. Finn would clam up. That only left Stella, and honestly, there was no one better. If she was concerned about what Stella might say, it was only because she knew Stella would be right. Sometimes she didn't want someone to prove her wrong, even if she knew she was, deep down in her core.

Stella refused to break the silence or provide AJ any release from the hook on which she dangled. AJ tapped on the steering wheel, her fingers drumming to some song she couldn't remember the name of, and the words spilled out. "I've met the captain of the ship a couple of times. Interviewed him, I guess you could say, and I'm going sailing with him tomorrow."

This time, Stella's silence wasn't for effect, but neither was it short-lived. She slammed her hand on the dashboard, coercing a jump out of AJ. "Wow, what? When did you have time to meet with him? *Twice?* I only knew about the first time, when you first saw his ship. You've been holding out."

"I know. Well, the other two times happened in the same day, once in the morning when I went to take another look at the ship. He said I could come back in the afternoon to meet Mr. Jackson, so I did. I got most of the story on the inn from Mr. Jackson."

"I thought you get most of the information from the Historical Society."

"Not technically. I mean, I got some photos from there, and they had information that corroborated Jackson's story. He's been the caretaker for a few years and has lived in the area his whole life. He remembers most of the history because he was a kid when the Ramseys still owned it."

"I guess I missed a lot not keeping up with you the last couple of days. And here I thought my bombshell of Adam was a big thing."

Stella sounded a touch hurt, and AJ couldn't blame her. They never purposely held things back from the other. "I'm sorry. I guess things happened so fast, and our schedules were off. I know I should have told you more when you called last night, but I was wiped from finishing the story."

Stella released a sigh. "It's been a busy couple of days for both of us."

AJ shook Stella's shoulder. "And the information about Adam was valuable. You may have stumbled on to something. I'm just not sure what."

"Right?" Stella seemed to forgive AJ her transgressions. "I knew there was something hinky there, but what could it be?"

"I don't know, but Ethan and Adam work together. It's how they first met, so I didn't feel comfortable going into it with Ethan there."

Stella slapped her forehead. "Duh, I forgot how you met Ethan. You know, the man has slipped into our inner circle. He's all charm and stealth. Most of the time, I like him, but sometimes he scares me."

AJ pushed her hair back and checked her rearview mirror, as if he could somehow still be watching them from his driveway. "It's like he's got an agenda none of us are clued in to. I'm sure I'm being paranoid. He is in security, it's ingrained in him to be spooky. He's so charming and such a gentleman, almost archaic in his attention to women. It's hard not to like him."

"He's also good-looking, all tall and dark, with a touch of Heathcliff, but I'm sure it has nothing to do with our liking him. And what about that accent?"

Both women laughed, everything out in the open. Stella stopped laughing first and turned a sharp look on AJ. "Wait a minute. What's this about sailing?"

AJ shook her head. She had hoped Stella hadn't heard that part, but Stella never missed anything. It just took her a minute to catch up. "Mr. Murphy, or Captain Murphy, I'm not sure what to call him, said I could do an article on his ship. I told him I didn't know anything about sailing, so he offered to take me for a quick sail."

"By yourself."

"Yes." The answer squeaked out. AJ cleared the mouse lodged in her throat. "I'm sure it's perfectly safe. Mr. Jackson seems comfortable with Murphy. He was invited to come along but had some family thing. If he had any concerns for my safety, he would have said something."

"We don't know anything about Jackson either, even though he says he's lived here all his life."

"True, but why would he lie? Unless I've stumbled upon some huge drug-smuggling ring, what is there to be afraid of?"

"Oh, I don't know. There are still things like serial killers out there."

AJ smirked. "Okay. So the idea did cross my mind." She held up her hand. "For an instant. I don't know what's up with this guy, or why he sails around on this old ship, but it's part of the interview process, to find out." She finished with a low mumble. "He seems harmless enough."

"Uh-huh."

Stella gave her a long look. AJ squirmed.

"So what time is this sailing adventure? It's unfortunate I can't invite myself along." Stella got deathly seasick just thinking about boats.

"Ten. I guess I can sleep in more than this morning."

"I want to hear from you no later than noon," Stella said. "One o'clock at the latest or I'm calling the Coast Guard, you hear me?"

AJ laughed and pulled up in front of Stella's house. "I get it. Let's catch up for dinner tomorrow or Monday. We need a plan for figuring out what Adam is up to."

"And we know asking him would be pointless." Stella got out of the car.

"Looks like the mysteries never end. I don't know how we got involved in so many so quickly."

"I guess the only answer is to stop being a reporter." Stella waved her hand as she turned toward the house.

Stella was right again. AJ's reporter instincts had sniffed out some intriguing stories before, yet she seemed capable of creating mysteries that weren't even there. Now she had to figure out which was which.

23

___

The sun played hide and seek with the heavy morning mist hugging the coastline, its streaks of light sparkling for a snapshot in time before disappearing, each time popping out with more vigor than the last. Soon the sun would control the day and chase away the final curtains of fog. Even with the lifting clouds, the morning's crisp light sharpened the edges of the firs, the cliffs and buildings, making everything appear closer, like a postcard cutout.

AJ was giddy, as if there was too much oxygen in the air. She hugged her sweater tight against the coolness, overlooking the tidal pools, but the rocks and pools could barely be seen. She had hoped to walk through the small puddles as she had as a child, but she forgot the tide would be in, swallowing the pools until it moved out again.

This was just a sailing lesson. She was excited, and not just for the opportunity to gain insight for her next article about the life and times of a historic sailing vessel. Yes, AJ wanted to gather all she could about the ship, its age, its purpose when it was first built, and the reason for keeping it restored to its original condition. Dozens of other questions ran through her mind too, but none of them explained the butterflies she could not bury. She wasn't sure she wanted to learn to sail, never having been out on a sailboat before. There had been the occasional whale-watching excursion on motorized boats, and a few parties on boats tied to the dock. One of those may have been a sailboat, but she couldn't count it if it never left the pier. Her parents weren't sailors—they enjoyed the ocean from the shore.

AJ took one last look and pictured her father moving around the rocks, pointing out starfish, sea urchins, and sponges, occasionally lucky enough to spot an anemone. But, covered by the churning water, the tidal pools could not offer AJ the peace she yearned for. She turned her back on the past and headed up the trail, past the inn, toward the dock.

At the point that revealed a full view of the small bay, AJ stopped to take in the sight below her. The ship took her breath away every time. She appreciated it more with each visit. She was a sleek vessel, and AJ could picture her on the high seas, cutting through the waves, her sails unfurled, racing ahead of the wind.

AJ arrived at the dock as Finn approached from the opposite end. His appearance stunned her with each visit. A bold visage, easily relaxed in tan cargo pants, the white shirt emphasizing his tanned skin, the collar open enough to display a hint of curls. She pictured him standing at the bow of the ship, the tall mast and sails behind him. An image of Ethan flashed, wearing his casual attire from the day before. A business suit fit Ethan better than a pair of jeans. Try as she might, she couldn't picture Finn in a suit and tie.

AJ felt his eyes on her, and she broke off her reverie to find him appraising her with a wide, slanted grin lighting his face, his eyes sparkling with merriment and perhaps a touch of mischievousness. She tried to stop the surfacing of a slight blush but wasn't sure she pulled it off.

"Beautiful." Finn came to a stop, a little too close.

"What?" AJ took a small step back but refused to look away.

He always seemed to find the right thing to say to keep her off balance.

Finn's smile crinkled the corners of his eyes. Judging from the fine lines on his face, she guessed that he smiled a lot. "The morning, it's a beautiful morning."

AJ scanned his face for any hint of guile. She saw none and couldn't argue the statement. "Yes, we've had a lucky stretch of good weather." Needing some distance, she pushed past him and caught the light scent of cedar again. She approached the gangplank, ready to take a step up, until Finn stopped her.

"It's proper to ask permission before boarding a ship."

AJ turned back to him. "I'm sorry. I guess I knew that. Permission to board?"

"Not today."

She shifted, one hand on her hip. "I thought you were teaching me to sail today."

"Aye, I am, but not on my girl. I don't want you breaking her."

"How am I going to learn without a boat?" AJ's irritation rose, concerned he was going to snake out of his promise of an interview. What game he was playing now?

If Finn caught the change in AJ's attitude, it didn't show. His smile never wavered, instead growing wider, if that was possible. He was having fun at her expense, and she played the role of unwitting dupe rather well.

"We'll use the other boat." Finn strolled past her to the other end of the dock, where he had been when she'd first arrived.

AJ followed him, her own long legs easily keeping up with him. "What other boat? I don't see any other boat." She pulled up short at the end of the larger ship. She stared at a small sailboat. A *tiny* boat. "You're kidding, right? This is a toy boat." AJ looked back at Finn. She didn't get the gag until she saw the abrupt change in his manner. Finn's smile disappeared, replaced by a more intense look, sweeping over the small craft and back at her. The instruction had begun.

"This, my dear, is a sailing vessel and, while she may be smaller than my fine girl, she's as yar as I could find and not to be trifled with on water."

Underneath his playful Irish lilt and colorful words, she detected his chastisement and prickled. "She seems small for the ocean. I'd assumed we'd be using yours."

"This is mine. I just bought her. She's perfectly suited for small hops along the shore and makes more sense than moving the big girl around. And it will be easier to learn the basics of sailing without becoming overwhelmed with all the sails and rigs." Finn tossed AJ's bag gently into the boat. She waited, unsure.

"She only looks small because she's sitting next to a large ship," Finn said. "She's seaworthy. I take the ocean seriously and wouldn't put us in any undue danger."

AJ stared at the boat. He was right on both counts. It was about sixteen feet in length—maybe not so tiny after all—and he wouldn't purposely put her at risk, not to prove some point. It would only put him in the same danger. "Let's do it, then."

She ignored Finn's hand and stepped into the boat, grasping the mast. The small craft swayed with the new weight. Finn loosened the ropes tying the sailboat to the dock and jumped down next to her, their bodies rubbing together as the boat steadied beneath them.

Finn tossed her a safety vest, donning one himself, barely rocking the boat as he repositioned the lines from the sail. "I'll get us out of the bay and then we can begin the lesson. You can watch and take in the beauty of the place as we head out. Things look different from the water."

Finn wasn't wrong. After raising the sails, he coaxed the craft out of port, shouting out where AJ should move and when she should duck. The boat tacked out of the small bay, heading for the deeper ocean. He told AJ to sit, and she relaxed against the side of the boat, watching the shoreline.

She had never seen the inn from this angle and was taken in by the charm of the setting. It was a perfect spot. The Westcliffe sat high on the point with the small bay off to one side, much deeper on this side of the point than on the other. AJ guessed there must be a bar running out from the shore, a few feet under the water, which created the pools on the far side. As the sails pulled them out to sea, AJ marveled that anyone could have found this place. It melted with the terrain around it, almost indistinguishable from the rest of the shore with the houses, trees, and green grass all blending together.

The sensation of the boat gliding through the water mesmerized her. The landscape diminished, the small craft moving faster as Finn worked the lines and the sails caught the full force of the wind. AJ turned to take in the sight of clear water ahead of her, with no point of reference as to where they were or where they were going. Only the shoreline behind them provided any guidance.

Finn dropped into the seat next to her, and his leg brushed against hers. She jumped and pulled her leg away. But his gesture wasn't on purpose; there was no place else to sit. She forced herself to relax to the calming tempo of the boat.

She slid him a glance and sat a little straighter. She half expected one of his signature grins, but he stared at her, all business. AJ smiled, a little surprised at her reaction to this side of the man.

"Are you ready for your next lesson?" Finn continued to watch her, his hand resting easy on the tiller.

"I think I'm waiting for the first."

"You've already had several, but I guess you weren't paying attention."

"I've missed something."

"Aye, but it was unfair. I told you to watch us head out. Things look different from the water. Would you be able to find port again from here?"

AJ smiled and pushed her short curls away from her face. "You're right. I couldn't see how anyone had found the bay. The inn blended in with the rest of the shore. I'm not sure I'd be able to find it again."

"So you have learned something after all. Now you need to learn reference points. You need to see the larger picture, the shore as a whole, the formation of the land and bays."

The lesson expanded to reading the shore, guessing depths of the water without instrumentation, and how to identify reference points. AJ honestly did pay attention, and some of the landmarks were obvious to her, but she found herself gazing at the small cliffs, rating each one against a climbers' scale. She might have to give one of them a try, change her routine. She did prefer the land to the sea, a high cliff to any good sail.

Staring at a particularly interesting cliff, trying to determine its location, she noticed it had grown quiet. She turned to see what Finn was doing, assuming he'd stopped talking to trim a sail or do something with a line, but she found him watching her. For the first time since they left port, something in the way he looked at her sparked an involuntary tingle. AJ looked away, wishing the boat was larger. The craft increased speed, forcing AJ's body against him as the boat leaned away from the wind. Finn had called it heeling, and AJ held on, enjoying the mist of the ocean spray, almost forgetting her earlier discomfort, until Finn released the sail, settling the boat.

"So it's time to learn a few things about the boat. I assume you know what a mast is and the difference between the bow and the stern, fore and aft."

She laughed. "Let's assume I know nothing. It will go much faster."

It did go fast, but AJ caught only pieces. There was so much to learn. Finn spoke of the sails, the rigging, and the wind, but she found that she wasn't interested in any of it. She enjoyed listening to him talk.

He loved the sea. That was easy to see. His voice became more animated the more he spoke. When he asked her to work a line or trim the sail and she fumbled at the task, his hands moved over hers to help guide her. She should have been paying more attention to what she was being told to do and less to the warm roughness of his skin against hers. But once she sensed a gentle shift of the boat and could hear the sail quiet as the wind caught the whole sheet, she laughed, pleased she had helped with the adjustment.

Finn laughed with her, his mood becoming more jovial as they sailed down the coast, never too far from the shore. He repeated instructions and drilled her on reading the land and various landmarks. AJ seemed to have a natural ability to read the coast now that she understood the basics, and she found navigation of more interest than the functions of sails. Yet AJ jumped anytime Finn called out an order, and she joked each time they had to duck under the sail, betting Finn one of them was sure to land in the water before they got back to dock.

"You're getting too much sun." Finn touched the tip of her nose.

AJ smiled at the unexpected gesture and touched her nose, testing the burn. "We've been out here longer than I expected. But I also thought I'd be on a larger vessel."

Finn's face showed no redness, his skin long tanned by the sea. He studied her, and she fidgeted under his intense scrutiny. She turned her attention to the boat, which seemed to have shrunk. Unable to keep her hands busy, she tucked them around her as if warding off the wind.

"You can see we had our hands full with this small boat. You would have learned nothing on anything larger."

"You're right." AJ straightened, pushed a loose strand of hair from her face, and rubbed her fingers along a polished cleat. "How long have you been sailing?"

Finn guided the boat, making sure it stayed in line with the shore. "Not long. Especially for being my own captain. We didn't live close enough to the water for me to learn as a lad, so I was much older before I ever boarded a ship. Once aboard, I was fascinated by how it all worked. The sails and the rigging, of course, but it was the navigation that interested me."

"Really?" She sat forward. "I like the navigation too. Plotting your course and seeing where it takes you. All the drilling you put me through on reading the land and the sea makes sense. I can see it's your specialty."

"Yes, and you should see me with a compass, a sextant, and a chart." He winked.

His mischievousness warmed her. "So tell me about your ship. Do you own her, or are you, I don't know, moving her around from one place to another?"

He hesitated a moment. "She's mine. I haven't owned her long, yet sometimes it seems as if it's been forever." His voice turned sad. His gaze turned to the water, and he seemed to drift into a different place and time.

The boat took an abrupt turn, and the sail narrowly missed her when it came about, forcing a small scream from her.

"Hey, I thought you were giving out warnings before doing that."

Finn had the decency to look sheepish. "Sorry, I wasn't think-ing." The grin reappeared. "You have fine reflexes."

"It's not my reflexes I'm worried about. I have no intention of going for a swim today." She repositioned herself, irritated by the surprise change of direction.

"Let's get back. You've learned enough for one day."

Not getting the apology she deserved, AJ turned the tables and got to the meat of her interview. "So how old is your boat exactly?"

"A couple hundred years, give or take."

AJ waited for him to expand, but he didn't. "And where was she built?"

"The shipyards in Portsmouth. England."

Again with the short responses. He had been so forthcoming with sailing and navigation. Now he clammed up. "I thought you said it was okay for me to write about the ship."

Finn sighed. "Aye, I did. I guess I got lost in daydreaming." Finn trimmed the sail and settled next to her, looking out to sea once more.

"The *Daphne Marie* was built around 1790, designed specifically for the Duke of Dunsmore, a man loyal to the King. She had a different name at the time." Finn searched the horizon as if the lost memory would appear at its edges. "I don't remember it anymore." Finn's manner changed when he talked about the ship, almost a reverence. "The name changed some years later with its new owner. It was meant to be a change in fortune for the ship, but it didn't work out that way." Finn busied himself with the sail again.

He was avoiding the topic, but it wasn't just devotion to the ship that distracted him. It was something deeper. A sorrow that seemed to touch him each time he spoke of the *Daphne Marie*. "Did something awful happen to the new owner?" AJ almost whispered it.

"A broken family and a man lost to the sea, never finding home again." Finn's sharp laugh unsettled her. "I guess the story isn't much different from the ones you've found with your old buildings. Perhaps the ship has something in common with them after all."

AJ wondered why an old story, as sad as it must have been, would be of such interest to Finn after hundreds of years. While he laughed about it, he seemed to find no humor in it. She wanted to ask why it seemed to affect him, but for some reason, she felt uncomfortable prying. She touched his arm and, realizing what she had done, pulled her arm back.

Finn looked at where she had touched him, and his smile returned. "Your innocent questions have gotten me recalling long-ago days and the harshness of life at sea. I think you'll find that the history of old ships carries many a sad tale for the captains as well as the sailors that worked them."

Finn turned the tiller, and the boat shifted starboard toward the water, forcing AJ to shift to the left to keep her body from leaning against him. "The *Daphne Marie* was built for a particular family, to provide transport to the continent, although it was also used for small cargo runs. The hold doesn't carry much, but it seemed to get the job done."

"Do you remember the name of the second owner?"

"No."

AJ waited for him to continue, but he didn't. "And how did you come about owning it?"

Finn's look became guarded. It should have been a simple answer. He ran his hand through his hair, kicked his foot against the hull. Then his grin returned. "You might say it was handed down through the family, an inheritance, if you will."

"Oh." His simple answer made her more curious as to what he wasn't saying and why he was so careful about answering. Perhaps Finn thought that whatever bad luck had happened to the second owner was connected to his own story, haunting him through the years. Melodramatic, maybe, but something had him less than willing to discuss the *Daphne Marie*. AJ wanted to explore that avenue in more detail without putting him on the defensive. She rose, needing to pace, then remembered she was on a boat. She tried to sit when a gust of wind hit the boat.

Suddenly, the sailboat pitched to port, and AJ cursed at Finn's untimely change of direction. She stumbled. Her arms reached out to grab something, anything, to catch her fall. All she saw was water, and the cold ocean waves reached up to engulf her.

24

The soft tinkle of a bell announced Ethan's entrance into the small, musty antique store. He stood just inside the door, unsure which way to go. There was no order to the place, with items haphazardly dumped into spots, forcing a buyer to sift through pieces to find anything, reminiscent of a true treasure hunt. Ethan's short phone conversation with the owner hadn't been enough for him to determine if the man had intended the illusion or if he was just lazy.

He picked his way through the shop and caught glimpses of a few original, timeworn pieces buried within other items you'd find in any trinket shop, their origins questionable. Then he found his way to the book section, and it was like walking into an entirely different store. The immaculate bookcases held aged books well organized into sections based on topic and alphabetical by author. Why one section of the store was well ordered while the other was so chaotic was explained when Ethan met the owners.

Edward and Tildy were an older married couple, and they claimed to have owned the shop for over twenty years. Tildy had once been a blonde, her straw-colored hair now tinged with streaks of gray, and her ample frame, softened with time, seemed to fit her. She flitted through the shop, rearranging inventory that didn't look any different after she moved to another section. Unsure at first if she had heard the bell, Ethan watched her move an antique washbasin before turning to make a path straight to him.

"Hello. Is there anything I can help you find? Or are you one of those who likes to peer through the collection to see what calls out to you?" Her high-pitched voice would grate nerves if she talked any faster. But her proud smile changed her entire being, and Ethan saw the woman Edward must have fallen in love with all those years ago.

Ethan smiled in return. "Today, I'm afraid neither. I called and spoke with your husband yesterday morning."

Tildy's smile faded, and Ethan could see the wheels turning. The smile returned, brighter than before. "Oh yes, I remember." She turned toward the back of the store. "Edward, Mr. Hughes is here. Leave that old book alone and come out." Her yell turned into a screech, like chalk on blackboard. She turned back to Ethan, chagrined. "Sorry, the old man is hard of hearing. Refuses to get a hearing aid. Sometimes I forget to go back and get him. I'm used to just yelling."

Ethan couldn't seem to stop smiling. For all her squawking, he found her charming, and was impressed she'd remembered his name. "It's no trouble. I take it Edward is the master of the books."

"Hasn't found a book he didn't like. People come from all over to review his collection. We could live on his book sales alone, but I do love to tinker." She turned and headed for the back of the shop.

Assuming he should follow, Ethan traced her steps, dodging the antiques. "You said on the phone you've been here a long time."

"Oh yes. We were born in the area. But we traveled a great deal. That's when Edward found his passion with the books."

A wiry man ducked through a curtained doorway, small reading spectacles perched on his nose, his head bald as a cue ball. The man wiped his hands on an old cloth, and he scratched his head. "Mr. Hughes, I would have called if I had found anything. You didn't have to drive up from Baywood."

"I had some time on my hands today, and the weather is perfect for a road trip."

Edward peered out the closest window, as if he hadn't seen anything beyond his books in days. "Well, yes, it does look like a nice spring day." He walked to the distant end of the counter and shuffled papers, finally pulling one from close to the bottom. He studied it. "I've spoken to a few dealers. Nothing has been ringing any bells with anyone."

Ethan's fists closed. He had to be close. He couldn't believe how elusive his target had become.

"Now, it looks like we do have one possibility, but it's going to be difficult to trace."

Ethan's spirits lifted. An opening. "Tell me more."

"There was an estate sale a couple of months ago, and one of the dealers remembered seeing an item that matches your description. It was the odd color of the stone that caught his eye, but it wasn't anything he collects, so he didn't pay it much mind. When I called about it though, he said he couldn't forget it. He was sorry he hadn't procured it, but the woman didn't seem interested in selling it."

"So she still has it?"

"No. Not anymore."

"I'm not sure I understand. She didn't want to sell it, but she no longer has it."

"Well, that's the way of antiques. The dealer contacted her on my request. Seems someone talked her into selling it after all."

Ethan sighed, fighting a wave of fatigue he hadn't felt since his younger days training for the guard. "Is there any way to track the buyer?" The question sounded hopeless. But it was out there —within arm's reach.

Edward shook his head. "The woman who sold it didn't get the buyer's name. But she did mention someone else asking about it."

The statement rocked Ethan. He *was* close. It *had* to be the item he was after. "Is it possible the buyer may have owned an antique store, and they were buying it for a store collection?"

"Possibly. But it sounded more like a private collector. My dealer said the buyer paid a decent sum for it. Most store owners look for deals. They want a higher margin."

A private collector would make it almost impossible to find. He could search for weeks for the smallest of clues.

"What about the *Antique Market*?" Tildy's voice pierced the air from across the room.

"That woman has the hearing of an owl. But she's right. It might be your best option."

"I'm not familiar with the name. Is that another store?"

"No. It's a trade paper, covers most of the Pacific Northwest. If your buyer was a collector, odds are they subscribe. You could put in a personal ad, describe what you're looking for. If they're serious, they'll see it. We all watch the personal ads."

He placed money on the counter for Edward to place the ad for him. Tildy received a kiss on her cheek for her brilliance before Ethan exited the shop.

A small glimmer of hope followed him out the door and into the afternoon sun. He let the optimism flourish on his drive back home. He had done what he could. Now he was back to the waiting game. He still had one other avenue, but that was proving to run aground as well.

25

The sea was black, a dark, silent void where nothing could be seen—a stark contrast to how blue it had looked earlier, with the sun sparkling on its surface. The icy water sliced through her. She wouldn't last long enough to be saved—she'd die of hypothermia before anyone could find her. The salty brine of the murky depths made her gag. Stark terror immobilized her—she could drown long before freezing to death. She was sure the boat had capsized and that Finn was lost somewhere in this void with her, although she couldn't see him. A deep sorrow joined her fear. Her mother would be forced to deal with another death so soon. Stella would be royally pissed at her stupidity. Even Adam floated into her consciousness. Would he even care if she was lost to the sea?

AJ searched the water around her. Nothing there. She shook her head to clear her mind, the effort slowed by the density of the water. She needed to find the surface. Something blocked her from turning, not allowing her to swim to safety. She flapped her arms, unable to find anything to grab on to, unable to pull away. Her legs were stuck, perhaps pinned to the boat—somewhere behind her. That was why she couldn't see the surface. She was unable to twist her body to look. Panic set in. She was going to drown.

As swiftly as the water had extended its icy grip, AJ was pulled away, as if a giant mechanical arm had reached down to pluck her from the depths. She had to close her eyes against the bright light. Her head rocked back as she gasped in a deep breath, then fell forward as she hacked up salt water. Fresh air burned its way back into her lungs. She couldn't understand why it hurt so much to breathe. She took in more deep breaths, each one more painful than the last, the salt burning her throat. More pain when someone pounded on her back. Then it stopped.

"Are you all right? Can you hear me? Slow down, don't gulp," said a muted voice.

She shook her head to clear her ears. All she could hear was the rushing of the waves, like holding a shell to her ear. She wanted to push her hair back, but her arms were trapped beside her and, unable to free herself, panic returned.

"Calm down, lass, you're safe. You took a quick tumble, but you're safe now. You need to take slower breaths, let the water work its way out. Try not to fight it."

The soft Irish lilt and calming words penetrated AJ's water-logged head and eased her panic. Her arms were tucked inside a soft, warm blanket. She had been saved after all. Finn rubbed her arms and covered her head with a blanket, or maybe it was a towel. Her hair was being dried. She opened her eyes again, fighting the sting of the salt water and the stabbing bright light. She could make out the edge of the sailboat, part of the sail, and the ocean beyond.

The boat was fine—it hadn't sunk. Behind her, Finn rubbed her arms and head, drying her off. She coughed some more. Finn's words made sense, and she slowed down, feeling better.

Then the shivering began. Finn's arms tightened around her and pulled her close. She accepted the warmth, leaning into it.

The trembling faded. She dropped her head back on his shoulder and let the sun heat her face.

AJ stayed that way until she could talk, her throat raw after choking out all the water. "How long was I in?"

He took a moment to respond. "You were never completely in the water. I caught your life vest before your feet left the deck, but the boat heeled over, which put your head, your arms, and a bit of your shoulders in the water. About a minute at most, probably less."

She popped up, hitting Finn's chin, surprising him by her quick reflexes. "That's all? I never left the boat? It seemed a lot longer than that."

Finn suppressed a grin. "Aye, it would have seemed longer to you. It happened quickly, but I have found the mind slows in times of danger. Makes you see things more clearly."

AJ's cheeks flushed. She'd freaked like some child for a whole minute, allowing panic to take over instead of logic. She should have been able to handle herself better, and the truth was difficult to hear. She stood, hoping she didn't send the boat reeling again, but it seemed sturdy enough. Planting her feet wider apart, she glared at Finn, who was fighting a grin. "I thought you were an expert seaman, a captain of your own ship. You almost sank a toy boat!"

As soon as the words were out, she regretted them. She was being peevish, and he had every right to toss her back into the icy depths, but she had been more scared than she wanted to admit.

Finn's grin widened. He leaned back against the hull, but he kept his voice gentle. "If I wasn't an expert seaman, we would have both landed squarely in the water with our toy boat sinking fast."

His gaze examined her so thoroughly, AJ reflexively pulled the blanket tighter.

"You've soaked the blanket through. Let's change it. There's another one here somewhere." He lifted the seat, revealing a storage locker underneath. "Ah yes, there's a couple more." Finn tossed AJ a fresh blanket and towel, taking the wet ones she handed back.

"I'm sorry. I guess I'm behaving like a child." Her sigh was shaky.

"You shouldn't feel foolish. It could have been dire if I hadn't been close."

He was placating her, but he looked sincere, so she acquiesced. She rubbed her hair with the towel, and when it was dry enough, tossed it with the other wet items next to the locker. She ran her fingers through the damp locks to put them in order for the sun to dry. She kept the blanket around her and sat next to him. "So, what happened?"

Finn laughed, and when AJ winced, he placed a hand on her hers and squeezed. "If I live to be a hundred, I will never see such a perfect combination of events like that again. When you stood, you stumbled on the lines, just as a wild gust hit us. The boat heeled sharp to port, giving you a dunking before I was able to catch you." He released her hand and looked past her to the shore, the crooked grin still wide on his face. "It could have happened to anyone."

"Really?" AJ was skeptical.

"Oh, aye, I've seen many strange misadventures on the sea. It's nothing to be embarrassed about."

AJ studied his face, looking for some sign he was lying to her, but other than his apparent amusement at her situation, his story matched her increasing recollection of events. "This is one for the storybooks for me. It was so weird how long it seemed when I was under." AJ played with the edges of the blanket. "I guess I owe you one."

"I'll try not to ask too much in return." Finn shifted the tiller, his focus returning to the sails, but AJ could see his attempt to suppress a chuckle.

AJ checked her clothing. The only item still damp was her

blouse. She removed the blanket and folded it, trying to remember where they'd left off in the interview. They had been discussing how he came to own the boat. If she didn't know any better, she would suspect the gust of wind, as he called it, was another diversion tactic. The one thing she did believe was how seriously he took the sea. He wouldn't risk something so dangerous just for a change in conversation.

"It looks like we have a visitor."

Finn turned the boat toward shore, and they entered the bay. The *Daphne Marie* sat tall and stately against the dock, as if everything they had said about her earlier was of no importance. While it seemed unbelievable that a ship so beautiful could possibly be the bearer of bad omens, she understood the concept. In researching the small artifacts she'd discovered through the years and the histories she'd uncovered, she'd learned that many people put stock in an item's ability to bring good luck or bad. Some even claimed the providence held to family lines, so the piece might bring bad fortune to their particular lineage, yet carry good luck or no blessings at all to anyone else.

"Is it someone you know? She seems agitated." Finn pulled in the sail, easily guiding the small craft toward the dock.

Stella wasn't so much agitated as plain irritated. Still shaken by her close call, AJ wasn't ready to face her. She couldn't fathom why Stella had come out to the inn until she looked at her watch. Almost two in the afternoon! She must have gotten worried, maybe even a little pissed, when she found the centuries-old ship and no one else around. AJ wasn't sure what had made her stick around, and she hoped Stella hadn't called the police.

"Yes, I know her." AJ tossed her blanket on the growing pile, then nudged the pile with her foot to a corner where they couldn't be seen, like a thief hiding evidence. But a glance toward Stella told her she didn't need to be worried. Stella had stopped pacing when she got a good look at Finn Murphy.

Stella's expression changed from annoyed to intrigued—and

then, looking at AJ, back to irritated. AJ tugged at her blouse and stood a little straighter, which proved difficult in the slow-moving craft with Finn preparing to dock. AJ had a great deal of explaining to do, again. She'd planned to come clean with Stella, eventually, and would have done it today. Too late for that. Stella watched Finn's every move, and AJ could guess what ran through her friend's one-track mind. AJ hadn't disclosed Finn's good looks, and she'd been out with him for several hours on a tiny boat. She reddened and scanned the boat for any last-minute housekeeping.

Finn maneuvered the boat to rest against the dock and addressed Stella with a full-on grin and his best Irish. "Do you mind taking the line, lass?"

Stella glared at AJ and seemed satisfied with her sheepish look. Turning back to Finn, she presented him with her most gracious smile and held out her hands. "I may not be able to get on a boat without losing my lunch, but I know how to tie one to a pier."

After tossing the line, Finn watched her tie it off and, nodding his approval, threw her the aft line.

AJ rolled her eyes. Stella wouldn't let her off easily. She searched for something to say to take control of the situation, but nothing came to mind, still a little fuzzy from the cold dip. Finn jumped onto the dock, but before facing Stella, he had the courtesy to turn and hold a hand out for AJ. She accepted his help, grabbing her bag before climbing from the boat.

"And who do we have here?" Finn accepted Stella's hand, but instead of shaking it, he bent his head and dropped a quick kiss.

"Stella Caldway. AJ's friend." Stella glanced at AJ, her gaze dropping to her hand. "Or so I thought. Where has she been hiding you?"

"I didn't know I was being kept hidden." Finn's smile was engaging, his curls escaping from place, as if he could master them to fall over his brow on command. He glanced at AJ.

"We've only met a couple of times. I believe I'm one of her stories."

"AJ mentioned a larger ship. You're the captain of this other one too?" Stella looked at the small craft and back to the larger vessel.

"It seems it's easier to learn to sail on a smaller boat. This is Finn Murphy," AJ said, finally finding her own voice.

"Well, he could have been this Mr. Jackson you talked about, but you don't look as old as I was expecting." Stella stared at Finn, who in turn gave AJ a questioning look.

AJ pretended she hadn't seen Finn's glance and kept her focus on Stella. "Weren't you going to call to check in?" AJ smiled, although it probably looked more like a leer, and she couldn't keep the nip out of her response.

"I tried several times but kept getting your voice mail, so I drove out. Didn't want anything to happen to you." Stella was still smiling at Finn.

AJ checked her phone. She had several messages from Stella. "I never heard the phone ring. We must have been too far away from cell towers."

"Uh-huh." Stella pulled her gaze away from Finn and gave AJ a closer inspection. "Are you wet?"

AJ blanked. Sometimes she hated Stella's powers of observation. Some parts of her blouse had dried faster than most, leaving light spots of dampness. She had no idea how to respond.

"It's the hazards from sailing on a small craft," Finn said. "We took a quick turn about, and AJ got caught in the spray."

Relieved by Finn's rescue, AJ tallied how much she owed him. For some reason, he kept covering for her, making excuses. "Well, now you know I'm fine." It got quiet, so AJ kept talking. "Did you want a tour of Finn's ship?" She pinched her nose and then remembered to turn to Finn. "Sorry. If it's okay with Finn."

"That would be grand." Finn turned to Stella. "Would you like to come aboard?"

"I'd love to." Stella gave AJ a wicked smile. "As AJ knows, I can get seasick standing on this dock. I don't want to tempt fate."

"Not everyone has sea legs, but I wish there was another way to show my hospitality," Finn said.

"Well, that's easy enough. We'll have to get together for drinks sometime."

"I still owe AJ an interview." Finn walked them to the other end of the dock. "I'm afraid the sailing lesson took away from all the questions she had planned for me." Finn stopped at the edge of the path and turned toward the women.

AJ still wanted to finish the story, but she was surprised at Finn's offer to continue a discussion he didn't seem happy to share an hour earlier. Maybe Stella was the key to getting Finn to open up. Right now, all she wanted was to get home, take a hot shower, and put the spectacle of her sailing adventure out of her mind. She turned to Finn. "Thank you for the lesson. I know I was a slow student. But I need to get home. I'll be in touch about the article." She turned toward the path, taking a few steps before calling back. "Are you coming, Stella?"

Stella stared after the retreating AJ. "I guess that's that." She took a moment to look Finn over. "It was nice to meet you, Finn." She paused. "You're a fine-looking man, Mr. Murphy. Be careful with AJ." She turned to catch up with her friend.

"Aye," Finn said as the women walked away. If Stella had meant her remark as a warning, and had it been another time, he would have found AJ to be an interesting challenge. These two could easily distract him from his goal. Guilt wrenched him, and he pushed it back, knowing full well that dwelling on the past would get him nowhere.

He turned back to the small craft to square her away after the trip, smiling at his remembrance of their morning. But his mood faded when he recalled the panic that overcame him when he'd almost lost AJ overboard. She could have slipped from his grasp. His breath hitched. He should have paid closer attention to the wind. The woman had beguiled him.

He had some time on his hands while he waited for news from his source. There wasn't anything keeping him from enjoying the company of two intelligent women. His lips twitched. If only for the conversation.

26

A t the parking area, AJ said little to Stella, simply promising to meet with her later. She raced out of the lot and drove, not to any place in particular, keeping her speed near the limits. She appreciated Stella's concern for her safety, but she had wanted to be in control of the timing to explain Finn, and she'd allowed it to get skewed. She needed to climb, clear her head, and work through the whirlwind in her mind, but the best climbing spots would be overrun with tourists this time of day. In the end, she found herself in front of her mother's house.

If she had planned on finding solace with Helen, she was mistaken. No one was home when AJ tried the door. Of course, it was Sunday. Her mother spent most of her time with Adam and the kids on Sundays and met with her own club groups on Saturdays. It was almost to the point AJ had to make an appointment to see her mother. But if she was honest about it, her own schedule wasn't any better. Just as she had been close to her father, the link between mother and son was as strong as ever in her family. Helen had bonded with Madelyn, even tolerated Madelyn's tendency for histrionics, and she never posed a threat.

She always conceded to Madelyn on decisions involving Adam or the children, her presence supportive from the beginning, tying the two together.

If AJ didn't have her own singular nature, she might have been jealous, but she never worried about getting time with her mother. Their relationship had always been casual, before and after her father's death. They spoke a few times a week, and AJ stopped by for morning coffee or, on the rarer occasion, after work to relax with a cocktail. But not today.

AJ headed for the library. She wasn't ready to review her tumultuous day with Stella. And if she went home, she'd be forced to relive her day with Finn, her embarrassing dip in the ocean, and the fact she walked away with little information. Or had she? She didn't know, and if she couldn't find a strenuous activity to block the restlessness, there was only one other option. Work.

The library would be open for another couple of hours, though she would have thought she had spent all day on the water. The quiet solitude of the library welcomed her, and she banished all thoughts of the day. Finn's command of the sailboat, his touch on the tip of her nose, then being pulled from the sea—wet, cold, and scared. AJ was grateful for the library's comforting aroma of paper and tattered covers. Although more sterile than a bookstore, where the smell of the books embraced her like a mother's hug, it was close enough.

In the far back corner of the library, something finally went her way. Her favorite stuffed chair sat empty, and she dropped her notepad and pen in it. She now owned this small corner of the world, at least for a little while. After combing through the history section for fifteen minutes, she settled back in the worn chair, notepad at the ready. She let the afternoon drift away, flipping through the small stack of books, each patiently waiting its turn.

The librarian kicked her out at five o'clock, and when she

walked out to the waning sunshine, she was restored. Armed with information on the history of sailing ships, AJ would be ready for her next encounter with the captain of the *Daphne Marie*. But there was one more task awaiting her before she finished her day.

She could have walked to Stella's from the library, but her renewed energy wouldn't last for the walk back, so she drove. The last two days had been a roller coaster ride, and she yearned for an early night of soup and bed.

She didn't bother knocking. Stella was home, and AJ knew exactly where she'd be on an early Sunday evening. She followed the stone walkway that traversed the perimeter of the house and slipped through a small wooden gate. AJ entered a private, flourishing garden, bordered by tall redwood fencing, a large fir tree, and two burgundy-colored vine maples. Trellises of vines and a variety of flowers backfilled the place, providing a scented seclusion from the rest of the world. Strings of white lights glowed throughout, complementing the intricately placed landscape lighting. The scent of peonies was strong and, to AJ, added a mystical ambiance.

The garden seemed to be working its charm on the lone soul ensconced in a chaise lounger, a fluffy wrap thrown around her, a half glass of white wine within reach. Stella's eyes were shut, and the thick shawl moved up and down in rhythm. AJ had made little noise when she entered the garden, but she wasn't surprised when the lounging figure spoke.

"You're late. Did you go for a climb?"

AJ threw herself into a large, padded wicker chair. She started to place her feet on the small adjoining footstool, and changed her mind, tucking her feet beneath her. The cushion enveloped her, and the last snippets of stress flowed out of her as she succumbed to the magic of nature. A small teapot sat next to her on a warmer, and she poured a cup of something smelling of ginger and jasmine.

"Perfect." AJ took a sip, leaned back, and closed her eyes in keeping with her hostess.

"I changed the tea twice already. Those warmers are useless. I hope my plants enjoyed the earlier attempts."

"I went to the library."

Stella nodded. "That makes sense."

The two women sat without speaking for some time, one not ready to talk, the other willing to wait. After a second cup of tea had been consumed, AJ let out a contented sigh and found Stella watching her.

"I was going to chastise you." Stella didn't wait for AJ's confession. "I thought about it all afternoon. Why you didn't tell me about him. Why you would leave out how young he was, how gorgeous he was. Why you seemed to be hiding him. Lots and lots of questions. But maybe you didn't see any of that." Stella sipped her wine, her gaze drifting to her garden. She pulled her wrap to her, twisting the edge of it with the one hand unattached to her wineglass.

Stella hadn't finished, so AJ poured more tea, relieved that Stella was letting her off the hook, at least partly. She wouldn't get away with all of it.

"Finn Murphy isn't just a gorgeous man. There's something underneath the tanned face and those stunning green eyes." Stella repositioned her wrap and poured herself more wine. "It's that piece of him running underneath all that maleness that has you intrigued. Maybe it's the story we both know is there. Even I know there's a story there, and I only met him for a few minutes. But I think it's the mystery of the man dragging you back." Stella's words lingered in the garden air.

Stella's quick assessment surprised AJ—she'd spent all of five minutes with the both of them. All the questions and doubts AJ had been ignoring bubbled up, and she tucked her feet in tighter, grabbing her tea like a protective amulet.

After a few seconds, AJ shook her head. "No. It's just the story.

There's a really good one there. I can feel it down to my bones. An old ship comes out of nowhere, with a captain who asks lots of questions but reveals nothing of himself. I just don't know how to crack it." AJ slipped a glance at Stella, a small grin over the rim of her tea. "And it doesn't hurt he's one hunk of a man."

"There you go." Stella stretched and pulled her wrap tighter against her. "Do you just find him attractive, or is it more visceral? Do your insides get all tingly and mushy when you see him?"

"Stop." She refused to agree to Stella's simplification of the situation. "It's not like that."

"Uh-huh."

AJ stared into the candle of the tea warmer, losing herself in the speckle of fire, not sure how to express her thoughts. She drained the last of the teapot, focusing on her next words, saying the only thing she knew to be true. "I don't know. I don't know him yet, and I know it sounds cliché, but it's like I've known him for years. He frustrates me with his refusal to answer questions or divulge anything about himself, yet for some reason, I feel safe around him, and I know I shouldn't. The more I dig, the less I know."

"And there's no tingly."

AJ sighed. "Of course there's tingly. Too much damn tingly."

Stella laughed. Not a small, "I'm with you there girl" laugh, but a deep gut laugh she couldn't stop. It spread uncontrollably to AJ, her laughter coming out in snorts, which made the two of them laugh harder.

The laughing continued until tears streamed down their cheeks. Stella finally held up a hand. "Stop. Stop right now." But when the two women looked at each other, they laughed again.

They fought for control, avoiding eye contact until they could pull themselves together, refusing to allow the slips of laughter still remaining to take over. Stella unwrapped herself from the chaise, disappearing into the house for a minute, returning with a wineglass and a new bottle of wine. Pouring a fresh glass for each of them, Stella returned to her original position, pulling the wrap back over her.

AJ settled back into the comfort of her own chair. "Well, I needed that," she said with a contented smile. "What keeps drawing me back to him?"

"You did get a good look at his face and the way those pants fit, right?"

AJ shook her head. "It's not that. I mean, it doesn't hurt, but it's not that. You hit on it right from the beginning. There's something beneath his looks and his Irish brogue that keeps pulling at me. I just can't pin it down. Is it the mystery?"

"Maybe you've finally met your match." Stella was already refilling her glass. "I do believe I'm going to get tipsy tonight."

"And maybe it's my innate curiosity and gut feeling telling me he's hiding something."

"Yeah, that's it. Blame it on your reporter's instincts, and we'll ignore all the tingly."

"That's a fantastic idea." AJ stood and grabbed her glass. "We'll forget about it all for the time being. How about you make us some dinner before you're too sloshed to find the kitchen?"

"By all means, let's bury it for now, if you want. But nothing stays buried for long." Stella took another sip of wine and leaned back against the chaise. "I've decided I'm still a touch mad at you. I'm thinking pasta. You know where the pots are."

AJ grinned and strolled to the kitchen. Dinner was a small price to pay to get back into Stella's good graces, and it gave her a little distance from the topic of conversation. She was finished with Finn Murphy and with her story on the ship, at least for one day. She had no time to dwell on a transient man nor the emotions he tugged out of her. Whatever they were.

27

The law offices resided in a stately brick building located in the more expensive north side of downtown Baywood. The town wasn't large enough to bear distinctive monikers for the various downtown sections, but, over time, the locals knew what part of town they were in by which street they crossed. The age of the street signs, the style of light fixtures, and general upkeep of the buildings defined each section of town. There was no official name for this area of town, and no one would ever find it written on a map. The locals referred to it as Northside. Not an extraordinarily original name, but, as with anything of this nature, the more people said it, the more the name took hold.

Early Monday morning, Ethan entered the Northside building. He had walked from his own office building, which was more centrally located. The walk took only twenty minutes with his long-legged stride, even with stopping to look in the windows of a few shops along the way. He resisted the coffee shops, though the scent of the fresh brew mixed with a whiff of baked goods almost made him stop. The coffee tasted so much better here. He could never seem to get enough and spent the rest of his walk plotting how he could take large quantities back with him.

He rode the elevator to the top, and his irritation grew. He shouldn't be the one tracking down Adam to garner results. Days had gone by without any word from him. Ethan understood the man had other clients, but he was paying good money for the research. He should have confirmed that Adam would be in the office at this hour, but no matter. He enjoyed the walk over, and his unannounced arrival at the office would leave a profound message for the man, whether he was in or not.

The elevator doors opened to a plush foyer of dark paneled walls, vintage cherry furniture, padded carpeting, and a guard dog receptionist. It didn't matter where you were, law offices, especially those catering to the more affluent families and corporations, were all the same. Ethan had to admit this particular guard dog was a fine-looking woman, with the consummate smile, the pleasant-enough hello, and a touch of frost in her stare, the perfect combination of aesthetics to keep unexpected visitors away from the talent. Unfortunately for her, no gatekeeper or security guard could keep Ethan from attaining his objective. That proved to be the case on this visit as well. Adam surprised the receptionist with his immediate agreement to have Ethan escorted to the back offices.

The lavishness of the lobby diminished as Ethan walked through the inner offices, but turned to opulence in the private chamber of a senior partner. Tall bookcases lined one wall. Plaques and expensive art ran along another, framing a granite counter holding both a small espresso machine and what looked like a well-stocked bar. But the focus of the room was the two remaining walls: floor-to-ceiling windows that looked out over the town. The desk, positioned in front of the windows, stood like an island between Adam and his clients. To soften the perception, a small sitting area with a leather couch and two matching chairs camped near the side bar.

Adam thanked the receptionist and smiled at Ethan, pointing to a chair across from a desk piled high with stacks of folders and papers, looking out of character compared to the uncluttered room surrounding them. "I know I should have called," Adam said. "I can't remember when I've been this busy." He spread his hands toward the mass of paperwork on his desk. "I can't seem to get ahead of it."

"I guess it's helpful I've come to you," Ethan said, his voice clipped.

Adam's smile slipped, allowing Ethan a glimpse of how tired the man was, an impression of a bad night's sleep. But Ethan knew the look of someone carrying trouble.

"I do have some information for you." Adam jumped up, grabbing a small cup from his desk, once again the perfect host as he headed for the espresso machine. "Can I make you something? Coffee, espresso, latte?"

Ethan's instincts were to decline, but he had walked by too many coffee shops. "I could use a good espresso."

"Top-of-the-line machine. Cost a fortune but worth every nickel. This is better than ten secretaries combined."

Adam worked the machine like a well-practiced barista, and the cup set in front of Ethan made his mouth water. He sighed when he took his first sip. He would need to get one of these machines. It would be worth it, even for his short time here.

When Adam returned to his chair, he sipped the brew, closed his eyes, and emitted a sigh equal to Ethan's appreciation. After a minute he refocused on Ethan. "I've been researching properties that might fit the bill, homes that have been around a long time, near the coast, all that. I don't know why it didn't occur to me sooner. Maybe because it's been closed for so long, no one gives it much thought anymore."

Ethan sat straighter, the espresso forgotten. "You're talking about the Westcliffe Inn?"

Adam slammed the espresso cup on the desk while somehow

keeping it from breaking. "Damn. If you knew the name of the place, why did you make me do all that research?"

"I didn't."

"Then how?"

"You bumped into Stella at the records office. She was there looking for information on the Westcliffe herself."

"How do you know that? Why would she be interested in it? Is it for sale again?"

"I was with her and your sister on Saturday." Adam's eyebrows rose. Ethan hastened to explain. "I wanted to see some antique stores, and AJ was the perfect guide. I suggested Stella come along, but that's not the point."

"Fine. None of my business, except for the Westcliffe piece."

"The topic of Westcliffe came up at lunch. Stella said she had bumped into you, and when she asked the clerk about the Inn, the woman already had the information at hand."

"Huh." Adam leaned against the chair. "What interest do they have in it?"

"AJ's doing a story on the place. It was my doing, I suppose."

"Yours? How's that?"

"When I first met your sister, she was having trouble coming up with her next article. I had just rented the McDowell place. When I discovered her interest in history, well, the idea came to me."

"Yes, I read her story. She definitely found her niche there. So now she's decided on a series."

"Seems fitting with the number of old buildings around here."

"And it so happens her next target is the same building you've been searching for."

Ethan couldn't ignore the number of coincidences piling up, and Adam gave him the opening to validate AJ's story. "She said she spent a lot of time there growing up, going to the tidal pools with your father."

Adam slapped his hand on the desk. "I knew it sounded familiar. Damn. I forgot all about it. They used to go off by themselves to play in those pools and talk about history. I went once, bored me to death."

"And you weren't bothered by the time they spent together?"

"Bothered?" Adam laughed. "I was so happy the two of them were out of the house. All I wanted to do was hang out with my friends, raise a little hell the older I got. Dad and I never had the same interests."

"Why all the friction between you?"

A shoulder inched up. "I don't see it as friction. Growing up, what older brother wants his sister hanging around? Especially a bookworm. Now, well, I have my own life, she has hers. If it wasn't for Mom, I'm not sure we'd ever find time to seek each other out. Probably won't after Mom goes. Madelyn and AJ don't get along, if you couldn't tell." Adam collected both cups and brewed another round. "Families. Don't get me started. Most of my business comes from families that don't get along. Why would mine be any different?"

Adam's mood lifted as he spoke of his family's dysfunction. He seemed to find comfort in his area of specialty. The weariness melted away. Placing the espresso in front of Ethan, Adam stood at the window and gazed at the city below. "Westcliffe Inn," Adam said. "Been closed for over thirty years now, which is when it was last sold."

Ethan tensed, waiting for the next piece to fall into place. "And the buyer?"

"As you expected. It was purchased by what looks to be a shell corporation. The only name I can find associated with it is someone by the name of Hensley, located in England."

Ethan stared into his cup. It was all coming together.

When Ethan didn't respond, Adam continued. "I did some additional digging. It's currently managed by an individual who handles two other properties close by, although those appear to be true summer rentals. The Westcliffe simply stands empty."

Already knowing the answer, Ethan asked anyway. "Who's the manager?"

Adam set down his cup and turned toward his files. The stack seemed in disarray, but he immediately pulled one out from the middle of the pile. Opening it, he ran his finger down the page. "A Mr. Leonard Jackson. I don't know the man, and couldn't find out much, but he was born here. Seems to run a variety of small businesses. Generally keeps to himself, from what I can determine."

Ethan smiled. Mr. Jackson. The name AJ had mentioned. So she had met with him, which would make sense if she were writing a story on the inn.

"Do you want me to meet with Jackson?" Adam asked. "See if I can find out anything more about the owners?"

"No. Give me a day to think over what you've given me." Ethan drained the last drop of espresso, not sure when he'd find anything this good again.

"I can check out this Mr. Hensley if you want."

"No. Leave it." Ethan's words, sharper than he intended, drew another lifted eyebrow from Adam. Ethan played it down. "Sorry. I've been tracking this for such a long time, I wasn't sure I'd ever find the place." He plastered on his best noncommittal smile. "I guess I'm surprised is all. I never worked through the next steps. I'll get back to you in a day or two." At the doorway, Ethan turned back to Adam. "Thank you for the coffee. I can honestly say it's the best I've ever had."

"Anytime."

Riding down the elevator, Ethan leaned against the wall and closed his eyes. His self-control had slipped for only an instant, but Adam had noticed. He should have been more prepared. But finding AJ mixed up in the middle of his investigation had put him off his game. He dared not speculate how she could impact the situation.

His task had been simple. Track the route the stone had taken.

Now he had brought more attention to his investigation than he planned. He had no way of knowing AJ would select the West-cliffe, of all places, for her next article—a series that he had innocently suggested. And now he had unwittingly aroused Adam's interest, and Ethan didn't think the man would leave it alone. It was going to put them all in danger.

AJ stood on the knoll, overlooking the *Daphne Marie*. The indigo bay sparkled with the conviction of another beautiful day. The gulls circled, searching for their morning feast, swooping down for some morsel before again rising high, the cackle of their voices easily heard as if in celebration for their string of good weather. Spring days grew longer, warming the ground and urging new growth, the promise of new things to come. Yet just as quickly, it could turn on you like some vengeful beast, enveloping the days in dismal downpours or continuous drizzles, shadowing the landscape in never-ending pewter. As any Pacific Northwesterner would do, she simply took advantage of spring's good nature and didn't ask questions.

Her morning climb had invigorated her, even if it left a small ache in her muscles. The price paid for taking a couple of days off. She was disappointed when Ethan hadn't come out to greet her. He had either decided to give her privacy, or he simply wasn't home. When he didn't appear, she missed the illusion of him being near, watching out for her, her own invisible bodyguard. It had been a long time since she had someone to look out for her, and it was comforting.

But nothing was going to spoil her day. She looked down at the ship and spoke to the ghosts of the inn in a light Irish brogue. "Not even Finn Murphy."

AJ hadn't planned on visiting the ship again so soon, but she had nothing else to do except work on her next article. The Westcliffe story was finished. Her next story sat floating at the Westcliffe's dock. She had made the assumption Finn would be there, working on the ship, whatever it was one did on a ship. What else did he do with his days?

She sauntered along the path with only her notepad and pen stuck in the back of her pants. AJ was confident, her homework on the ship complete. She was in her element, her smile contagious. The day too perfect for anything less.

"There's nothing finer than to find a smiling lass at your door on such a beautiful morn." Finn called out from the side of the ship, his brogue heavier than normal.

"And aren't we laying it on thick this morning." AJ looked up, hands on hips, her infectious smile in place.

"Aye, I couldn't help myself." Finn strolled to the gangplank, wearing his trademark slanted grin. His light blue shirt was open halfway down his chest, as if he had thrown it on before becoming aware of her arrival. A silver chain lay against his sun-darkened skin, a small pendant hanging from it. He buttoned his shirt enough to cover the medallion. "You're welcome to come aboard."

AJ wasn't sure if he was being polite at the intrusion or if he was truly pleased to see her. Striding onto the deck, she surveyed the ship as if seeing it for the first time. Her legs swayed with the slight undulation of the deck, the light waves rolling the ship. She hadn't noticed the nuances of the ship on her first visit, as she had been so uptight at the time, but today, she sensed each movement—the ship was alive beneath her feet. Turning away from

Finn, she moved to the mast, laying her hand on it, working her hand over the hard wood warmed by the morning sun. AJ peered up, trying to make out the top so high above her.

"Would you call this a sloop? It was the closest type of sailing vessel I could find."

"Close enough."

"And I noticed four gunports on your port side, so that makes a total of eight guns?" AJ looked back at Finn, her face earnest.

"Aye, you've done your homework." Finn walked past her, close enough to brush the edge of her shirt with his own. "And this over here is the rigging to hoist the sails. The main sail here runs aft of the mast. There's also canvas on the bowsprit. Fully rigged, she can outrun any ship, even against the wind." Finn's pride was evident, master of his small kingdom. His gaze roamed the ship before it fell back on AJ.

"And do you have guns on board?"

"You are a thorough one." Leaning back against the hull, Finn cut to the chase. "She's been leaned down in order to run fast, as much weight as possible removed. Just enough cargo for me. As I mentioned when you toured the ship earlier with Mr. Jackson." When AJ didn't respond, Finn moved to the doorway that led belowdecks. "You said navigation was of interest. Do you want to see how it's done?"

He hadn't answered her question, but she was eager for another look below deck. The stairs were narrower than she remembered, and she was relieved when they opened to the large room. The old brass lamp still sat on the table, emanating a low glow, lighting the room in soft amber tones. Finn stood at the chart table, where he had lit another lamp and spread new charts over the top of the one that had been open—the chart AJ had wanted a better look at.

Hiding her disappointment, AJ joined Finn at the table and looked at the charts. She had expected old charts, tattered corners, aged-stained paper, but the charts in front of her were modern and looked new. She had been sure the one on the table a few days ago had been older than what lay in front of her now. Light reflected from the instruments lying on the charts. They too looked new, like something purchased in the last few years, but AJ wasn't fooled. She marveled at how well the antiques had been preserved through the years.

"What a magnificent compass. How old is it?" AJ moved it around to watch the ball tilt. The casing was made of silver filigree. Interlaced curves and lines ran along all four sides, and when AJ closed the lid, she saw the small fine threads form an elaborate "M" in the center. She reopened the box, turning around the room, watching the needle move as she did.

"Old enough. You could say it's been kept in the family."

Setting down the compass, AJ picked up the sextant, a larger metal object. Its shape formed an odd triangle, with mirrors and a moving arm. She turned it around in her hands, unsure how to properly hold it. "I know this is used for navigation but never understood how."

"That's easy enough." Finn slid behind her, his arms reaching around her. The sudden move made AJ squirm, but Finn stepped in closer, trapping her next to the table. "You wanted to learn. Hold still and I'll show you."

AJ went still. He stood behind her, encircling her, moving her hands to more appropriate positions on the sextant. This time, she caught the smell of pine, the scent strong from a hot summer day. She refocused her mind as Finn raised her arms to eye level.

"You hold it like this so you can look through this line. You want the horizon in line with this lower mirror." Finn moved AJ's hand to a crosspiece. "You move this arm so you can capture an object in this second mirror, until it lays over the top of the horizon on the first mirror. It can be any point in the sky. During the day, it would be the sun. At night, it could be the moon or a particular star. The final step is to look at the number at this mark."

AJ looked through the mirror, trying to stay focused on the lesson, but the room was too dark. Her body swayed back as she lined up an imaginary sun. Her back pressed against Finn.

"Are you paying attention?"

Realizing she was daydreaming, AJ stood straighter, bumping her head on Finn's chin. "Of course, but I'm sure it's easier to demonstrate outside."

Finn laid the instrument back on the table and stepped away. As he did, the coolness of the room returned, and she missed the heat and spice emanating from him. The room went quiet. AJ allowed time to expand, waiting for Finn to say something, but he was busy looking for something in the chart storage boxes—maybe some old charts rather than the new ones he'd sprawled on the table. Other than some of the food stores, the charts were the only modern objects on the entire ship. Looking at the table, she touched what looked like a simple ruler, also very old.

"Where did you get all these antiques? They look new, but I know they can't be. They have marks from the original makers." AJ's voice sounded loud as it broke the silence.

"Why all the interest in some old gadgets? I thought you were interested in the ship." Finn plopped a few charts on the table but didn't open them.

"Yes, but navigation is part of the history. Besides, I'm an antique collector of sorts, and I can usually tell original from fake. These are what we would call gently used rather than new, but it's pretty obvious to me these are old." AJ ran her hands over the compass again, as if she had some connection to it.

Finn said nothing for a while, and AJ didn't have to look to know he was assessing her again, as if seeing her in a different light. When he responded, his voice became deeper. "Now I understand the interest. I didn't know I was talking to an expert." He moved close, the distance he had put between them instantly gone, his arm touching hers. "Do you want a lesson on reading the chart?"

AJ stepped back. For the first time, what she saw wasn't the captain of a ship or the jaunty Irishman. She saw a man in every sense of the word, and she wasn't scared or intimidated by it. Instead, she was drawn to it. "Maybe another time." Her voice came out like a squeak. She cleared her throat. "It's all interesting, but you're right, the story should stay focused on the ship." She turned away, looking around the room for another topic. She moved away from the table—and Finn—and took a last fleeting look at the edge of the chart that lay under the others. She could swear it looked much older. She was touched with disappointment and assumed it was the loss of not seeing the older chart.

Finn guided AJ back to the stairs. "You've seen most things of interest on your last trip here. The best part of the ship is on her deck."

AJ followed Finn and drank in the sunshine, allowing the fresh air to clear her senses. When she looked back to Finn, she knew they had crossed some line, but she didn't know how it happened or what it meant.

"What else can I show you?"

She had danced around it enough. It was time to get to the point of it all. "I could use something more about you. And a little more about what you know about the ship's background. I have more than enough about the basics of the ship, but there's no real story without the history."

Finn leaned against the railing and studied her, then glanced toward the open sea. He exhaled long and slow before turning back to her, his voice reluctant. "Aye, all right. It's a story you want, there's a story I can tell." He paused. "But it comes at a price."

AJ sighed. She had been waiting for his response after two days of failed attempts, but she wasn't expecting another foray into her personal space. She refused to be daunted by his tactics. In fact, she was growing accustomed to them. There was a slight edge to her response. "And what price this time?"

Finn laughed. "That's the spirit." His hand moved in slow motion as it touched the tip of her shirt collar. "Nothing so dire. Dinner."

AJ blinked. "Dinner?"

"You do eat on occasion, don't you? I mean, you are skinny, but I assume you must eat eventually."

"We prefer to call it trim, and I eat at least every other day." AJ strolled to the gangplank, not wanting to appear rushed. She turned before leaving. "Tomorrow night. There's a place in town called Joe's. Think you can find it?"

"I'll manage."

"Is seven okay?"

"Aye." Finn's slanted grin returned to his face.

The grin shifted them to their old routine. "You're not squirreling out of this one. I expect a story. Even trade."

"So I assume this means you're paying."

AJ shared her most withering smile before turning away. She could still hear his warm laughter as she walked to the path. A smile rested on her lips, and she told herself she wasn't giddy, just happy to get her story.

FOR THE THIRD time in almost as many days, Finn leaned against the rail of the deck and watched her walk away. Each time she left, he found himself more curious, although he knew it would come to no good—he had enough intrigue in his life. But now, of all things, he wasn't only being investigated by a reporter, but one who also knew her history and antiques. If that wasn't risky enough, he still wasn't sure how she was connected with her brother. If she had an ulterior motive, or if they had some game of their own, he couldn't see it. While it appeared to be coincidental on the surface, he needed to confirm it.

He wished he'd had met her sooner. Her interest in antiques

could create a new avenue in his search. He went back to work, his mood light from his short break. When he passed by the mast, his hand touch the hard wood, rubbing up and down as AJ had done less than an hour earlier. A small twitch played at his lips. Giving the mast one last pat, Finn grabbed a bucket, "Looks as if you could use a rubdown mate."

29

F ar above the *Daphne Maire*, a man watched two figures exchange their goodbyes from a point of land that jutted out over the small inlet, where the ship sat tied to the dock. The point was unreachable by road. A narrow walking path revealed the secluded spot, which dropped into a spectacular view of the coast, if you knew it was there or if you had searched for one, as Ethan had done.

After his brief meeting at Adam's office, and with the address to the Westcliffe tucked in his pocket, Ethan drove to the coast. He couldn't drive straight to the inn as it wasn't visible from the road, and he didn't know the layout of the place. Unsure of who might be there and not ready to make his presence known, he looked for a vantage point. He had driven the road several times in search of a place, but the area was heavily wooded. On his fourth pass, inching along the road in his Escalade, he caught sight of a small path at the edge of the woods and decided it was his best and only option.

He parked a small distance away in a small patch of dirt, as he had seen others do, then searched for the path. Ethan had trouble spotting it at first, as the trailhead was small and partially covered by bushes, but once found, he slid easily onto it, disappearing from view.

The path meandered through thick firs, occasionally opening into small sections of knee-high grass, forming tiny meadows before being swallowed once again by the trees. The path was worn and led to the coast, and at first he wasn't sure if it would be close enough to glimpse the inn. But the path was more direct than Ethan expected, turning only a couple of times to work its way around small sections of tiny ponds that collected the spring rains.

The trail remained in the forest to the end of the path where, a few feet from the point, it opened to a small patch of barren ground, a perfect setting for catching sunsets. The spot revealed an unencumbered expanse of the rugged coastline, both north and south. He looked down from the point, following a line of pelicans, dark shadows hugging the waves, directing Ethan's sight to what he came for. From here, he had a bird's-eye view of the Westcliffe and the small inlet to the south of the inn, where the *Daphne Marie* rolled along the dock.

From where he stood, Ethan could make out the two figures walking onto the deck. He recognized AJ—her lithe figure and brown tresses easy to spot—but he didn't recognize the man who followed her from below deck. He didn't need to. He knew everything he needed to know by looking at the ship—one he had caught mere glimpses of before, the eighteenth-century sloop that arrived either before him or shortly after, as if they had been chasing each other through the centuries.

Ethan frowned when the tall man reached out for AJ's collar, the move all too intimate. If he remembered correctly, AJ had said the ship had been there only a few days. She left the boat, the parting not as personal, so perhaps Ethan had misread the earlier gesture. He hoped so. He didn't want AJ involved in this, not any more than she already was.

Retracing his earlier steps, his return to the car was quick. He waited by the road, in the darkness of the forest, until enough time had passed for AJ to have driven away.

The inn's condition surprised him considering how long it had sat empty. He couldn't remember what AJ and Stella had said about the upkeep, if they mentioned it at all. He had been so shocked to hear the Westcliffe name that he had stopped listening, and now it seemed as if a crucial part of the conversation had been missed. He did, however, remember the discussion about the tidal pools.

THE ROCKY PATH dumped its visitors into the lap of the pools. The tide was either half-in or half-out, Ethan wasn't sure which, leaving enough of the rocks and puddles in view to know this was the place. The cove wasn't large. Dark emerald firs dotted the shoreline, intermixed with large rocks, leaving a spotty path of sandy shoreline here and there, the gentle surf mixed with the cries of circling gulls. If you looked from the right spot, you could catch a glimpse of the northern-most point of the inn's dormer, the only sign of civilization. Small shore birds hopped among the rocks, darting away as a wave rolled in and stirred the pools, dancing back to see what treasures remained behind. Beyond the pools, the rest was all ocean. When Ethan arrived, with the sun high in the sky and no clouds in view, the water was more blue than gray.

One didn't require much imagination to see how a young AJ could have thought this place magical—alone with her father. The two of them exploring the pools, the older man teaching AJ about history and antiquing. Ethan swallowed the small pang of regret at not having such a childhood. He didn't live his life dwelling on the past like an old codger. His life was about the future. Curiosity abated, Ethan turned to the path to deal with the current situation.

He strode to the ship. This confrontation was a long time in the making, but he was wise enough not to board without the captain's consent.

"Permission to come aboard." Ethan looked the ship over. It was well cared for, but there were signs of slow aging and a long time at sea. The gunports appeared empty, but the light scarring of wood suggested they had been used at least once. He tried to remember a time when they would have been fired, but before he could muse on it any further, he felt the presence of the captain.

"Aye, it's about time we met," Finn said as he considered his visitor. "Permission granted."

Ethan wasted no time boarding the ship, taking a long, hard look around the deck before resting his gaze on the captain. He could see why AJ would be intrigued. It wasn't his looks. Although any woman would find this man pleasing, there was more to it. His pleasant manner, the casualness of his bearing masking the tight control, the slow, lazy grin, and his Irish brogue, all culminated in the engaging man before him and would make this man likable to either gender. But he hadn't become a ship's captain with his pleasantries.

While Ethan took stock of the captain, he could see the man was doing the same in return. The man's gaze had never left Ethan since boarding. The slow assessment gave no indication to the bearer's thoughts, and Ethan could picture the man at cards. Perhaps that was how he made his living. A con man. Yes, that description fit.

"The name is Finn Murphy," the man said, but made no sign of shaking hands in greeting. "I believe you've been chasing me."

Ethan mulled over the name, then gave his head a slight shake. "Not so much you as the item you seek."

Finn gave a slight nod, and his smile disappeared. He put some distance between them, moving to the side of the ship, grabbing a line to rework the rigging. His fingers nimbly retied the rope through a deadeye bolt.

"The ship looks ready to sail. You must believe you're close." Shortening his long strides, he strolled around the deck, taking a closer look at the condition of the vessel. He couldn't tell whether his statement was true or not. Finn probably always kept the ship ready for sail. But the man's response confirmed Ethan's impression.

"I believe in being prepared." Finn finished working the lines, not looking at Ethan. "You didn't tell me your name. Do I know you?"

Ethan came back around to where Finn worked, watching the man finish the rigging and move to the next deadeye, removing the line and rubbing tallow onto the bolt.

"I don't think we've run in the same circles. I'm Ethan Hughes."

Finn worked the lubricant into the deadeye. "No, the name doesn't sound familiar. How is it we haven't met before now?"

"We got close one time before, but trouble plagued us."

Finn stopped his work to look out to the bay. "Ah yes, I remember now. That was you."

Ethan looked away as well, not wanting to resurface the memory. "We must be getting closer."

"Aye." Finn brightened. "That must be it. It's about time, don't you think, that we put this all to rest?"

"Perhaps. Depending on who gets to it first. It sounds like you've engaged a man to aid in your search."

"You know about that." Finn set down the bucket of tallow, giving his full attention to the ropes.

"It only makes sense. I've done the same." Ethan wanted Finn to know he was nipping at his heels, keeping the pressure on.

"I would have expected as much."

"How do you know AJ?"

Finn stopped working, the rope dormant in his hands. The thumb of his right hand rubbed the rough edges. "What a small world it remains, after all this time." The words almost escaped with the wind. "She's doing a story about the ship. I assume you know she's a writer."

Ethan moved closer. He'd almost missed Finn's first remark. "She did a story about the house I'm renting."

"She's an incredible woman. Intelligent. But like a bulldog. Never lets go of a mystery."

Ethan laughed. "She is persistent." He turned more somber. "I would hate for it to lead her into jeopardy."

Finn returned to work, retying his last knot. "She seems more than a match for either of us."

"Caution is in order. Neither of us will be here long."

"I know how to treat a lady. Not that it's any of your business." Finn's voice hardened. Dropping the rigging, he turned to face Ethan, the smile on his face not as pleasant as when Ethan had first arrived.

Ethan stared back. He wanted to press further, but this wasn't the time. Still, he couldn't resist one last shot. "I wasn't sure, based on who you work for."

He knew Finn had tracked his ascent to the top of the path. Ethan's mood had turned dark. He'd finally met the man he had been so curious about. It had to happen at some point. In the end, it didn't matter. He had no rational idea how to change the man's mind about which side he was on. No, it was more a sizing up of his competition, and in that, he found he had a formidable foe. He would have expected as much.

But something else bothered him, more than any other time. This journey had already been long. He suspected it wouldn't end by finding the artifact, and he was prepared for that.

What he hadn't been ready for was AJ becoming entangled in it all. He had to find a way to extricate her from this dangerous road. She had to be kept away from Finn at all cost, or her life as she knew it could change forever.

The question was how the devil to do it. She couldn't be told the truth. Ethan laughed. Who would believe it? No. There had to be another way.

———

AFTER ETHAN LEFT, Finn closed the lid to the small bucket of tallow and carried it below. He grabbed a glass and a tall bottle filled with a soft tawny essence, falling into the closest chair. He poured himself two fingers of Jameson, the finest of Irish whiskeys, and let the fire move its way down his throat. A gentle warmth rolled through him, and he closed his eyes. He hadn't thought he would ever meet him, the man in the shadows. Even never having met him, there had been some comfort knowing he was there, just out of sight, a fellow traveler alone in a strange land. And now, they were so close.

A flash of soft brown curls disrupted Finn's daydreaming. He remembered AJ's spark as she asked her questions, ready to drink in his answers, and rather than be satiated, his responses urged her on to more inquiries. This Ethan was right. Their search had become too complicated, and through it all, AJ had unknowingly found herself a bodyguard.

He took another swallow and let it seep deeper. Ethan's last words still troubled him. He hadn't been able to respond because, at the heart of it, he couldn't argue the point. This was not the first time he questioned his path. But it was a waste of time, and undoubtedly a waste of good whiskey. He fooled himself each time a new possibility erased the storm clouds, as if he had a choice.

Putting the bottle and glass away, Finn grabbed the bucket of tallow and returned to the deck.

30

AJ knocked on the age-scarred door, surprised by how solid it was. It seemed to swallow the sound of her rapping knuckles, and she wasn't sure anyone would hear her banging. She was glad for the large overhang protecting the front porch. Spring had shaken her mighty sword, and the rain had been pounding for the last few hours. She searched for a chime, but the door opened before she could find one.

"Good morning. It's lucky for you I was walking by the entrance. I would never have thought to look for you at my front door." Ethan held the door open for her. "I'm glad I didn't have to worry about you climbing in this weather."

AJ removed her raincoat, trying to keep it from spattering the floor, and hung it on the proffered coat rack. "I didn't mean to bring the weather in with me. I hope I'm not intruding so early in the morning."

She followed Ethan through the short maze that led to the kitchen, surprised by the changes since her last visit. The walls, still needing a new coat of paint, had been freshly washed, the draperies cleaned and pressed, the windows buffed to a shine, although some were now rain-streaked. Ethan had created a sparse bachelor house, and she was curious how it would look when finished. "You've done some work. The place is coming along."

Ethan poured two large mugs of coffee and directed AJ to the small kitchen table. "Furniture here and there, some cleaning. My biggest adventure has been with the lights. I'm fascinated by the new selections. It's like bringing sunshine into the house, even on mornings like this."

"The magic of LED." AJ smiled at Ethan's slide into domesticity, another side of this man she hadn't expected. "I'm sorry to drop in. I climbed yesterday, but you didn't seem to be home."

"I had an early appointment. The view would have been better yesterday." Ethan pointed toward the picture window, and the backyard beyond, the ocean masked by the piercing spring storm.

"Some days it's not so bad watching nature take its course. But it's so isolating."

"Isolation can be some people's comfort."

"Or their first step into madness."

Ethan laughed. "Your articles are making a cynic out of you."

AJ laughed in return. "I suppose they are." She fiddled with the napkin and brushed her hair behind her ears. "So, what have you been up to?"

Ethan paused before answering. AJ hadn't meant to pry. She had come to see Ethan as an old friend, even though they hadn't known each other long. Now here they were, coffee buddies, swapping their daily activities like she did with Stella.

"I'm afraid I've been a slug since our outing to Chilton. You seem to have found time to get some sun."

AJ bent her head to sip the coffee, hoping to hide her surprise at the question. "I've been working on my next article. It's been keeping me outside. I've been lucky with good weather."

"That's right. The Westcliffe, wasn't it?"

"Yes." She wasn't sure if she should mention the ship, but why not? He'd eventually see it in the paper. "I've expanded it some."

"How so?"

"There's an old sailing vessel moored at its dock. It would make a nice companion article, something to mix it up."

"The vessel is part of the inn? That's strange, with it being empty for so long—if I remember your discussion with Stella correctly."

AJ squirmed. She hadn't wanted to get into the details. "I'm not sure they're connected. It appears the captain happened to find the bay and, like you, seems to like his privacy."

Ethan refilled their mugs. "Well, I'm not your brother, but I can't help but hope you're being careful with all the new men dropping into your life. You never know about strangers these days."

AJ found it interesting he lumped himself into the group. "I think I'm a fairly good judge of character. I haven't been misguided in my assessment of you."

Ethan's eyes opened wide in mock hurt. "Good God, I hope not. But I did have a character reference from your brother."

"Not exactly my standard of reassurance."

"There you go, being tough on him again." Ethan held up his hands to stop AJ's retort. "I know, there's history that's not of my concern. The point is, Adam had already performed some due diligence for our working relationship. It's different from someone who happens to appear one day."

A shudder slid through her at Ethan's choice of words, at her memory of the ship, and how she had discovered it through the fog.

"Are you chilled? I can get you a wrap."

"No. I'm good. You're always looking out for me. I do appreciate it, but I'm okay. The captain has been elusive in sharing information on his ship, but he seems safe enough. Do you remember Stella and me mentioning a Mr. Jackson?"

"Yes, I think so. He's a caretaker or something?"

"Right. He takes care of the inn. He's been in Baywood his whole life, and he's been helping this Mr. Murphy—that's the captain—so it's pretty safe." AJ resisted another shudder, remembering her dip in the ocean and the strong arms that held her from falling in.

"So what's he doing in Baywood?"

Damn. He was becoming a better investigative reporter than she was. He seemed to know all the right questions she had no answers for. She took a long sip of coffee, staring out at the darkness, hard to believe it was morning. "I don't know. He hasn't said."

"I see."

Two simple words. They said it all. And once again, Ethan amazed her with his ability to get straight to the crux of the matter. "How dangerous can it be? He's sailing around on an eighteenth-century ship. It kind of sticks out." She tried to keep her response light, not wanting to sound defensive, but looking at Ethan's face, she hadn't come close to selling it.

"Look. I'm in security. I can't help but be cautious and point concerns out to you. I know we haven't known each other long, but I feel protective. I can't explain it. You need to be wary of someone who can't tell you what he does or why he's here."

"I get it." AJ touched his hand. "I appreciate the concern. I promise to be careful. One more interview is all I need." She tried a shaky laugh. "I'm not writing a book, just an article. I don't need much more."

Ethan touched her hand in return, a gesture so fleeting, it left AJ positive she had imagined it.

"I hear you have another article ready to go."

Samuel's words made AJ jump. She had been so focused on her writing, trying to guess what story Finn had to share, that she hadn't heard his footsteps behind her.

"Sorry." Samuel laughed. "Didn't mean to spook you. I wanted to touch base. You've been in early and back late these days. I never get to see my star reporter."

AJ smirked. "Star reporter for bringing in some historical series."

"The key word there is series. And this historical stuff about the city, the readers eat this shit up." Samuel patted AJ on her shoulder and leaned over to read the screen. "So this one is about a ship? Is this something docked at the marina?"

"No, it's currently docked at the Westcliffe."

"Hmm. That's your second article right, the old inn. And this ship is there. What's the connection?"

"I guess there isn't one. I mean, I thought there might be one, but it doesn't seem to be panning out." Adam's interest in the Westcliffe, while surprising, still didn't connect any dots to Finn or the ship. "The story about the ship seems interesting enough, and since it's right there by Westcliffe, it could work."

Samuel rubbed his hands together. "This is perfect. It's a nice break in the lineup of buildings. You'll need to find something similar we can slip in between the next two buildings you work on. Do you have the next ones picked out?"

AJ didn't. Her whole focus had been on Westcliffe and the *Daphne Marie*, and, if she was honest with herself, the captain. "Still picking through them." She hated lying to Samuel, but the small fibs were becoming habitual. She had some time— these two articles would run over the course of two weeks. Plenty of time. "I wanted to get this last one nailed down first."

"Sure, sure," Samuel said. "Just don't lose your momentum. You've got a great thing going for us here." He turned to leave and said, "Uh-oh. Wasn't he here a few days ago?"

AJ turned, a smile on her face, expecting to see Ethan, even though she had seen him earlier. The smile disappeared, and she groaned. *Adam.* "Yes."

"I've seen more of him here in a week than, well, I'm not sure I've ever seen him here before."

"You haven't. I'm sure this won't take long."

"Oh, I don't care about that, just a surprise is all." Samuel headed back to his office, nodding to Adam as they passed each other in the aisle.

Adam's run-in with Stella at the government offices flashed through her mind again. This might be the time to ask him about Westcliffe—but she sensed something different about him. His suit was a rich dark gray, perfectly tailored and fresh from the cleaners. His shirt was lightly starched, his tie always a perfect match for the suit, his shoes polished. She had to give Madelyn credit, she always kept Adam looking the part. It wasn't Adam—if left on his own, he would live in Dockers and Tommy Hilfiger.

Then AJ saw it. Adam looked tired. No, more than tired—

simply exhausted. He carried a sunken look his polished corporate suit couldn't hide, and she could only remember seeing him look this drained one other time. Shortly after her birth, their youngest child, Charlotte, had picked up a viral infection, forcing a few days in the hospital. Madelyn and Adam had both run themselves into the ground caring for their first two while taking turns at the hospital with Charlotte. Adam had looked strung out from little sleep and too much stress—like now. If she didn't know Adam better, she would be more concerned. But her mom would have called if this was a family problem. This had to be something else.

"You're becoming a regular visitor," AJ said.

Adam's laugh sounded forced. "Yeah, give me a desk." He strolled around the room, refusing to look at AJ. He seemed to take in the layout of the office, turning this way and that, seemingly interested in the place for the first time. He hadn't bothered with his first visit, but now it seemed to take his entire focus.

He wanted something. Adam didn't show his discomfort like most people. He hid it by becoming all lawyerly and feigning interest in things around him. Rarely did Adam have interest in anything other than his immediate universe of career and home.

"I never paid attention to how a newspaper worked." Adam finally looked at AJ, but he wouldn't hold her return gaze. "Guess I expected printing presses or something."

"Printing presses are in the back, but we only print twice a week. And they roll at night."

"It's awfully damned quiet in here."

"We're not Portland, and even there, I doubt it sounds like newspapers did in the old days, with phones ringing constantly and reporters banging away at typewriters." AJ turned away from Adam, already tired of the small talk, picking up folders and tucking them away in a drawer. "Is there something you needed?"

"It's Madelyn." Adam blurted it out.

"Madelyn." AJ stopped the shuffling. She wasn't fond of her, but she didn't wish her any harm.

If Adam noticed any note of concern in AJ's voice, he didn't show it. "You know she's the committee chair for the hospital's annual charity event. This year, it's raising money for the children's center. A new remodeled wing or family center, something like that."

"Oh. No. I didn't know." AJ went back to rearranging her desk, her concern abated. "It must be a lot of work for her."

"I guess that's why she's given me a task this year."

"You?" AJ had to smother a laugh. "That doesn't sound like you."

"It's an important cause. The children's center is critical for our area. We're so far away from the bigger cities and hospitals."

Adam's voice held a note of earnestness, and it silenced AJ. Neither he nor Madelyn ever spoke about the scare with Charlotte, but a family center would have meant the world to them back then. "You're right. I didn't mean to belittle your efforts. It's good of you to help out."

"That's okay." Adam leaned against a desk, a slight twist to his lips. "We're looking for items for the silent auction."

She wasn't sure what he could possibly need from her. "Uh-huh."

"Well, you buy antiques, and I know you sometimes resell them. I was thinking you might have something you could donate."

AJ sat back, calling herself all kinds of stupid. She had never considered donating any of her purchases. "I never thought of that."

Adam brightened. "So maybe if you had, oh, I don't know, maybe a piece of jewelry or something."

"Jewelry."

"Yeah." Adam played with his cuff links. "You know, there are lots of women at these things, and we have several well-to-dos coming in from Portland and Salem. Women love jewelry." He forced another laugh.

AJ mentally sorted through the items she had at home, something she wouldn't miss. "You're right. Jewelry would be the best, although I have a couple of interesting things the men might like."

Adam pushed his hands into his pockets and rocked back on his feet, but it didn't look natural for him. "I would think jewelry would catch the eye of the women in the crowd."

"Hmm." AJ searched her memory. "I don't know if I have anything. I'm not much of a jewelry collector."

The magical strings holding Adam up snapped, his shoulders slumping. He seemed to lose his focus. With a tired expression, he tried again. "Oh, well, I didn't know if maybe you picked something up recently, or you know." Adam reverted to a quick look around the office again, avoiding AJ's intense stare. "Or anything."

She thought about getting Adam a chair before he fell down, but didn't want to extend his visit. Instead, she stared at a spot on the wall, just past his left shoulder. There was a necklace she had acquired about a month ago. She never sought out jewelry, but as soon as she had seen this particular piece, it called to her. A stone so unique, she had pushed the woman into selling it to her for a pretty penny. She tucked it away as soon as she brought it home, meaning to research the piece, but had forgotten about it.

"I did buy something a while back, but I'm not ready to let it go," AJ said. "I'm still checking to see if it's authentic." Hope flickered, then died in Adam's eyes "But I'm sure I can find something equally splendid for you. When do you need it?"

"I don't know. Madelyn never gave me the date. I can't keep track of those things. She just asked for the donations. Maybe a week or two, I'll get back with you. Thanks. Madelyn will be thrilled. Thanks again." Adam finished in a fluster, and he scurried back down the aisle, talking to himself.

"What the hell?" AJ said aloud. This was an Adam she had never seen before. He had to have an ulterior motive. Madelyn might have gotten Adam to help with the charity event, but, if anything, Adam would have called, refusing to demean himself with an actual visit. More likely, he would have asked Joyce, his assistant, to contact her. Joyce was the one who called about plans for their mother's birthdays or the holidays. It was so much easier for Adam if he didn't have to talk to her.

Normally, AJ would have picked up on the jolt of a story beneath his hollowed look and unusual behavior, or at least would have once again questioned his interest in Westcliffe. But she had more crucial things vying for her time, namely one ship's captain she would be meeting for dinner. She reviewed her list of interview questions again, hating to admit that Finn intrigued her far more than a simple story. Ethan's words of caution echoed, and she wondered if there might be truth behind his concern. She should talk to Stella about it, but she wouldn't have time before dinner. Had she found the time, Stella would have known and been able to tell her friend, that she had already fallen through the looking glass.

THE AFTERNOON DRAGGED, the hours endless since AJ had left his place, and the time divulged no answers to Ethan's dilemma. He slumped in his office chair and propped his long legs on his desk. He gazed out the window but could have been sleeping. Eyelids partially closed, his body draped across his chair like a marionette, its strings snipped. But his muscles were taut, his pulse beat rapidly, and an underlying sharpness hid like a lounging cat, waiting to pounce on an unsuspecting meal that wandered too close. His thoughts churned through the time line, trying to pinpoint his next course of action.

Ethan couldn't believe Finn had taken such a risky path by soliciting help from an outsider, yet it could prove the wisest course. He hadn't gotten this close in the past, but his mission was to watch and follow, to gather the intelligence. It took all of Ethan's resolve to resist doing more. He tired of the chase.

With all the hunting, this was the first time a third party became so entangled in the plot. Well, there was one other time, but Ethan had closed the door on that memory. The part he was willing to recall was the local authorities' interest in their mission. He never fully understood how they became involved, but he had been able to extricate himself from the scrape, and in doing so had helped the man he had been following, the man he now knew as Murphy.

This time was different. He had the damnedest of luck to meet a reporter, someone with a natural gift for sniffing out a mystery in a story, particularly one with an equal passion for history. He had walked such a tightrope with her, only to discover she had been the one to find Murphy, another man who had been so careful to stay out of the public light. It was finally all coming together, but in a way Ethan would never have thought possible, and for the first time, the outcome was moving out of his control. There had to be a way to get AJ away from Murphy.

It might be possible. And there was only one person with the ability to help.

J oe's Place was busier than AJ expected on a weeknight, and seating was limited. She slowed when the hostess moved toward a secluded booth toward the back of the restaurant. She preferred to sit out in the open with more people around her, but the only other choices were by the front door or the kitchen, so she took the proffered table. The bar area might have been better, but it was even busier with the lingering work crowd.

It didn't matter. They were in a crowded restaurant. She swept away Ethan's nagging words.

She fidgeted at the table, rearranging napkins and utensils on the table, but she didn't have to wait long. Finn entered, wearing a dark green shirt that set off his tanned skin and green eyes. He had exchanged his blue jeans for a pair of black ones, and several women watched him cut through the restaurant. He focused on her, and she cursed the tingle. AJ went back to fingering the utensils and moving the condiment tray to the back of the table, wishing she had invited Stella.

Finn slid into the booth with his typical aplomb, his smile warm, the normal mischievous grin tucked away. "Am I late?"

"No. I just got here."

"Good. I lost track of time, and Jackson was late in picking me up."

"Jackson brought you? Where is he?"

Now the slanted grin was back. "I didn't invite him to dinner. My story is just for you."

AJ blushed. "He's not waiting out in the parking lot, is he?"

Finn shook his head and sat back, his gaze admonishing. "No, that would be rude. He had an errand to run before going back home."

"Oh." AJ looked through one of the menus the hostess had left and wondered how he planned on getting back to the ship.

Finn moved his menu away. "So what would you recommend?"

AJ ordered for both of them, and while they worked their way through dinner, Finn asked her about the town, prying out pieces of personal information along the way. Once again, the questions focused on her, but she didn't mind. She found herself talking about the special bond with her father, and her casual rapport with her mother. But when the conversation turned to talk of her brother, AJ became taciturn.

"You're touchy when it comes to your brother."

"Not all family gets along."

"But you have a small family, and with your father's death, well, I would think you'd grow closer."

"Yeah, well, it didn't happen. I guess instead of bringing us closer, his death released us to our own paths." AJ grew quiet. "I never understood it before, but Dad was the one tying us together. You usually expect the mom to be the glue."

Finn shook his head. "I still have a hard time grasping the discord. I know brothers and sisters can try each other's patience growing up, but there should be something deeper, a loyalty if you will."

AJ laughed, but the intensity in his gaze stifled it. "I guess it doesn't always work like that. Do you have siblings? You seem to have a pretty narrow look at it."

Finn sent her a lightning-fast flinty stare. Before he could answer, the waiter came to take their plates, and once he was gone, the moment left with him.

"So now I know the topic of your brother is best avoided. Is there any other subject I should sidestep? Current relationships perhaps."

"The trade for dinner was a story. Not my story, but yours."

"Aye, it was." Finn sighed and sat back. "A comfortable sofa and warm fire would make for a better telling, but a good cup of coffee will have to do."

STELLA SIGHED and stretched out on the chaise. She loved her patio. The whole day melted away as she laid her head back, allowing the aromatherapy to loosen the knots along her back. Her clients had dragged her through a roller coaster tour, constantly changing the requirements for their next house. She needed a huge pantry and a room for crafts. He wanted a home office and a big backyard. Then she fell in love with a house with a small back yard and a smaller kitchen, but she loved the master bedroom. He was enamored with one that had a small outbuilding made into a shop, and Stella would bet a year's salary he would make it into a man cave before he would ever consider putting a tool in there—the man was a priss.

A mercurial client usually enthralled her, and this was where she excelled in guiding her clients to the house they needed, helping them look past the things they thought they wanted. But for some reason, these clients grated on her. She didn't know why and didn't care. She wanted to get away from them and call it a day.

Stella had planned to call AJ to meet for happy hour, but all she could muster was finding her way to her patio. Better than a hot bath, and so much easier for drinking wine. She preferred her little white lights artfully arranged throughout the garden to any candlelit bathroom. No fuss, no muss, and they came on automatically at dusk. And she never worried about soap suds in her glass. No. She took a sip of wine and melted into the soft padding of her lounger. Nirvana.

So when the doorbell rang and the knocking at the door commenced, she cussed at the intrusion. She rarely received strangers at her door—the "no soliciting" sign took care of most of them. She cursed all the way to the front door, all her peaceful calm erased, as if the last hour never happened. She hated that.

The angry response she planned for her unwelcome visitor evaporated when she saw Ethan standing in her doorway. Her smile was immediate and natural, but it faded in light of his stern and agitated look.

"Good evening, Stella." Ethan managed a small smile for her. "I don't mean to intrude without calling first."

Stella stood aside for him to enter. "I was relaxing in the back. It looks like you could use some time back there. It's been a helluva day for me."

Ethan followed her to the patio where Stella pointed him to the stuffed wicker chair. Once the chair swallowed him, she handed him a glass of scotch, then refilled her wineglass. "I believe I heard you say you liked a good scotch. I don't drink the stuff myself, but this should be well aged. For the price, I have to assume it's top shelf." Stella returned to her lounger, hoping to retrieve some small essence of her tranquility.

Ethan sipped the scotch. "It's good."

Stella would normally have launched into some inane chatter to fill the silence, but she sensed they both needed time for the alcohol to take effect. She needed to reclaim her Zen, and as much as she would enjoy his company, there was no hope this was a social call.

That was unfortunate. Stella was getting used to his stoic nature, his stern and broody look that could transform with a twinkle of a smile. She was comfortable watching him sip his scotch and letting him be the first to break the silence.

Ethan looked around the patio. "You have a beautiful garden. I'm sorry I'm ruining what looks like a relaxing evening."

"You haven't ruined it yet, but it looks like you're planning on changing that."

Ethan set down the scotch and folded his hands. He leaned forward and tried to smile. "I have found myself in a dilemma, and I was hoping you could help."

FINN SIPPED his coffee and set it on the cleared table. Nothing between them now except their cups and the tale he owed her. He was lucky to have gotten AJ to share as much as she had of her own story—her happy childhood, her interest in history. If only he had met her earlier. Jackson was a good enough guide around town, but who wouldn't prefer the company of a beautiful woman? Her refusal to talk about her bother and her animosity toward him surprised Finn. But knowing what little he did of Adam, he could sympathize. Yet it always dismayed him when some brothers and sisters didn't get along. His gaze slid to hers as she waited for him to begin, her questions set aside for the moment.

"The ship was built in 1790. I think I told you that."

AJ sat quiet and unmoving.

It was purchased by a duke who was very powerful at the time, but as was the way back then, power, who had it and how it was used, was unpredictable and ever-changing. The duke eventually lost favor and, with it, much of his fortune, or so it was said. So he sold his ship for some coin and a promise of an errand to be run. Now the man who bought the ship was new to the sea, with only a touch of experience in his youth. He thought he had fallen into grand luck and would be on his way to new adventures. In some wicked way, he was, just not one of his conception."

Finn stopped to sip his coffee, tilting the cup toward him, staring into it as if the dark brew held some of the story, like tea leaves telling of one's future. He gazed into the cup as he continued. "This new captain was soon to set sail on his first maiden voyage on his fine new ship, when he was approached by a man of the duke's. The ship hadn't even seen its first sail with the new owner, and the marker for the promised errand was being called in. The captain was disheartened for it to be his first sail, but if he could get this business out of the way, full ownership would be his.

"So a fortnight later, he took on cargo that was said to be owned by the duke, and he brought aboard a mysterious passenger that never showed their face, who was given the captain's own quarters. The cargo and the passenger were taken to a port off the northern coast of France, which at the time was turbulent with revolution. Once the voyage had ended, the ship was his, complete with papers showing his ownership back to the day the coin was delivered.

"Feeling good, the deed done and the ship fully his, he never questioned the date of transfer and sailed to a few small ports on the continent before turning the ship for home."

Finn stopped again, his coffee pushed aside as he searched AJ's face. "Is this the type of story you were looking for?"

AJ nodded and laid a hand on his arm, seeming transfixed by the tale he was weaving. Finn stared at her hand, then took it in his own, keeping his grip gentle and warm. He turned her hand over and looked at her palm, running his fingers over it, then he stroked the lines on her wrist. "I once knew someone who could tell the future by looking at your palm. If only the captain had listened to her."

AJ looked as if she was going to respond, but when she glanced up at him, her words vanished. She pulled her hand back, rubbing her palm where Finn had touched it, and she smiled, encouraging him to continue.

"When the captain returned home, he discovered he had been duped. All his earthly possessions had been spirited away, and he was wanted by the law, charged with conspiracy. The papers and the date of transfer reflected the captain's ownership, making him responsible for the transport of illegal goods. He was told his family had been taken and placed under arrest pending his return. A viscount, in charge of the matter, presented a deal to the captain. If he would entertain another voyage, all would be forgiven and his family restored. The passage being asked of him would not be easy and, in itself, seemed fantastical. Yet the captain could see no other way out for his family and agreed to the impossible journey."

Finn locked eyes with AJ. She was thoroughly enchanted, either by the story or his telling of it, he wasn't sure which. "So, as the story goes, the captain left on his journey to save his family and return honor to their good name. But no one ever saw the captain again nor heard what became of his family. The ship sailed off one day, never to be seen again."

Finn pulled his cup back to him, grimacing at the taste of his now-cold coffee.

AJ stared at Finn. "That's it?"

Surprised, Finn brushed back an errant curl and leaned back into his chair. "What do you mean?"

"Never to be seen again? But you're sailing on the ship, so it must have been seen again. I can't end a story like that when it's obvious the ship wasn't lost at sea."

"I tell you a perfectly good story, and now you're nitpicking over the details."

"Are you telling me the story was made up?"

"No, it's not made up." Noticing the looks they were getting from the other tables, he lowered his voice. "At least not that I'm aware. I should have said the ship was never seen again in their lifetime. Of course the ship resurfaced. Obviously. It was the captain that was never seen again. I forgot you were looking for historical facts."

"Well, you don't have to say it like facts are a bad thing." AJ's whispered voice grew agitated.

Finn laughed, partly to put the story behind him, but mainly because this woman could so easily lighten his mood. She had such a strong desire to learn, an ability to listen without interruption and to call foul when the story didn't add up. Fascinating. She reminded him so much of…someone else. He abruptly stood. "So we're even now. My dinner paid."

"Where are you going?"

"Let's go for a walk. It seems like a nice evening, and we've been sitting here for far too long."

Once outside, Finn took AJ's hand, placing it through his arm, and they strolled along the street like a young couple, enjoying each other's company on a cool spring night. AJ pointed out spots Finn might find interesting and answered more questions about the town. The conversation never touched on anything personal, and Finn sensed AJ relaxing her guard until he stopped. Her face registered surprise when she looked to the side and spotted her own car.

Finn looked down at her. "Could you take me back to the ship?"

AJ stared back at him. "Sure."

"So you believe AJ's in some kind of trouble?" Stella seemed doubtful and waited for Ethan to go over it again. When he didn't, she prodded him. "I'm not sure I follow. Why do you think this Finn Murphy is bad news?"

Ethan ran a hand through his hair. She was a tough one. He had known it was going to be difficult, a long shot at best, but this was the only course of action he had time to pursue. All he could do is try to convince her. "You know my job is in security." Ethan paused, searching for the right words. "I've run across information about some stolen property." He slid a glance in Stella's direction, making sure she was paying attention. "I believe there are a couple of men looking for the property."

When Ethan didn't continue, Stella prompted again. "And these men are in town. And what, Finn Murphy is one of them?" Stella sat a little straighter in her chair, her eyebrows crinkled.

"I don't have proof, but he is new in town."

"It's the start of tourist season. There are lots of new people in town, including you. Coastal homes will fill with all kinds of people, some for the whole season."

"I agree, but this Mr. Murphy has been spotted around town asking questions and meeting with people not prone to tourist routes." He couldn't say anything about Adam. That was certain to drag Stella, and possibly Adam, into his problem. He only needed Stella concerned enough to get AJ out of the way without asking too many questions. A fine line indeed.

"That's pretty thin." Stella leaned back in her chair and appeared to be mulling it over. "His boat isn't exactly subtle. Wouldn't a thief want to blend in more?"

"Normally, I would say yes, but on the other hand, who would suspect someone who is so noticeable? I believe you've met him. He's very engaging."

Stella smiled. "You got that right. He'd stop any woman in her tracks. I can't believe AJ would fall for that."

This wasn't working—he should leave. Instead, he rolled the empty scotch glass around in his hands. He caught the scent of lilacs and let his gaze roam over the garden, taking in the small white lights and dark green foliage. He lifted his glass toward Stella. "Do you mind?"

"Not at all."

Ethan poured himself a second glass and, while he was up, refilled Stella's wineglass. As soon as he sat, the answer came to him. He didn't need to *convince* Stella. All he needed was a tinder —a spark to set the fire. Let Stella fan the flames. He wasn't sure there was enough time, but Stella had a fertile imagination. The seed of doubt might result in full bloom faster than he could predict.

"I'm not worried about AJ falling for the man." Ethan let the words hang in the air for a few seconds. "It's a little worrisome with her being around him if we're not convinced about his reason for being in town. Did AJ mention why he was here?"

She shook her head. "No. I don't think he's told her. She's had difficulties with him telling her much of anything. That's what got AJ hooked—she thought there might be a story." Stella stood, checking the padding of the chaise. She patted the pockets on her slacks and sweater.

She had taken the bait, but she seemed to have lost focus on their discussion. "What are you looking for?" he asked.

As soon as he said it, Stella found her cell phone and dialed. "It wouldn't hurt to see where AJ is. We usually call each other before bedtime to share our day. Let's see what she's up to."

Ethan waited while Stella listened to the ringing. He hoped her mind was a thousand miles away, working through the doubt, the questions with no answers. He heard AJ's voice, but Stella hung up.

She frowned and redialed. Again, AJ's voice was cut off as Stella closed the connection. "It goes straight to voice mail. I haven't heard from her all day."

33

The inn was a little creepy in the dark. AJ had never been out here this late. Looking past the inn, beyond the vacant darkness of the Westcliffe, she caught a slim sliver of moonlight as it commenced its nightly journey, casting its shimmering reflection off the ocean. She turned off the engine, as it seemed impolite to sit with it idling, waiting for Finn to get out. Once the car was quiet, its lights gone in a wink, the darkness enveloped them, leaving AJ to second guess her motives.

"Peaceful, isn't it?" Finn's voice registered barely above a whisper.

"Definitely quiet. And dark." AJ kept her voice low to match his, as if in reverence to the night and not wanting to disturb any strange beasties prowling outside.

Finn laughed softly. "And dark. But not as quiet as you think. Can't you hear the ocean?"

AJ cocked her head, a fox listening for its prey, and she smiled. "Yes, faintly. You must be attuned to it."

"Aye, at times it's like the blood in my veins. Come take a look at it." Finn was out of the car faster than she could respond.

Unsure she had a choice, she followed him toward the inn and the path to the dock, matching his quick strides. She was about to call out, asking for him to stop, but Finn paused at the turn in the path. He seemed captivated by the sight. AJ joined him, and they stood quietly, looking down at the bay.

The faintest of glows lit the small inlet and left part of the ship in the moonlight, the other half in dark shadows. She imagined what the ship would look like with a full moon, the shadows crouched in the recesses, waiting for darkness to return. The *Daphne Marie* rocked against the dock as if someone had whispered her name, and their soft breath had moved her.

"I have something to show you," Finn said. He led AJ down the path to his ship and across the deck to the stern.

AJ peered up, dazzled by the vast number of stars, and without the glare of city lights, the Milky Way stretched across the evening sky. On her early morning climbs, most of the stars were swallowed by the predawn light. This sight invaded her soul.

"It's beautiful." AJ pulled her sweater closer, the light breeze giving her a chill.

Finn moved closer, perhaps to block the wind. "Are you familiar with your stars?"

"No. I know the main ones. The Big Dipper, Orion, Cassiopeia."

"And the North Star?"

"Yes, I think so."

Finn fell silent. He rubbed the rigging, even now checking for frays. "You were interested in the navigational instruments I have."

"They were amazing pieces." AJ couldn't hide the awe in her voice. She could still picture the compass, her fingers skimming across the silver filigree to finely etched *M* that marked the owner.

"Tonight is a perfect night to show you how they work."

AJ let the silence deepen. She wiped the hair away from her face, her eyes locked on the blackness of the sea. When she turned to him, she shared her most dazzling smile. "Yes, let's see how those things work."

"MAYBE YOU SHOULD TRY LEAVING A MESSAGE." Ethan remained calm, lounging in the wicker chair, but his stillness was tightly controlled. "Maybe she's on the phone."

"Maybe." Stella pulled at her lip. She hadn't spoken to AJ since yesterday. She didn't say she had any plans, just wanted to finish her articles. AJ often went dark when she was on a story, falling into them, not coming up for air until she was done. That was all this was. She redialed straight to voice mail again.

"It's AJ. If you've got a story to tell, leave it at the beep." AJ's weak attempt at reporter humor.

"Hey, honey, it's me. Just checking in, haven't heard from you in a while." Stella sounded tired. "Give me a call as soon as you get this. I've got some info for you. It's important."

Stella dropped into the chaise. She pulled her wrap around her and looked at Ethan. They hadn't known him more than a couple of days before they had gone antique hunting with the man. But he knew Adam, which seemed to make everything all right, even though AJ would never listen to anything Adam had to say. On the surface, the only difference between him and this Finn Murphy was the lack of a personal reference. Stella wasn't sure what was going on, if anything, but she could see the lines of worry on Ethan's face.

"Maybe we're rushing to conclusions here," Stella said. "It's not too late. She could be working, or maybe she went to dinner with someone. Or maybe she's with her mom. AJ mentioned they hadn't visited much lately."

"Can you call her?"

"AJ's mom?" Stella shook her head. "Not without creating a panic. No. I've left a message. There isn't anything more to do until she calls."

They sat in silence. Ethan stared at some point in her garden, his eyes unfocused. Stella couldn't guess how often he allowed that to happen, comfortable enough to check out, not be in control. For some reason, the unguarded look didn't suit him.

He had brought his concerns to her, and Stella racked her brain, trying to remember what AJ had told her about Finn, but it was hazy. She had been meeting with him about the inn—no, the ship. Mr. Jackson was the expert on the inn, but Stella didn't know anything about him either, other than being born in Baywood, decades ago. If Jackson was any kind of trouble, he would have been in the papers, but AJ hadn't found anything. A person couldn't do something in this town and not create some interest, not in a town of this size.

Then there was Adam. He had been looking at the records for Westcliffe, but that didn't mean he knew Finn or even knew about the ship docked at the inn. She couldn't picture Adam going out there. He wasn't a hands-on kind of guy, yet he had gone to the records office on his own instead of sending one of his clerks to do it. She was going around in circles trying to connect the dots.

"I'm sorry I laid this at your feet." Ethan sat straighter in his chair, his gaze soft but fully engaged. "AJ is fine, even if we can't locate her. I only meant to share some caution until we know more."

"Well, I can't argue with someone who's watching out for us. We'll check in with AJ in the morning, and she can tell us about her interview with Finn."

Ethan rose. "I'll see myself to the door. I'll be sure to lock it before I leave."

Stella laughed. "Have you thought about being a personal bodyguard?"

Ethan's raised one eyebrow. "What makes you think I'm not?" With a slight bow of his head, he disappeared into the house.

A minute later, the front door thumped shut. She poured herself another small glass of wine and pulled open a blanket, the wrap no longer providing the warmth she needed. She snuggled within its deep folds and questioned Ethan's visit. He said it was only a suspicion, but he had come to her rather than the police. She hadn't asked—maybe he was already speaking with them.

She tried calling AJ one more time and got the same response. But she could be an alarmist. She needed AJ's cool head to explain everything in the morning. She breathed in the floral scents of her garden, yearning for the tranquility she'd never quite achieved before Ethan's visit.

AJ WAITED on deck while Finn went below to retrieve one of the navigational instruments. She didn't know which one and didn't entirely care. Other things played at her mind. The air was warmer in the bay and away from the wind, but she still pulled her sweater around her, a reflexive action, nerves reacting to the path she chose.

She hadn't heard his silent approach until he was right behind her. He stood there, not moving or saying anything, and AJ finally turned to find him staring at the sky.

"What are you looking for?" AJ whispered. It seemed wrong to disturb the silence.

"We could use the moon as our navigational aid, but I prefer to use stars. They seem more stable to me, the moon more, I don't know, mercurial."

"I don't think I've ever heard anyone talk about the moon that way before." AJ tensed for another lesson, as if sailing hadn't been enough of a failure.

"Oh aye, the stars each have their place in the night's sky, tucked into their constellations, each with their own heavenly purpose." Finn searched the heavens and pointed to a group of stars. "Take Bootes, for example."

"Which one is that? I haven't heard of it."

Finn turned her head, shifting it to the left. "See that bright star? It's Arcturus, the brightest in Bootes, and there are two small arms that run lateral, and five less bright stars forming an elongated shape."

"Oh, the kite. The long part always looked like a kite to me."

Finn chuckled. "Okay, I can see that." He tilted AJ's head straight up. "Now what do you see?"

AJ laughed. "The Big Dipper."

"Ursa Major. Most people only see what you call the Big Dipper, but the constellation is much larger." Finn grasped AJ's hand and guided it to the right. "If you follow the stars, you can see the head." He slid her arm downward. "And the legs of the great bear. It doesn't matter the constellation or the grouping of stars, each one can be depended upon by their mates."

When he dropped AJ's arm back by her side, the chill of the night air skimmed across her, and she moved closer to Finn, still looking to the night sky. She was so close, Finn's breath rustled her curls when he spoke.

Finn's fingers arched from left to right as if in their own dance, his voice a whisper. "The moon, however, is ever-changing, moving from new to quarter to full as it dances across the sky."

AJ took her eyes off the slight figure of the moon and backed up a step to look at Finn. "Why, Mr. Murphy, you're a romantic."

"No one has accused me of that before."

"You can't fool me with your Irish blarney. Anyone who talks of the night sky like you has the heart of a poet." AJ smiled and returned to her spot near him. "Whether you're willing to admit it or not." She touched his hand and removed the sextant from his grip, trying to remember how to hold it. "So show me again how those stars can help guide us."

"All right, straight to business it is. You need to find two things, your horizon and a point in the sky. So what point would you like to use?"

"Let's use Arcturus."

"Aye, good choice, Bootes it is." Finn placed his hands on her shoulders, turning her so she faced the sea and the constellation. "Hold up the sextant."

AJ held the instrument, and Finn moved her hands into the proper positions. She tried to remember her first lesson, but she couldn't focus with his body pressing into her back, the warmth transferring heat to keep her warm. The smell of cedar invaded her senses. She tried to focus on his words.

"Now look through this hole here while you find your horizon and slide this bar until you see Arcturus come into focus here."

AJ fumbled with the slide, becoming accustomed to it. He bent down to see what she was looking at, his face so close to hers, the touch of his hair tickled her neck. An internal flame enveloped her, rising from her core and spreading outward. "And then what?"

His lips played at the curls touching her ears. He was so close, maybe he could pick up the scent of lavender from her shampoo. His arms slid back up, pointing to a spot on the sextant. "You look at the scale here to determine the degree mark." He stayed close and turned her to face him. "The mark is critical." His eyes no longer on the instrument or the horizon. They held AJ in place, searching.

All she heard was a loud pumping sound, the beating of her heart as she held his gaze. Her body responded to his closeness, the heat emanating from him. She wished she wasn't holding the sextant, the only thing preventing her from reaching up to test the softness of his hair. Her mind became foggy, her voice thick. "The mark is critical. And then what?"

She moved closer. He took the sextant from her fingers with one hand and drew her in with the other. He leaned down and took her lips with his own. There was nothing hesitant in his kiss. His tongue immediately parted her lips, searching for a response.

He didn't have to wait. Her hands free to explore, they slid up his arms, tracing the muscles beneath them. Hands moved around his neck, and she pulled him closer, her tongue seeking his. She softened against him, the sextant lying at their feet, forgotten. Finn's hands moved to her waist and pulled her closer until there was no space between them, only the hardness of his chest. His fingers played at her neck before they cupped her face. He pulled back from the kiss.

She saw wild yearning in him. The fire that spread through her burned bright in him, and she pulled his head down for another kiss. And she whispered, "Show me more."

Finn swept her up and carried her toward the stairs. Her laughter echoed through the narrow stairway as they made their way below. AJ held on tight until they reached his cabin and he dropped her to her feet in front of the bed. There was no question about what came next. She was all in now. A deep longing fired her blood when she realized how long she had been waiting for this moment.

She kept her eyes pinned to Finn's as she unbuttoned his shirt. Her hands slid across his chest and down his arms, peeling the shirt from him. A medallion hanging from a black cord grazed his chest and caught her attention. Her mind stopped for a split second when she saw the stone within the medallion. Something scratched along the surface of her memory.

Before she could bring it into focus, Finn's fingers brushed the underside of her chin, tilting her head up. His kiss trampled her curiosity. Her blouse slid away. She felt the coolness of the room, like a feather brushed against her skin, before it was replaced by the rising heat of Finn's embrace.

AJ pushed Finn away, far enough to open the belt at his waist. Her fingers were swift as she moved to the button of his jeans and the zipper, yanking his pants from his hips. Finn stopped her progress, tossing her onto the bed and pulling her own pants from her.

AJ's laughter returned. A deep throaty laugh. Finn stripped his pants off. As her warm gaze roamed upward, his brown locks dropped forward over his brow. The mischievous grin spread across his face. Her laughter turned to a wicked grin of her own as he perused her with an equally long look. She screamed with delight as he jumped onto the bed, her lips devoured.

Her mind reverted to its most primitive state. AJ drank in the full scent of him, the touch of his skin, his muscles. His hands seared her, roamed over her. Searching. His kisses like the wings of a butterfly one minute, molten lava the next. She reveled in the strength of his body as he lay on her, his fingers finding the right spot. Her body lifted in response, his lips light against her throat, his kisses more demanding. AJ closed her eyes, holding on tight as Finn slipped inside, and, guided by the stars, they danced with the moon.

J woke as Finn pulled on his shirt. Their first time together had been followed by two repeat performances, each slower and more intimate than the last. AJ blushed at the memory, smiling as she watched Finn dress. When he finished with the belt, he turned toward her and smiled in return.

"I didn't want to wake you until the last minute." Finn leaned over to kiss her. "I imagine you need to get to work."

"Hmm. At some point." Her voice was rough from sleep, her body warm in the sheets. AJ rubbed her thumb across his cheek. She felt the hitch in his breath, and her smile turned to an impish grin.

"Oh no. You, dear lass, could make me forget my whole day." Finn pulled back.

"Would that be so bad?"

"Not at all, but I have a meeting, and you must have something to do at that paper of yours." Finn buttoned the rest of his shirt. The chain flashed an instant before it disappeared from view, and she was hit with a feeling of déjà vu. It faded when Finn grabbed another kiss.

"What are you doing this afternoon?"

AJ stretched, looking around for her clothes. "I don't know. I need to finish the story on the *Daphne Marie*. It won't take long."

Finn helped in AJ's search, tossing pieces of clothing at her. "I'll leave the room to you. I'm afraid all I have is an old-fashioned chamberpot behind the door." And with his signature grin, he disappeared.

"Great." She took a long look around the room and moaned, speaking to a now-empty room. "Well, we all have to pee."

Once on deck, fully dressed, finger-combing her hair as best she could, AJ looked for Finn through the light drizzle. She spotted him where they had been watching the stars the previous evening, holding the sextant, running his hands over it. This time, AJ allowed the tingle free range to spread through her, giving lightness to her steps and a permanent smile to her face. She wasn't one bit sorry for the previous night, regardless of what happened next.

"Is it okay?" She stepped next to him, her concern for the antique unmistakable. "We didn't break it, did we?"

"No." Finn turned it over. "Maybe a new dent on this one side." His fingers rubbed the spot. "It still works fine."

"Thank God. I wouldn't want to be responsible for damaging such a beautiful antique. And you still owe me a navigation lesson. You've cheated me out of them. Twice now."

Finn pulled her to him. "Oh, and it was all my fault was it?" His kiss was demanding, and AJ's body melted against him. "You have the ability to drive all good sense from me." Finn pushed her back.

She already missed the warmth of him. "Do you need a ride to town?"

Finn hesitated. "No, Mr. Jackson should be here any minute." Finn looked at the instrument in his hand, rubbing the new dent. "But I do have the afternoon free."

Finn's fingers moved back and forth on the sextant. AJ

refused to take the bait, but it would have been simple to give in. She'd stay with him all day if she could. "Well, I'm sure you'll find something to entertain yourself."

AJ turned and walked to the gangway. She gave him a parting smile, pleased to see his own smile—not a grin, but a genuinely warm smile. She ran down the gangplank, only slowing as she moved up the path, giddy from lust. All she needed was a little time to herself. Her pace increased. AJ was almost at a run by the time she reached the lot. She had to call Stella.

Once safe inside her car, she threw her head back and grabbed the steering wheel. It started slowly, like a wave spreading out along the sand. It hurt as it moved up her chest, the air exploding out of her. She laughed. Shaky, then stronger, unable to erase the grin. Now that she was alone, she recognized the emotions, surprised to find similarities between them.

She is five feet from the top of a climb, hair blowing in the light breeze, small trickles of sweat dripping down her face, her muscles calling out to her, vibrating from the fatigue, and she pushes through the pain and discomfort. With a last blast of adrenaline, she pulls herself over the ledge and drags herself into a sitting position. She gazes at the ocean, a peaceful sensation swells through her, emanating out from her center, and for just that moment, with the light from the sun announcing the day, the warmth upon her skin, the welcoming cries of gulls, the world is perfect.

Breaking from the spell, AJ pulled out her phone and pushed the familiar number.

The voice sounded groggy and disoriented. "This is Stella."

"You sound awful. Did you fall asleep on the patio?"

"AJ? Thank God. Are you all right? You shut off your phone, you never do that."

"Are you available for lunch? At the café."

3 5

The bar was dark, as any good bar should be, a local joint near the heart of the city that catered to the serious all-day drinkers. The men, and sometimes women, whose lives had run aground, much like the scattered, dusty old pictures of the shipwrecks dotting the walls of the dingy bar, found their comfort here. The one place no one judged. The Shipwreck spoke as much to the clientele of the aged establishment as it did to the ships immortalized on the walls.

Adam looked out of place, nursing the glass of scotch in front of him, but he wasn't the first man dressed for business that had found his way to the Shipwreck this early in the day. He sat at the bar, his tie loose, and not alone—two other men sat like bookends at either end of the bar, staring into their own drinks. Adam's discomfort grew, an uneasiness that pushed at him, making him more distraught as he considered his situation.

This was how men like him created a life in this bar. They start with one problem and find a way to deal with it. But the way they deal with it creates another problem, which leads to yet another, and before they know it, they've created a web of lies so thick they can't see their way past them. They get drawn in so deep, they end up in a dive like this, dragged into despair.

Adam's problems might have seemed more manageable if he had picked a more high-class joint in which to drown his troubles. But there was a greater likelihood of being recognized in the nicer places—if they were even open at this hour. And it wouldn't look good for a lead attorney at a major law firm to be seen drinking like a midday regular. No, this was much better. He wouldn't make a habit of it. Besides, he wasn't here to drown his sorrows. He was here for a meeting, and with his newfound resolve, he lifted his finger for another round.

He was well into his second scotch when the man appeared next to him, wrenching him out of his reverie. Adam looked into the rugged, tan face of the man, the impatient eyes dark and unforgiving, and his nerves receded under the stony emerald glare.

The man stared at the almost-empty glass of scotch in front of Adam. "Drinking away your morning, I see." Finn sat next to Adam, turning to the bartender. "I'll have a pint of something dark, and get my friend here another."

"I don't need another. I need to get back to work after this."

"That's all right. You can walk it off. We won't be long." Finn gave the room a slow scan before settling back on Adam. "Have you found what I'm looking for yet?"

Adam shook his head. "Not yet."

"What's taking so long? I thought you said you knew who had it. I'm spending good money for you to get it."

"It's not as easy as you think." Adam spit the words out. His anxiety and the scotch were getting the better of him. "It wasn't where it was supposed to be. Not anymore."

A FEW BLOCKS AWAY, at the small café in the building of the

Baywood Herald, AJ and Stella were lucky to snag a table. The lunch crowd was at high peak, a time they both tried to avoid. But Stella had a short window, and neither had the patience to wait until after work.

"So tell me where you disappeared to last night," Stella said. "I know you think Ethan's concern is unwarranted, but he doesn't seem like someone who rushes to judgment." She fussed with the cellophane protecting her plastic utensils, finally jabbing the fork through the plastic with brute force.

AJ patiently worked the plastic of her own utensils, retrieving her fork to spear the salad in front of her. "I'm not questioning Ethan's warning about the thefts in the area. I'm sure they're real, but Finn doesn't have anything to do with it."

Stella peeked at AJ and confirmed she was overworking her casual demeanor. She didn't need to be told where AJ had spent the evening. "So tell me how things are with your captain."

"He's not my captain. Good grief, you make it sound like, I don't know, more than it is." AJ talked into her salad bowl, bent over her task, not once looking up.

"But that was who you were with last night. And I know of only one reason why you would have turned off the phone."

AJ's shoulders slumped, and her hint of a smile wouldn't go away. Stella sighed. "I don't need the details. Well, yes, I actually do, but I only have an hour. Just give me the highlights for now."

AJ blushed. "It was one night, and I'm sure the only night." She finally looked at Stella. "He promised me a story if I took him to dinner."

"Well, that seems harmless enough. But you ended up on the boat."

"Sounds like you already know enough." AJ relented after a few more stabs of salad, laying out her entire evening, the dinner, the interview, driving Finn back to his boat, and finally, the speed-reader's version of the events that followed.

Listening to AJ recount the evening, Stella heard the excitement in her voice, the sound they all got from the first rush of lust. She nodded along, supplying all the appropriate responses, the uh-huhs, the reallys, and the go-ons. But she could also see Ethan's eyes as they laid out his suspicions and the concern that emanated from him. "I don't know. That sounded pretty passionate, enough for there to be more than one evening."

"He hasn't said how long he's going to be here, but I get the impression it won't be much longer."

Stella waved a forkful of salad. "Then I say get as much as you can, as fast as you can."

AJ choked on her salad. "It's been way too long for you. Whatever happened to the Realtor you met, what, about a week ago?"

Stella smiled like the Cheshire cat. "We talk." She pierced a tomato, looked it over, and popped it into her mouth. "Let's stay focused on you. What about Ethan's concerns?" And for the first time, Stella saw conflict in her friend.

FINN'S BEER wasn't nearly as dark as he liked, but it was better than the weak yellow piss people usually tried to push on him. He took his first taste as Adam's words sank in. The mug hit the bar with a thud, his desire for the brew now gone. "What do you mean it's not there?"

"Not there. They sold it. Some estate sale a few weeks ago."

"Are they sure?" Finn racked his brain. It must be close or he wouldn't have found his way to Baywood, nor would he still be here. "Maybe you didn't give them the right description."

"They knew exactly which piece I was talking about. I barely said a few words, and they described it to me perfectly."

Finn reined in his growing temper. There had to be a way to track it. "I can't believe they sold it, like some piece of second-hand goods."

"From what they told me, they hadn't planned to sell it at all.

The old lady living there was their grandmother, and she died a few months back. The family was selling some of her collections but had hoped to keep a few pieces of the nicer stuff."

Finn's patience waned, but it was better to let people talk, divulging too much as they rambled. He couldn't do anything about the lost piece, other than to find out what happened and work through another plan to recover it. He took a long swallow of beer, the taste as bitter as his disappointment.

Adam stopped talking, peering into what was left of his third scotch. He had either disappeared into his own demons, or the drink had been too much. Finn waved the bartender over and ordered a cup of black coffee for Adam.

They waited for the coffee, each man an island, the silence the only string keeping them connected as they each considered their own problems, the answers not forthcoming. Finn had disliked this man from their first meeting. A bartender from another bar, who was also connected to a local poker crew, had introduced Adam to him. All Finn had been told was that Adam was a local lawyer who knew the lay of the land and was looking to make some extra cash. Finn had guessed a gambling debt was involved, but it wasn't his business. Finn didn't care, he just needed a job done, and there was no one better for the job than a lawyer.

Finn didn't think highly of men who gambled away their fortunes. This man had a wife and children, yet risked their future for the call of the cards. But Finn understood why men threw caution aside, attempt a taste of adventure to animate their perfectly dull lives. Once lured into their new life, they found themselves caught like a bug in a web—the more they tried to climb out, the tighter the snare. Only Finn's awareness of the game kept him from clinging to a barstool in the middle of the day.

He turned to the man beside him. Adam cupped his hands around the mug of coffee, bent over it as if the rising steam was enough to clear his brain. And maybe it was. Finn could see the alertness returning. Though Adam still glared into his cup, his eyes were more focused, his body straighter. Still, Finn waited, allowing the man to finish half the mug before continuing.

"So you said they didn't plan on selling all the pieces."

For a minute, Finn wasn't sure if the man had heard him. Adam sat still, a far away expression masking his face. Then, like a man frozen in time and suddenly released, he raised his mug to his lips, taking a long slow drink, and motioned to the bartender for a refill.

Adam waited for his coffee, took a quick sip of the hotter brew, and turned to face Finn, his eyes clear and sharp. The lawyer was back. "The granddaughter had kept several select pieces from the collection. She had hoped to keep something of her grandmother's most treasured items."

Adam paused for another sip of coffee, then pushed it away. "They were going to shut down early and close the sale. They had made what they needed to cover the debt. The rest of the stuff would be moved to small thrift stores or antique shops or, I don't know, maybe dropped off as donations." Adam shook his head and laughed.

"What's so amusing about this?"

When Adam looked back at Finn, the vacant eyes had returned, just for a moment, before regaining their focus. "My luck. You know the saying, if it wasn't for the bad luck...well, that's how this went as well.

"The granddaughter had walked outside to remove the sale sign when a car pulled up. A woman got out and said she'd tried to get there earlier but had gotten turned around. The grand-daughter understood. I had a difficult time, for that matter—the place isn't easy to find if you aren't a local. Anyway, she felt bad closing the sale after the woman had such trouble finding the place, so she let the woman look around while she finished closing."

Adam shook his head again. "If she had told the woman no, I'd have your piece right now."

Finn lowered his head and turned the pint in front of him, wanting to finish it in one long swallow. They had been so close.

"The woman saw the piece in the collection case and talked the granddaughter into selling it, for a more than reasonable price. While she hadn't planned on selling it, nothing was holding her to it, and this woman had been so enraptured by the piece, she saw no reason not to sell it. And that, my friend, was that."

It was Finn's turn for silence. He was tempted to finish his pint, perhaps even a second one. He could call this stool his own for the afternoon. Positioned away from the entrance, he could ignore the day and join the other poor souls melted onto their stools, with no direction and no one to go home to.

Adam sighed. "Look. I haven't stopped the search, and I might have an angle on who the woman is."

Finn snapped out of his stupor. "Who is she? How can I find her?"

Adam raised his hand. "No. You need to be patient. I can get you what you want, but I need a little more time."

"But if you know who has it, I can take care of it easily enough."

Adam shifted in his seat, glanced at the man at the end of the counter, then scanned his surroundings with clear disgust. "No. From what I've uncovered about this woman, it would be better if we take a more subtle approach. I'm not sure money will sway her, but you never know." Adam sat straighter, the scotch cobwebs falling away. "Give me some more time. I'll get the piece for you."

Adam was right. He could mess it up, barging into an unfamiliar situation himself. He needed to remain patient. "All right. But I won't wait much longer. I'll give you a day, two at most. Don't make me come looking." Throwing some money on the bar, Finn strode out, leaving Adam to mull over his next move.

36

AJ picked through her salad, her appetite fading. Ethan's suspicions hammered at her. She had no reason to doubt Ethan's expertise or his information, yet she hadn't seen anything questionable in Finn's activities other than not sharing his purpose for being in Baywood. "I don't know. I guess I should be worried, but I'm not. There's nothing there, not anymore." She pushed the rest of her salad away. "Maybe I'm too close."

"Maybe," Stella said. "What exactly did you talk about at dinner?"

"In the end, not much. He has a way of turning the conversation away from himself, not unlike Ethan."

"They do seem similar in not talking about themselves."

"But I did get enough about the ship for my article, and some history on one of its earlier owners," AJ said. "Another sad account of shattered dreams and dysfunctional families. History is filled with so many of those, I guess no one is interested in happy endings."

"Which, I may point out, is not much different from today. Although, I prefer a storybook ending."

"That's you. Ever the optimist."

"Well, someone has to be, and I'm happy to carry the burden."

AJ reviewed the events of the last several days in her mind, tracing back all the times she had been with Finn or seen him. She didn't think anything nefarious was going on, but something didn't want to let go. She played with the plastic covering her cookie, rolling her fingers over the lumps and bumps of raisins, staring through it, until an image emerged.

She pictured the chart table and the edges of the older chart, hidden under the newer ones. If she had been able to see it, her gut told her it would have provided the answers she needed. She had concluded there was no story with Finn or the *Daphne Marie*, but now here was Ethan with his questions. Questions she herself asked just a couple of days ago.

"What?" Stella asked, breaking the silence. She always seemed to know when AJ was troubled by something.

"Have I been so blinded by the mystery of him, I'm not seeing what's right in front of me?" The question came out in a harsh whisper.

Stella placed a hand on her friend's arm, her own voice not much louder. "We don't know anything, only Ethan's suspicions."

"And that's not good enough to at least give it some credence?"

Stella pushed her plate away. "Isn't that what we're doing?"

AJ shook her head. "You're right. I don't know what to think. I've gone back over every minute I could remember seeing him or being around him. The only other person I've seen him with is Mr. Jackson, and we haven't found a drop of anything to even suspect he's up to no good, let alone point to him as being the town's fence."

"What about Adam?" Stella packed up her trash. "Who hired him to check out Westcliffe? Or is that a coincidence?"

AJ leaned against the table, lunch trash still in hand. She had forgotten about Adam. "I don't know how to figure that one out. Not without asking him. I'm not sure how to go about it."

"You're a reporter. Can't you tie it back to your story on the inn? I did see him at the recorder's office."

AJ mulled it over. "And you were there, what, checking it out to help me with the story? That will make him suspicious."

"And if he's not in the right mood, we'll have to listen to the old client-attorney privilege spiel."

"Let's go. You need to get to your appointment. Maybe I need to visit Finn again. See if I can get him to open up."

This time, Stella barked out a laugh, causing a few heads to turn. "And we know the best way for that to work."

AJ reddened and hurried out in front of Stella. She pushed through the door with her head lowered and didn't see the man until she bumped into him.

"AJ, I've been looking for you."

Ethan, as always, had a smile ready for her, but this time with a furrowed brow. His eyes were a shade darker than normal, and a questioning concern lurked in their depths.

"Hey, Ethan." Stella pushed AJ farther out the door, away from the entrance. "We just finished lunch, and I have to get to an appointment."

Ethan glanced at Stella. "Have you talked to AJ about my concern?"

"Yes, but she still has reservations. As do I." Stella searched her bag, finally picking out her keys. She turned and, catching AJ off guard, hugged her tight and whispered in her ear. "Listen to what he has to say, but use your own judgment. And be careful either way." Stella let AJ go and searched her friend's face, looking like she wanted to say something else. "Call me later, honey."

Before turning away, Stella pointed to Ethan. "You owe me a dinner for ruining my quiet evening."

AJ saw the concern reflected in Ethan's thin face. "I hear you have questions about Finn Murphy. Do you want to come into the office?"

"Let's walk instead."

The pavement was damp from drizzle that had turned on and off all morning. The clouds had lifted, although the gray skies refused to go away entirely. She shrugged. "I won't melt if it starts to rain again."

AJ led them down the street, making Ethan match her slower stride. She let the silence hang between them like the hovering clouds, waiting to see if his words would drown her in more doubt.

"I know it's not my place to look after you. I don't want you to think that's what I'm doing."

AJ stopped at a window to peer into a vintage furniture store. She focused on the small ornate globe sitting atop a scarred wooden pedestal. Ethan's face reflected in the glass. He appeared ready to say something, and, not wanting to hear it, she walked on.

She waited until they passed a few more stores, then gave him a break. "So tell me about, what is it, a thief?"

"I handle security for some affluent residential properties and there has been concern about some thefts in the area. They aren't your everyday robberies. They appear to be more organized, going after the more high-end items."

AJ gave him a wry smile. "Isn't your security supposed to prevent thefts from happening?"

Ethan smiled back at her. The worry lines above his brows disappeared. "The thefts weren't at the homes I secure."

"Ah." AJ resumed her window shopping.

"I do keep informed on possible threats to my clients and monitor the police reports."

"That makes sense. I knew you were in security, but I never knew how it worked. You know, what you really do all day."

"Well, there is more to it than sitting around waiting for an alarm to go off." Ethan steered her across the street, where there were more stores for her to look at.

AJ didn't miss the fact that, although she appeared to be leading Ethan, he was the one directing their walk, leading her toward the stores and away from the residential sections. Neither was it lost on her that Ethan always knew where to be, anticipating a person's needs. She had first noticed it while they were antiquing, and he mastered it with a subtlety she was sure was lost on most people. His knack for observation explained why he was in security, or maybe his job resulted in his keen senses. She assumed he was successful in his work, but it occurred to her she didn't know him any better than she knew Finn.

"I'm not the police," Ethan said. "I don't catch criminals, but when I hear of things like this happening, I do keep a watch out for possible suspects, in case they try to get close to my clients. Or my friends."

AJ searched his face for deception but saw only the stamp of deep worry lines and the clarity of meaning, and the look meant more to her than his words. "And you believe Finn Murphy fits the bill as a possible suspect."

"He's new in town, and he has the means to leave quickly, under the radar."

"Because of his ship."

"Yes." Ethan came to a stop in front of the Baywood Herald.

"But you don't know for sure. No proof of any wrongdoing."

"No. But his arrival time matches, and he doesn't seem to have any specific reason for being here."

"Baywood is a tourist location. Most people don't have a reason to be here other than that." AJ kept the hope out of her voice. Stay neutral and focus on the facts. She was a reporter, after all.

"That's true." Ethan paused, searching for the right words. "It's the timing. Do you know why he's here, AJ? Did he give any good reason, other than just passing through?"

AJ stepped back, pulling her arms around her. This was too much. It couldn't be true. He was not a thief. She turned to look around, not focusing on any one thing. The rain returned, a light drizzle, almost imperceptible, but she pulled the hood of her jacket over her head, giving her shelter and privacy from Ethan's penetrating gaze. She needed time, but all she could see was last evening, lying warm and safe in Finn's embrace. Could she have been that wrong about him?

She looked past the brim of her hood, where Ethan waited for her. Sometimes she wanted to knock the quiet patience right off his face, but this wasn't his fault. He was trying to be helpful and was concerned for her safety. She had to give his worry some credence.

"You're right, Ethan. I don't know anything about him. He hasn't told me why he's here, other than visiting." AJ squeezed his hand. "Thank you for being such a good friend. I know you're trying to look out for me, and I'll take what you've said to heart. There are more questions here than answers, there's no arguing that."

She could just as easily have been speaking of Ethan, who never said why he picked Baywood of all places. There were larger cities for a security firm to set up shop, and it never occurred to her to perform a little research on him. All it took was some time with Google. She surprised them both by leaning in and planting a firm kiss on his cheek. She squeezed his hand again. "I'm sure you'll get to the bottom of it." She left him standing on the street, staring at the closed door of the *Herald*.

37

AJ stared at the monitor. She had been staring at it for the last hour, unable to concentrate. Any minor amount of work she had accomplished had been rote, mundane. She kept getting pulled back to the same questions, the same person. She couldn't avoid it any longer and found she didn't want to. He had asked what she was doing this afternoon. It should be enough of an invitation. She should have asked for his number.

She shut down her computer, grabbed her bag, and looked around the office. No one paid any attention to her—too busy with their own articles. Samuel was off on one of his advertising campaigns or searching for a breaking story. AJ loved this place and couldn't picture working anywhere else. Just not today.

Her drive to the inn was quick. It was a comfortable commute, and she imagined returning home at the end of the day to sit on a porch of her own while she looked out to sea. It wouldn't be like the people in her articles. Obsessed individuals who spent their long days and nights looking out at this same body of water, waiting for something or someone to appear. She wouldn't be waiting for anyone. She would be able to enjoy the peace it offered.

AJ's nerves jangled as she pulled to a stop, hoping she hadn't made a mistake by returning and that he would be happy to see her. Leaving her bag in the car, she tucked her keys into her pants. She brushed back her hair, trying to keep the light wind from blowing it across her face, unsure of her decision to return, until she saw the ship.

Finn was on deck and appeared to be working on the sails, removing the rigging that bound the sails to the masts. He could be performing routine maintenance—or preparing to leave. She wouldn't know the difference. He paused in his task to stare out at the ocean, and she wondered if he was daydreaming. She hoped, with some embarrassment, that he had been thinking of her.

When she'd spied on him long enough, AJ raced to the dock, this time welcoming the tingling sensation, the anticipation of his greeting. When she neared the gangplank, she could no longer see him, but she could hear him working. It sounded like he was whistling, but it might have been the wind.

"Permission to come aboard."

ADAM DIDN'T RETURN to the office after meeting with Finn. Most of the alcohol had worn off, but he wasn't yet a hundred percent. Joyce would know something was wrong, and he didn't want to have to conjure up another lie. Not today. So he drove for a while, no destination in mind, until an urgent need to go home flooded through him. He needed to be with his family.

Disappointment greeted him when he opened the door. The silence in the house confirmed no one was home. He set down his case and keys and, like a robot returning to its charging station, made his way to the study, pushing off his shoes and falling into the welcoming arms of his recliner. He pulled the comforter around him. The clean scent made him smile. Madelyn must have washed it.

The end had been so close. He pictured his hands around his prize. Could see the moment when Finn gave him the last envelope that would see Adam clear. He swore an oath that he would never put his family in this jeopardy again. Not on his watch.

But the last piece evaded him. And though he knew he should come clean to Madelyn, his pride held fast, blocking any logical thought. The more he ran through it, the more he knew he was still in the game. Suddenly, the safety of his study became a prison. Instead of being comforted by his surroundings, his home became a glaring beacon for everything Adam could lose.

A slow panic rose through him, and sweat covered his body with a soft sheen, dampening his shirt. The last time he felt this sensation was when he fretted over the bar exam. He had more at stake now, and that alone flamed the fear, like a virus feeding on its host. It pushed him to a decision. There was one final risk he had to take. An irrational idea—a horrible notion— but it was the only solution.

"PERMISSION TO COME ABOARD."

Finn heard the words, but it could have been a hallucination. She had been on his mind after all. Perhaps it was the wind. He dropped the ropes he had been working on, checked the gangway, and found her looking at him, a cautious smile on her face. He returned his own broader smile, warm and welcoming.

"Aye, a sight for sore eyes. Someone to take me away from the misery of my work," Finn said.

"I wasn't sure if I should come back so soon." AJ roamed the deck, crossing to where Finn had been working on the sails. "You mentioned you had no plans for this afternoon." Her fingers played across the canvas.

"And I'm glad you did." He had hoped she would stop by, knowing she shouldn't. He'd struggled with his own desire to see her again and kept busy with work to stop himself from seeking her out if she didn't come back on her own.

Finn sat next to the rigging. He turned his face to hers with the idea of showing her how it worked. Before he could speak, her fingers, light as air, brushed against his cheek, and she leaned down to place a soft, warm kiss against his lips. A sense of urgency ran through him.

He fell into her gaze. She ran her hand over his cheek again, a light touch on his hair. Surprising him by taking the initiative, she leaned in to place her lips on his once more, this time more forcibly. All thought vanished. He pulled her to him, searching for her tongue already playing at his lips.

He swept her up and carried her below, enjoying her throaty laughter. This time she held him tighter, planting warm kisses along his neck as he tried to make his way downstairs without dropping her, and for a second, he pictured taking her right there on the stairs.

AJ wiggled out of his arms as soon as they entered the cabin. She peeled off her sweater, flung it across the room, then followed with her blouse, the pants, and the rest. Stark naked on the bed, she inched her way toward the carved headboard, that wicked smile on her face.

Finn fumbled with his pants. A small voice in the back of his mind made a meager attempt to stop this reckless behavior, but the passion that had lain dormant since she had left a few hours earlier silenced his fear of regret. Her face reflected his own desire. He slid onto the bed. Her arms embraced him and pulled him down, and with equal passion, they let the *Daphne Marie* rock them sweetly into the afternoon.

THE VIEW from the large bay windows revealed an expansive sky, dotted with evaporating puffs of marshmallow clouds. The sun reflected off the ocean, trying to ward off the dark clouds lining the far horizon. A storm was coming.

Ethan stood in his living room and weighed his options. He had done all he could to protect AJ, but something tugged at him, traveling the length of his back. He was familiar with the sensation, a bad omen. He was missing something.

He knew time was growing short. He'd experienced it before when they had gotten close, but that wasn't what triggered his sixth sense. Ethan was as far away from finding the object as he was to knowing what bothered him. Perhaps he should make another visit to Finn Murphy. No. It would be better to follow him, but Murphy's location in the bay made that difficult.

The realization of his next move rocked him. He needed to trust AJ if he expected her to do the same of him. Maybe he wouldn't have to tell her the whole truth, just enough to convince her to help him. Then she might fully comprehend the risk Murphy represented. His plan didn't provide any insight into what was nagging him, but it gave him the satisfaction that he had something to do beyond staring at the sea, as beautiful as it might be.

Now he had to find AJ.

AJ OPENED HER EYES. The shadows creeping their way across the room told her that it was late afternoon. Finn slept beside her, his face soft and boyish, and she wanted a glimpse into his dreams. His long lashes were a touch darker than his brows, and his wavy mane lighter, almost a match for her own curls. Her eyes traveled to the soft, downy hair on his chest, and she started to run her fingers across it until she spotted the medallion.

It was a silver Celtic cross, all arms equal distance in length, a circle encompassing the intersecting lengths. Embedded inside the circle was an unusual stone. She had seen it before—where?

Finn stirred beside her, and her gaze moved back to his face. He watched her, his eyes dark and sleepy. AJ brushed the hair from his face and placed a soft kiss on his lips.

"This is a most pleasant way to wake from a nap," he said. His voice was husky from sleep.

AJ rolled to her side, resting on her arm. "I have to admit, I don't mind playing hooky from work."

He pulled her back to him. "I'm glad I've been able to be a distraction for you."

She rested her head against his chest and sighed in contentment. "Yes, you've definitely been that." His chuckle resonated in her ears. She touched his medallion. "Where did you get such a beautiful cross?" He stiffened for an instant before pulling her closer.

"It's an old heirloom." He rolled over, trapping AJ beneath him, the cross grazing her breasts. Finn grinned. "And there will be no antiquing aboard ship today, madam." He kissed her on her forehead and more passionately on her lips.

AJ forgot about the medallion as Finn demonstrated his personal techniques for creating alternative distractions.

An hour later, as AJ dressed alongside Finn, the medallion long forgotten, she broached the question that had nagged at her when she had first arrived. "You were working on the sails earlier. Was it maintenance or something else?" She tried to keep her tone light.

Finn looked at her, his gaze soft but determined. "Where did you think this was going to go?"

"I don't know. I guess I hadn't thought it through."

He ran his hand over her shoulder, and the tingle burrowed

straight to her core. He cupped her breast, his hand warm through her shirt, but she backed away.

"You knew I wasn't going to stay."

"I know."

"It's not someplace you can go."

"And, what, I'd drop my life here and go with you? I don't even know what you do." AJ lost the battle to keep her voice light. She turned away and searched for her shoes. "I didn't want this to happen. To leave it like this. It's not your fault—it's as much mine."

She took another full look at him, knowing it could be her last. His tousled hair, his green eyes still dark with something she couldn't name. She laughed out loud and could see it unsettled him. "Look at the two of us. The clichéd, star-crossed lovers." AJ was happy to see his grin return. She was on safer ground. "It's silly to ask if I'll see you again."

"One never knows what the future holds."

He held the grin, but with effort, and she had no words to respond. Before she knew it, he was next to her, pulling her to him once more. She lifted her lips to his, closed her eyes, and held on as his tongue searched for hers. She let him consume her. To burn his touch and his smell into her memory, accepting this last token before he disappeared, lost to her forever.

AJ broke the connection and stepped away. She looked back before walking through the door. His arms dangled by his sides, a simple smile all he seemed able to give her. He looked so alone. She turned and ran up the stairs.

38

Driving home, AJ tried to ignore the sense of loss. Finn was a man on a ship, no better than a traveling salesman. Her rash actions were more Stella's style of free love. AJ had been the one looking for the stable guy, a good job, nice car, not too close to his mother. Someone not-Adam. She snickered. There was no question she'd found someone unlike her brother. She couldn't picture either of them ever getting along.

But Ethan seemed to get along fine with her brother, and Ethan was nothing like him. It surprised her to think Ethan and Finn would get along. They shared so many similarities, yet she had fallen for Finn.

Fallen for Finn!

The realization slammed her, but she had no other explanation for why she kept coming back. She could have completed her article days ago. She didn't need Finn's tall tale.

AJ struggled with her internal revelation the rest of the way home. At the door to her apartment, as she fought with the sticky lock, the sight of the Celtic cross flashed in her head, as did the unfamiliar stone that resided at its core. The recollection crashed into her like a rogue wave, and she dropped her bag on the floor, sprinting through the apartment to her bedroom.

She stared at the large antique jewelry box that held center stage on her dresser. The box, one of AJ's most treasured possessions, had been a gift from her father a few months before his death. She opened it and the smell of the wood enveloped her, a scent that would linger with the box until its last days. Warm tears fell as she remembered her father and all he had taught her.

She wiped her eyes and lifted the box's top shelf, filled with the items she wore through the week. Jewelry lay piled in the lower half of the box. AJ loved how the mix of necklaces and bracelets melded together, her own treasure chest of jewels. She rarely searched for antique jewelry, uninterested in the stones that caught everyone else's attention. From her experience, they tended to be overvalued. But every once in a while, she would find something unique that called to her, and it ended up in this box. Someday she would research each piece to see if there was a history to discover. Jewelry from estate sales rarely came with their own provenances.

AJ lifted out each item one by one, knowing which piece she was after. She pulled out several before finding an earring and its matching partner. Each earring was fashioned in silver, in a type of circular pattern she didn't recognize. Nor could she determine the origin. Inside each earring was a small stone. AJ looked closely at the stone and recognized it as the same stone in Finn's medallion. Its marbled coloration was identical. She had no idea what kind of stone it was. She had never seen anything like it before.

Except...

AJ laid the earrings aside. After moving aside another piece or two, her hand clasped a silver necklace. The chain was heavier than most, which was why she would never wear it, but she could appreciate the workmanship in each link. But it was the stone she was interested in. It lay in the center of its own silver pendant, the circular design matched the earrings. The setting differed from Finn's cross, but there was no denying it. The shades of blue, yellow, and gray were too distinct. It had to be the same type of stone.

An overwhelming desire came over her. She had to show this to Finn. He would want to see this necklace. The stone seemed too uncommon not to be related.

She placed the other jewelry and matching earrings back in the box. Closing the lid, she allowed herself a few seconds to run her hands across the top. Then she raced back to the living room, grabbed her bag, and took a look around her apartment. Something seemed different. She shook it off and walked out, slamming the door behind her.

ETHAN ARRIVED at AJ's door late in the afternoon. He had tried her office first, but the staff said she had left early. He wasn't sure where she would have gone, perhaps to Stella's, but it made sense to try her at home first. With his mind focused on what he would say to her, he hadn't paid attention to the door until he reached for the knob and discovered the door was already open, a small crack providing limited visibility. Worried, he leaned his ear to the door but heard nothing discernible.

Maybe she had left in a hurry and hadn't noticed she didn't close the door. But AJ didn't seem that careless.

Ethan peered through the half-inch gap of the open door but couldn't see much. A bookshelf of some kind, a slip of wall, a painting, and nothing more. A quiet curse slipped from him. He should have thought to bring his gun with him. The clock ticked away faster and faster. Never mind the consequences—he knew them all too well.

Bracing himself for what he might find, Ethan pushed the door open. There was no one there. He was sorry he didn't have time to take a closer look, to marvel at how AJ had surrounded herself in books and antiquities. No time to appraise the large book sitting by what must be her favorite chair, a small afghan hanging across one arm.

Ethan sensed someone in the apartment just before a sound came from one of the back rooms. Perhaps AJ was home after all and for some reason had left the door ajar. But he didn't believe that, not of the woman he had come to know. He could picture Stella leaving a door open, but not AJ.

Allowing himself one last recrimination for leaving his gun behind, Ethan searched the shelves of knickknacks for something he could use to mount a defense. He spied an old letter opener next to a matching inkwell and pen, all made of silver, discolored with age, pieces that had tarnished over the years and had been polished a thousand times. Ethan picked up the letter opener and tested its strength. It was well made. He had been in enough knife fights, and this small relic was all he would need, unless, of course, the intruder had a gun. Nothing he could do about that. He crept down the small hallway toward the noise.

The last door was half-open. It had to be AJ's room. His doubts resurfaced. If she was home, he would be feeling pretty stupid in a few seconds. He had no choice now but to announce himself, leaving him vulnerable if it wasn't her behind the door. He took a small step and opened his mouth to call out—

An arm and leg flashed by the door. Not AJ's. He tucked the letter opener into his sleeve, out of sight but available if needed, and slammed the door open. He was ready for anything—

Until he saw the person's face and the mess in what could now be confirmed as AJ's bedroom.

Drawers had been opened, ransacked, and haphazardly shut. Pieces of garments remained visible where they had been crammed back in, as if left behind to mount a protest against their rough handling. The bed was scattered with purses, belts, and jackets. Boxes, their contents of letters, old watches, and what must have been hundreds of buttons of various sizes and shapes had all been dumped on top of the clothing and accessories. But it was the dozens of seashells, some broken from being tossed without care onto the bed, that enraged him, knowing they must have been treasures AJ had collected with her father.

Ethan took it all in within seconds, and he turned to the man who had created the destruction.

"Adam. What are you doing?" Ethan tried to keep his question level. The man looked demented, running his fingers through a large pile of jewelry that had been dumped on the dresser. An old wooden box had been turned upside down next to it.

Adam looked up, dazed. He didn't seem surprised to see Ethan, but he said nothing—just turned his attention back to the jewelry.

Ethan tried again. "What are you doing here, Adam? Where's AJ?"

Adam picked up a bracelet, turning it over as if appraising its value. Ethan struggled to maintain his patience. He didn't have time for this, but he needed to know why Adam was here. He was about to ask a third time when Adam finally seemed to register him.

Adam had the decency to look ashamed at his behavior. He let out an audible sigh, his voice a croak. "I'm looking for a necklace."

"A necklace." Ethan blanched. "What kind of necklace?"

"One with a colored stone. Yellow and blue, marbled with some gray." Like a defeated soldier, Adam sat on the bed.

"AJ has the necklace?" Ethan's words were barely audible.

Adam stared at Ethan, his voice equally quiet. "You know about the necklace?"

"How do you know AJ has it?"

Adam looked at his hands, turning them over, then scanned

the room as if he might find a place he hadn't torn apart in his frenetic search. "I tracked her from the last owner."

"How did you find it so quickly?" Ethan found no reason for pretense now.

"My client had most of the details. It was really a matter of finding where everyone was living now." Adam returned to his search through the detritus from the opened boxes. "It's not hard to find people anymore, unless they're looking to disappear. Then it can be trickier, but not impossible."

"Under my nose the whole time," Ethan said, mostly to himself but loud enough for Adam to hear.

"You're looking for the necklace too?" Adam moved back to the wooden box he had turned over, slowly sifting through the pieces lying tangled in a heap on top of the dresser. He stopped and looked at Ethan. "Your interest in Westcliffe—you thought that was a connection to the necklace?"

Ethan had taken Adam's place on the bed, trying to work out where AJ would have taken the necklace. She'd have no reason to hide it. By itself, there was nothing special about it. The stone wasn't any known element, not precious to anyone unfamiliar with it. The word shot through him. *Westcliffe*.

"I wasn't sure. The location was convenient and the inn closed. It was worth checking out." Ethan calculated his next steps.

"This looks like it could be the stone, but it's not a necklace." Adam picked out a couple of small items from the pile that had been discarded like yesterday's trash. "Earrings. That's not close enough to a necklace, is it?" The disappointment was thick in Adam's voice, and he pushed the pile away from him.

"Do you know where AJ is?" A cold sweat worked its way over Ethan, and a sickening sensation prickled him. When Adam didn't answer, Ethan became more forceful, turning the man to face him. "AJ. Do you know where she is?"

Adam shook his head. "Not sure. I got here just as she was

leaving, almost ran into her as she ran out the main door. I didn't think she'd be home...at least I was hoping she wasn't. I have a key, so I let myself in." Adam was talking fast now. The words seemed to stumble out of him. "My client isn't going to be happy."

"Finn Murphy, is that your client?" Ethan barked the question.

"Yes." Adam stepped back, finally seeing the rage in Ethan's face—and something else. "How did you know that?"

"Come on, we need to pay Finn Murphy a visit. We can't waste any time." Ethan ran to the door.

Adam followed. "Where are we going?"

"To Murphy's ship."

"He has a ship? How did I not know that?" Adam trailed behind Ethan, seeming to take two steps for every one of Ethan's, although Adam wasn't much shorter. "Why are we in such a hurry?"

"Because AJ is in grave danger."

Ethan sprinted to the Escalade. He was behind the wheel, putting it into gear as Adam fell into the passenger side.

"Was it something I did?" Adam said.

Ethan's only answer was to floor the SUV, leaving marks against the pavement as it hurled itself down the road.

39

AJ drove the long route back to Westcliffe. She needed time—she had no idea what to say to Finn. She wasn't looking for any promises or commitments. She couldn't, wouldn't, go with him. She knew close to nothing about him, had no clue what he did to earn a living, whether he had a family. She let up on the gas, almost hit the brakes. *My God, please don't be married.*

She hadn't forgotten Ethan's warning, and while in the throes of passion and lust, she wasn't thinking clearly, but she would know if there was something morally wrong with Finn. There was a mystery that floated around him. His silent reveries, his refusal to talk about his family—it was clear there was a past he wasn't comfortable sharing. AJ didn't know what he might be running from, but for a reason she couldn't explain, she was convinced to her bones he was not a bad man. He was not a thief.

By the time she parked in the lot, she didn't know why she had considered this a good idea. She had simply snatched the necklace and raced out of her room. What would she say to Finn? She had no reason to ask anything of him. While her heart tugged at her, AJ's pragmatic side, the side her father had instilled in her long ago, would not let go. She wasn't there for any other reason than wanting to share the necklace with him.

The necklace had been in her lap the entire drive, her hand caressing it while driving. After she bought it at the estate sale, she had spent that first afternoon looking it over, trying to see if there was anything special about it. Carved into the back were some initials or words in a language she didn't know, but it wasn't unusual for treasured pieces to have the names of loved ones engraved into metal for eternity. After her initial inspection, she had placed it in her treasure box along with the matching earrings and summarily forgotten all about it.

Now, a couple of months later, a mystery ship appeared with a captain who had stolen her heart, and they each had a necklace with a unique and rare stone. She shook her head and retraced her steps to the path. Her father's voice rang in her head about history and facts and truth. The reasons she had become a journalist.

AJ slipped the necklace over her head and tucked it under her sweater. As she reached the dock, she had her story all figured out. Finn would know what the stone was, and he would be able to provide the information she needed to give history to the necklace. Satisfied she was able to rationalize her visit, she couldn't hold back her smile as she strode to the ship.

ETHAN PUSHED the Escalade to its limits on the city roads, ignoring speed limits, and they spilled onto the small country road that led them to the shore, never slowing down. His mind raced. So much time spent in his search. The years that had gone by. Now, AJ's involvement in this plot was unthinkable. He had no hope of recovering the necklace—not here, not now. He would need to continue the mission at another time. His driving force now was AJ's safety.

The SUV shuddered as Ethan took each turn, his eyes darting to the rearview mirror, hoping not to find any carnage behind them. The fear in the man beside him clung in the air, but Ethan had no time to slow.

ADAM BRACED HIMSELF, one hand white-knuckled around the door handle, as though he could jump and live to tell the story. His other hand pushed hard against the dash, waiting for the impact. His eyes, large and unblinking, watched with horror the near misses with passing motorists, and the flash of terror from one poor soul who had thought to cross in the middle of the street before falling back from the speeding tank.

Finally, they escaped the city. But if he had been expecting some respite from the speed, he was out of luck again. Trees rushed past—any one slip would hurtle them into a large fir. Images flooded past him as quickly as the trees. Adam tried to organize the facts from the last few days, but his well-honed legal mind failed him.

He couldn't believe he had gotten himself into this mess. He would never, ever go near another poker game. Not even for fun. His card days were over. He clamped his eyes shut and prayed to any gods that might be listening, promising to stay on the straight and narrow if they would guide him out of this disaster. There were other ways to get the rest of the money. If he survived the day.

Adam's eyes flew open when the SUV braked hard, lurching to the left and back to the right. He had to see what was going to kill him, and his sigh of relief rolled through the vehicle. A flash of a deer, eyes as wide as Adam's, escaped into the dense trees and tall grasses.

"You've got to slow down, man."

Adam's words dissipated into the silence as the Escalade picked up speed. When Adam forced his eyes from the road to sneak a peek at Ethan, he couldn't recall ever seeing a man with equal parts of anguish and deadly determination, not even with the desperate men he counseled at trial. Adam knew that this was when a man became the most dangerous—when he had nothing left to lose.

THE SHIP ROLLED against the dock. Darkening skies cast long shadows of the *Daphne Marie* along the pier. The sky had been clear when AJ parked, but in the bay, the fog appeared to be rolling in.

At the gangway, AJ called out for Finn, her resolve diminishing the longer she waited for his reply. The ship was quiet except for the light creaking sounds protesting the restlessness of the waves, creating an occasional bumping and rubbing of the ship as it kissed the dock. Still no response from Finn. AJ edged up the gangplank until she could see the whole deck. She called out again. "Finn, are you here?"

AJ hadn't anticipated the fog. She hugged her arms around her, though she didn't feel any chill. Maybe he wasn't here. He may have gone somewhere with Mr. Jackson. Her spirits fell, and the heaviness of the silver chain tugged at her. She waited another minute before yelling louder, now inches from stepping onto the deck. "Finn, I just need a minute."

A rustling sound came from below, and someone moved quickly up the steps.

When Finn's head popped up, AJ's stomach took a slight dip. Even in the fading light, she could see his crooked grin.

"AJ, what the devil?" His smile faded. He looked around, and confusion replaced the welcoming grin. "Why did you come back?"

AJ had been hoping for more of a welcome. It had been foolish to run over. "May I come aboard?"

Finn took another look around the deck and walked to her, the pleasure to see her once again on his face. "You don't have to ask. You're more than a guest now, I should think." He held out an arm to her. "Sorry for the poor welcome. I was just surprised by the change in weather."

When she stepped onto the deck, she extended her own hand. He grabbed it, pulled her close, and gave a her long, hard kiss, as if they had been parted for days instead of an hour or two.

This was the welcome she had been expecting. She gave in to his warm lips and strong embrace. How wonderful it would be to have more of this in her life. She took what she could before taking one step back.

Finn grasped her shoulders and looked her over. "I didn't dare hope to see you again."

AJ shrugged despite the heaviness of his hands on her. "I didn't either, but I found something I wanted to show you."

"And what might that be?" His voice was no more than a whisper with a note of urgency. He looked around the ship. "The fog is moving in quickly. Show me what you brought."

She reached into her sweater and pulled out the necklace. She waited for Finn to say something, but he just stared. Unsure how to read Finn's expression, AJ went with what she had originally rehearsed. "I wanted to show this to you. It looks like yours. The stone is so unique. I was surprised when I saw your medallion."

Finn's hand shook. He turned AJ's hand, trying to move the stone into the light. "Where did you find it?"

"At an estate sale. I've only had it for a couple of months now, maybe less. The woman who owned it had recently died." AJ touched Finn's hand, still clinging to her own. "Her grand-daughter didn't want to sell it, but, I don't know...I saw it and I needed to have it." She let the necklace drop from their hands and brushed her hair back. "I don't usually look at jewelry, but it

was as if it had called to me or something." She quiet[e]
hadn't meant to share so much. "Silly, isn't it?"

Finn stared at the pendant, then looked at her, a look of wonderment on his face combined with a glimmer of something else. Finn pulled her to him, holding her tight. AJ melted into the embrace, smiling with a small amount of satisfaction that he was happy to see her *and* the necklace.

40

The SUV slid to a stop in a parking lot. Within seconds, Ethan launched himself from the driver's seat, racing toward a building tinted with orange from the fading sun. It took Adam only a few seconds to see where they were.

The old Westcliffe Inn. He hadn't been here in ages. The last remnants of sun ducked behind the clouds, leaving the front of the inn in shadows, the fading light playing tricks, making the inn appear as it had all those years ago. Adam never had the same interest in this historic old relic as his father had, nor had he found any curiosity in the childish wanderings of the tidal pools. When Ethan first mentioned the name of the inn, Adam hadn't put it together. It wasn't until Ethan told him of AJ's interest that he remembered.

Adam ran through the possible scenarios as to why they had come here. Struggling to disengage himself from the seat belt, he needed to follow Ethan. He pulled free from the seat and spotted AJ's car. Adam moved faster, muttering to himself. She'd better not be collecting what was owed him. After all the work he did, he wouldn't be cheated out of his final payment.

"Why is AJ here?"

But Ethan was out of sight and probably out of earshot. When Adam found the diverging paths, he wasn't sure which way Ethan had gone—until he looked to his left and pulled up, gasping, as he got his first look at the ghostly ship below. Now he'd seen it all. Ships were something he knew about, and that ship looked like it had just floated out of history.

Although there was no fog at the top of the cliff, thickening tendrils of mist surrounded the ship, as if attempting to hold it in the palm of its vaporous hands. Adam shivered. He spotted Ethan halfway down the path, running like the devil himself chased him. Adam raced after him, the ghostly hounds of hell snapping at his heels. He didn't know why, but he was overwhelmed with an urgent need to find AJ.

FINN STEPPED BACK FROM AJ, her face full of questions. She held on to him, her fingers grasping his shirt, and for the first time since his mission began, doubt crept in. He wasn't sure of his next step, but he understood why the mist had returned. AJ's story had given him chills. Her love of antiquing, Adam being her brother, and that Adam had discovered she had the necklace. Finn knew AJ well enough that he understood Adam's dilemma in procuring the necklace. How would he have explained why he was searching for the necklace without revealing the weakness that had put him in Finn's employ?

Everything made sense now, except for AJ being the one to find it in the first place. On the surface, it appeared to be a coincidence, but knowing what he did about the stone sent chills racing to his core. His concern for AJ doubled as soon as he saw the pendant, and his first reaction had been to pull her to him and hold her fast.

"Do you think it's the same?" AJ's face reflected the mystery of it all, her love for history and antiques shining in her eyes. "The earrings weren't as obvious with the smaller stones, but the size of the stone in the necklace, I was sure I was remembering it right."

Finn's eyes refocused on her scrunched face, trying to put a puzzle together. He looked back at the necklace lying against her sweater. "Earrings?"

"The stone. Is it the same?"

"Aye." Finn let out his breath. It seemed as though he'd been holding it for decades. The fog thickened around them. "I believe so. I didn't know there were earrings." Finn pulled out the cross from beneath his shirt. "It's very old."

"I thought so, but I've never seen anything like it before. When I first saw your medallion, I remembered the stone, but I couldn't recall where I had seen it."

Finn sighed and pulled AJ against him once more. He didn't want to let her go.

But he had no choice.

"You and your stories. You would be intrigued by this one."

"What's wrong?" AJ tried to pull away.

"I wish we had more time." Finn whispered his words against her head. He turned them around as if they were dancing, holding her head against his chest. He wanted to etch this moment in his mind, to carry it with him forever. "I need you to go, AJ."

By THE TIME Ethan had slammed to a stop in the parking lot, he had it all laid out. He would follow his training. It was the safest way. He knew his goal and must follow each logical step to achieve that goal. His emotions could not play a part in this. They would only create mistakes, and there was too little time for any error in judgment.

Had anyone been at the path leading to the dock, they would

have heard his heavy sigh. He had been daring the ship to still be at dock, but any relief was swallowed by the sight of the dense fog enclosing it. He didn't slow as he turned the corner, pushing hard to reach AJ, the necklace now an afterthought.

Adam called out behind him, accompanied by faint footsteps, but he pushed it all away. Adam no longer mattered.

As Ethan neared the ship, he saw her. For the briefest of seconds, an immense relief washed over him, but it was fleeting. AJ was standing with Finn, his arms wrapped around her in a tight embrace, lovers standing in the twilight without any knowledge of the danger around them. But Finn knew. He knew too damn well. So why wasn't he making AJ get off the ship?

FINN CONTINUED his slow dance with AJ in his arms, wishing this moment didn't have to end. Had he not been turning, he would never have seen Ethan racing down the dock, another man behind him.

Finn kissed the top of AJ's head, and she tried to pull away, but he held her tight, stroking her back. There was no way he could get AJ off the ship. Not now. Not without Ethan getting on board. The stakes were too high. He couldn't sacrifice everything he'd worked for after the hardships he'd endured these last months.

He worked through his thinning options and kept circling back to the one thing that might work. He had no other option. His gut wrenched as he made an internal promise to keep her safe.

WHEN ETHAN APPROACHED THE DOCK, he was surprised to hear Adam close behind. It must be the runner in him.

"What's wrong?" Adam panted, still several footsteps behind Ethan. "Why are you in such a hurry? Are you sure AJ is in trouble?"

"Yes, unbelievable danger." Ethan's voice was soft, as if winded, but in truth, he meant it only for his ears. He refused to slow as he came upon the ship, the fog so thick it seemed to frame the figures standing on the deck. "You have no perception of the peril."

Ethan stepped onto the gangplank and called out. "*AJ!*" But the mist swallowed his voice.

AJ found the strength to lean away from Finn, looking into his melancholy face. The necklace didn't seem as important as the idea of saying goodbye to this man. She wanted to know more about him. His secret wall had just began to crumble.

The look in Finn's eyes woke AJ out of her trance. She stood straighter, catching the change in him and noticing the thickening fog for the first time. "What's wrong?" AJ pushed away, but Finn refused to let go. It was no longer a loving embrace.

"Do you trust me? Honestly trust me?"

AJ stared back, confused. The answer seemed easy at first, but his darkening face made her rethink the question. "Why wouldn't I trust you?"

His dour expression conflicted with the uncertainty in his reply. "I need to know if you trust me. No doubts. I need to know." His voice was firm and unwavering, his eyes beseeching her to tell him the truth.

AJ searched her mind and heart for a consistent answer. She didn't have enough information to provide one. The question wasn't fair. His impatient gaze traveled over her face, desperate for her response. Down deep, her instinct told her this man meant more to her than she could imagine. In truth, it was a simple question. "Yes," she said. Again, with more conviction. "Yes, I trust you."

AJ heard her name. Someone on the dock called out to her. She turned her back to Finn, his arms still around her. Through the mist, she made out the form of Ethan at the bottom of the gangplank. Someone ran up the dock behind him. It looked like Adam, but why would he be here?

Finn's arms tightened their grasp around her, probably a response to Ethan's sudden appearance. She had been comforted by the embrace, but when she tried to step away to greet Ethan, Finn's hold grew tighter. Her first reflex was to struggle but Finn relaxed behind her, and her body responded in kind. She stopped struggling, expecting to be released.

Instead of freeing her, Finn reached for her necklace with one hand and held his medallion in the other. How similar they were.

Ethan called out again, panic and desperation in his voice. Adam called out as well, and again she questioned why Adam was here. Something must be wrong. Her confusion grew as she looked down at the arms encircling her, at the two necklaces, finally back at Ethan, her welcoming smile fading when she saw his terror-stricken face. What could have happened? Time slowed. The mist made it almost impossible to see past the ship.

Ethan stepped close enough for the words to be clear. "Stop, AJ."

Stop. Stop what?

Ethan screamed louder, "Step away, AJ. Step away."

She struggled to move out of Finn's arms. Something was wrong. Maybe Ethan was still concerned about Finn and some illicit theft ring. She knew Finn had no part in anything like that. She wanted Ethan to know it was okay.

But that didn't explain Adam. Maybe something had happened to Mom.

All the different possibilities rushed in, creating a wave of fear. Finn's arms tightened more. She couldn't breathe. Her fingers plucked at his hands. She had to step away, clear her head and get to Ethan. What was wrong?

"Let me go."

Finn's lips brushed her ear. "No. It's too late. Trust me."

Ethan yelled again, his voice muffled. He seemed to fade in and out of the condensing fog. She couldn't hear anything, but she could still feel the warmth of Finn's arms, holding her tight against him. Ethan's eyes grew wide in alarm, a silent cry shaping his lips.

AJ pulled far enough away to see the look Finn gave Ethan, a smile she had never seen before—not fully triumphant, but tinged by another emotion AJ couldn't place. Finn lifted his medallion to meet her pendant, his arms still refusing to release her.

She looked back at Ethan. He backed up, resignation engraved on his face, a deep look of sorrow. For the first time, she doubted Finn. His arms tightened again as if preventing her from melting away, and she looked down.

Finn touched the stone of his medallion to the stone in her necklace.

She tensed. Something was terribly wrong. The fog was so palpable, almost impenetrable. Shapes became distorted. She found it difficult to breathe. Terror gave way to bewilderment as Ethan faded away, and the ship disappeared into the mist.

———

THANK YOU FOR READING

Thank you for reading *A Stone in Time*. Follow AJ and Finn's journey in Book 2 of the series, *Keeper of Stones*.

Stay connected to Kim to keep up with new releases, book signings and other treats through her website: www.kimallred.com. Join her newsletter at: https://www.kimallred.com/contact. Connect on Facebook: https://www.facebook.com/kimallredwriter.

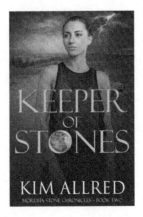

KEEPER OF STONES

CHAPTER ONE

The white sails, tied tight against the rigging, leaked enough flap to flutter in the light breeze. Tails of ropes swung in unison with the rolling of the waves, rocking the sloop tied to its moor. AJ Moore stared up past the sails and rigging to the sky as she watched the clouds. It was rare to see blue skies this time of year, or so she'd been told. Ireland wasn't considered the Emerald Isle because of its sunny warm days.

"Step away, AJ. Step away."

Two months, and two hundred years from her future, had seemed an eternity since the fog dissipated, leaving her disoriented, confused, and finally disbelieving. She was no longer in Baywood, Oregon. If Finn could be believed, which was not one of his strong points, she was in Ireland, and the year was 1802. The year of Napoleon, a mad king on the English throne, and continual wars—certainly no place for a twenty-first-century woman.

Finn's strong arms encircle her, warm and comforting. The light touch of his fingers skims her sweater, reaching for her stone necklace.

AJ sprawled on the deck of the ship and watched the clouds float by, her skirts spread out around her. Her daily visits to the ship had become a ritual since the day they'd arrived through the fog. It wasn't as if the ship could take her home. It had been in her future, jumping with her and Finn to this new time, and it was a link to what she knew.

Desperation fuels Ethan's voice as he calls out to her, his face struck by terror. Her brother, Adam, echoes the alarm, stretching his arm out to her. He never cared about her before.

AJ shook her head to erase the memory like an old Etch A Sketch board. With the wood slats of the deck hard and unforgiving underneath her, she turned her focus to the clouds. The images shifted, first a turtle and then a horse. A hawk marred the forms, its flight breaking her concentration.

She couldn't shake the daydreams. It was going to be one of those days. The ones that led to a bout of depression. Stella would kick her ass for feeling sorry for herself. Stella believed in one day for self-pity accompanied by as many glasses of wine required to get through the night. Then move on. AJ had to believe that her friend would consider her current plight an exception to the one-day rule.

The thickening fog distorts Ethan's shape and muffles his voice. AJ can't hear anything but a rushing sound, like holding a seashell up to her ear. Finn's warm arms grip her tight. She strains to make out Ethan's face through the haze, his alarm barely visible, a silent cry forming on his lips.

She squeezed her eyes shut and sucked in a breath of cool morning air, pulling her woolen wrap tighter. The late spring sun couldn't break through the cold winds blowing in from the sea. The flashbacks didn't come as often, but when they did, they hit her with a force as strong as the day the world as she knew it disappeared. The only way through it was to relive it and deal with the aftermath.

With his arms ensnaring her, Finn touches the stone of his medallion to the stone in AJ's necklace. Ethan and the dock fade into the whiteness of the mist.

The sounds of footsteps snapped her back, and she turned her head to find the familiar dark shape set against the morning light. She threw an arm across her forehead to cut the glare from the sun and forced the tension from her muscles.

"I didn't mean to disturb you." Finn's voice was soft and distant.

She waited, but he wouldn't say anything more, not until he could determine her mood. She rolled her head away and swallowed the thickness clogging her throat. "It's all right."

"I need to make a trip to town. I just wanted you to know where I went."

"I thought you were going tomorrow." She tried to hide the bitterness. Her body ached with the need to go with him, to see other people.

"We need oats. The horses will be expecting their grain." He shuffled his feet. "And I thought I could take some of the extra loaves with me."

She couldn't hold back the smile. When she first tried her hand at baking bread, it had been a dismal failure. Finn went to town regularly to keep them supplied in fresh baked goods. Boredom eventually set in, and she focused her attention to the task. She became so adept at baking, she couldn't see the counters or tables for the number of loaves covering it, more than the two of them could eat. Finn took them to town, either to pay back the baker who supplied them in the beginning or to trade for other goods. She never asked.

"We could use some other staples. Flour and sugar. Cinnamon if you can find it."

"All right. I'll be back before supper." He waited.

She kept her head turned, staring blankly at the rigging until she heard his footsteps recede. She tired of these days where the past wouldn't let go. The last two months had been filled with anger, depression, and then curiosity about her new surroundings. She went days without speaking to him at all. In the end, she cried, letting him hold her and soothe her and tell her it would be all right. She even fell back into bed with him, trying to find any comfort she could, remembering her life before this. After all he had put her through, her heart tugged whenever she saw him, even when they had an incredible fight and he knew to stay away.

She bolted upright when she heard the hooves hitting the dirt path leading away from the cottage by the sea. Everything he did focused on her needs, her moods. It had taken two weeks before she caught on. And then she had pushed him, tested him. He never disappointed. She knew her guilt at her own mood swings would never compare to his guilt at bringing her back in time with him. It was done, and she needed to stop punishing him for it. They must discuss the future.

Standing to watch Finn disappear from sight, she brushed her skirts that fell two inches too short and tugged at the sleeves that stopped short of her wrists. Her question of who owned the well-made dresses that hung in her wardrobe had been met with a grunt from Finn. She sighed as she turned toward the rock-edged bay that protected the cottage from winter storms. Finn promised they would leave soon, but he never mentioned a destination.

Turning her back to the sea, she walked to the vegetable garden. Chores came before her daily cataloging of discoveries within the cottage. Unique household items written down with an old quill pen on any bits of paper she could find. All antiques, in her mind. She couldn't abandon her passion for the old or the love of history her father instilled in her. She wanted to remember everything she could when she found her way back home.

She grumbled at Finn as she pulled carrots, the fresh earth settling her. Through all her anger and tantrums, particularly during the first week of being completely inconsolable, he was there. She hadn't known him very long before the time jump, as she called it, but she discovered her feelings for him still remained. During the days they didn't speak, she watched him, the crease of worry on his brow with long stares out to sea. He spent infinite hours working on the old house, tending the horses and maintaining the ship. She watched him from the window, from the garden, and even from the ship, where she might magically disappear back to her own time. With all he tried to do, she couldn't help but harbor anger at what he had done. She resented him for rebuffing her questions of how they came to be where they were, a place he seemed intimately comfortable with. He refused to speak of the stones.

"You need to get settled and understand how things work here. Then we'll talk about the stones." Finn kept to this line, refusing to budge.

"You owe me more," AJ retorted with the same response, always to his retreating back, stomping her foot or kicking something for emphasis. She couldn't help herself—she was a reporter after all. Or used to be.

From the garden, she paused in picking lettuce and sat among the vegetation, letting the warmth of the sun wash over her as her hands dug into the soil, a worm inching its way over her fingers. She wasn't one for gardens, that's why she loved her apartment. No fuss, no muss. But she loved Stella's flower garden, the odd-shaped paper lanterns swaying in the evening coastal breezes, and she longed to see it again.

The day of her arrival in Ireland, when the mist had faded, her first glimpse of Ireland had been the single dock, the hillside covered with spring flowers, dotted sporadically with elm trees and oaks, and the well-tended cottage. Then she noticed nothing at all when the impact of what had happened grabbed her and threw her down the rabbit hole.

Over the next few weeks she had examined the land, the cottage, and the sea, all nestled together in its own world. She witnessed the remoteness and desolation that matched her own spirit. Eventually, she came to appreciate the beauty, the imagery, and the tranquility that softened her anger and tamed her fear.

Grabbing the lettuce and carrots she'd pulled from the garden, AJ made her way back to the cottage. It was time to leave this land and figure out how the stones worked. Whether Finn was ready or not.

"The meal was exceptional." Finn refilled the wineglasses and sat back, his long legs stretched out in front of him, hands resting on his stomach.

"Thank you." AJ sipped the wine and glanced at him over the rim of the glass. She couldn't ignore the presence he made. He wore simple trousers and an old woolen shirt, and though they fit loosely, she had seen his muscles flex when he started the fire. A tightening in her core nudged her as she remembered her hands moving over his warm skin and hard muscles. He smiled at her, a slow, lazy grin softening his square jaw. As if on command, a lock of his sun-kissed brown hair slid over his emerald eyes, almost black in the low light. The tingle rose up, and she averted her gaze.

"I thought we might go for a ride tomorrow." Finn stared at his glass, his finger moving slowly around the rim as if the suggestion was nothing more than a casual thought.

"Oh." AJ lowered her head and stood, carrying the empty plates to the counter. It wasn't that she didn't like horses. They were fine as long as she stayed on the ground. Her first riding adventure required two weeks of recovery before she agreed to make a second attempt. She refused any further lessons.

"You need to know how to ride. It will be noticeable if you shy away from them." A hint of a smile creased the corners of his mouth. "You really are getting much better." He busied himself with breaking off another piece of bread.

She rolled her eyes as she swept the last of the bread away from him. "Now you're just lying."

Finn grinned at her. "Aye, I'm ashamed I had to do that, but if it works, I'll do my best not to make a habit of it."

She couldn't hold back her own grin, even as she fought the growing panic of getting back on a horse. With the table cleared, she plopped down to finish her wine and mull over Finn's suggestion. He refused to take her anywhere in the two-person carriage she had seen in the barn, forcing her to stay within walking distance of the cottage.

"I'll try. It would be easier if I could straddle it like you rather than sitting sidesaddle."

He shook his head. "That would bring more attention than not riding at all. If you would promise to ride each morning, I would be agreeable to shorter sessions."

She gazed toward the window, dusk settling over the hills shaded black against the sky. He offered a decent compromise, a way to discover what lay beyond those hills—a history she only imagined. She had decided only hours before it was time to leave. This was her opportunity to meet the challenge, to see if she could blend in. She met his waiting gaze. "All right. I can't stay here forever. I need to find a way home."

Later than evening, AJ sat at the oak writing desk in their bedroom, hunched over bits of paper. She dipped the quill into the ink, pushing to finish the words that had bounced around in her head all day.

"Come to bed. We have a long day tomorrow." Finn pulled the covers over his broad shoulders and turned toward the wall.

She finished the last few words and extinguished the lamp. Her bare feet scurried over the cool floor the fire never seemed able to warm. She missed the bunny slippers Stella had given her last Christmas. As she jumped into bed, the idea of rubbing her cold feet against his legs was difficult to squash.

For the briefest of moments, she reached to run her hand down his back, to feel the solidness of him, to remind herself she wasn't alone. He would be accepting of her touch even though his back was to her. It was his way of giving her space. She pulled her hand back and rolled to her side, waiting for sleep to come.

Finn's embrace tightens when she shows him the old antique necklace with the odd marbled stone. One that happens to match the unique stone set in his Celtic cross medallion.

Her anxiety flares as she struggles to move out of his arms. She plucks at his hands, scratching at the arms that tighten around her like steel claws. A sheen of sweat glistens on her brow, and she strains against the restricting body. She can't breathe. If she could just break free, clear her head, and get to Ethan.

The thickening fog distorts Ethan's shape and muffles his voice, but the soft words float to her. "Step away. Step away."

With his arms still ensnaring her, Finn touches the stone of his medallion to the stone in AJ's necklace.

She tenses. Something is terribly wrong. A rushing sound fills her ears as she watches Ethan fade.

The mist consumes the ship, and the dock disappears, spiriting Ethan and Adam away. AJ's skin prickles as an invisible force reaches deep inside her, pulling her as if the hand of Kronos reached inside her, grasping her spine and ripping it out.

It couldn't be real.

The muscles of Finn's arms constrict around her. The mist smothers her like a lead blanket, heavy and unmoving. She peers through the thickness of the fog, but there's nothing there.

Blinded by a bright, impenetrable whiteness, she reaches out to steady herself, but she can't raise her arms. Her head dizzy, her stomach reeling, she wants to retch. She closes her eyes as the world drops away, her stomach spiraling with it. Her head rests against Finn, his body a rock. At least that's something. She isn't alone.

Any comfort she might feel in his embrace evaporates. She struggles but can't wrest herself from the straitjacket that binds her. Her eyes snap open.

She calls out, "Finn." The vortex consumes the word before it takes shape. Her senses scream, and when she knows she's going to vomit, the fierce tug pulling at her lightens. The mist slowly dissipates, and Finn's arms, while still around her, loosen their grip.

AJ blinks to refocus. The mist disappears to reveal the mast of the ship, the deck, and then the railing. The sun breaks through to chase away the remaining fog. Her breath escapes in a rush as the dock reappears. Something isn't right—Ethan and Adam have vanished.

A well-kept house made of wood and stone sits a few hundred yards from the dock. Finn's warm fingers circle her wrist, his thumb rubbing gently against its raging pulse. His words roll over her, soft as a gentle breeze, "Do you still trust me? I have a story to tell you sweet lass."

AJ shoved the covers from her, sitting up and clutching her nightgown. Her breathing was hard and fast, pounding against her ribs. She counted to ten, then repeated it two more times before her heart rate slowed. She wiped her brow, sticky with sweat.

She whipped her head toward Finn. He reached for her before he turned in his sleep. Her nightmares were either becoming quieter, or he was getting used to them. When they'd first arrived in this time period, he would shake her from them and hold her tight. Now he barely stirred.

She lay down, leaving the covers off to cool her body. After a few minutes, she dragged them back over her before turning to her side, her knees pulled up, waiting for the darkness to give way to light.

Thank you for reading *A Stone in Time*.

Stay connected to Kim to keep up with new releases, book signings and other treats through:

Her website: www.kimallred.com.

Join her newsletter at: https://www.kimallred.com/contact.

Connect on Facebook:
https://www.facebook.com/kimallredwriter.

ABOUT THE AUTHOR

Kim Allred lives in an old timber town in the Pacific Northwest where she raises alpacas, llamas and an undetermined number of free-range chickens. Just like AJ and Stella, she loves sharing stories while sipping a glass of fine wine or slurping a strong cup of brew.

Her spirit of adventure has taken her on many journeys including a ten-day dogsledding trip in northern Alaska and sleeping under the stars on the savannas of eastern Africa.

Kim is currently working on the next book in the Mórdha Stone Chronicles series and her upcoming new sizzling romance series—Masquerade Club.

To stay in contact with Kim, join her newsletter at https://www.kimallred.com/contact/, follow her on Facebook at https://www.facebook.com/kimallredwriter/, or visit her website at www.kimallred.com.

Made in the USA
Las Vegas, NV
26 June 2023

73928908R00184